# Praise for Brian Pinkerton

'Quite simply, one of the best thriller guys you can find.
No nonsense, no bloat, just thrill.'
Mort Castle, editor of *Shadow Show: All-New Stories in
Celebration of Ray Bradbury*

'An entertaining retelling of a classic SF invasion
story along the lines of *The Puppet Master* or
*Invasion of the Body Snatchers.*'
*Booklist* on *The Intruders*

'Filled with memorable characters and turbo-charged
with a breakneck pace... a visceral plunge into
paranoia and terror.'
Jonathan Janz, author of *The Siren and the Specter,*
on *The Intruders*

'A terrific entry into the sci-fi paranormal genre that fans
will love to read. A story with a surprising amount of
heart and humanity at its core.'
Emerald Reviews on *The Intruders*

'Millions tune into a virtual reality program while society
collapses around them in this thoughtful cyberpunk novel
from Pinkerton [that] builds to a clever, desperate climax.
Fans of stories centered on the conflict between the
virtual and the real will find plenty to enjoy.'
*Publishers Weekly* on *The Nirvana Effect*

'*The Intruders* by Brian Pinkerton is my favorite book of
the year so far... I cannot recommend it more.'
Josef Hernandez, A Reviewer Darkly

'This is a highly entertaining read full of horrors and heartbreak. The adventure is fast-paced and the invasion is unique and scary.'
Outlaw Poet on *The Intruders*

'This is such a gripping novel that I was hooked from the first page...an amazing science-fiction dystopian story.'
The Strawberry Post on *The Nirvana Effect*

'Incredible...easily one of the best dystopian novels I have read this year... the author beautifully maintained the momentum till the very end, which led to an explosive climax.'
Rajivsreviews.com on *The Nirvana Effect*

'A dizzying compilation of action scenes and moral quandaries... Pinkerton wields fast pacing and an entertaining, electrifying plot.'
*Publishers Weekly* on *The Gemini Experiment*

'Part spy thriller, part SF adventure, Pinkerton's latest is a fast-paced and action-packed novel with well-developed characters that will have strong YA and adult appeal.'
*Library Journal* on *The Gemini Experiment*

'*The Gemini Experiment* is a thrill ride filled with twists and turns that keep the reader guessing and entertained all the way to the stunning conclusion. Brian Pinkerton has created a wonderfully constructed story, frightening in its believability...an exceptional read.'
Cemetery Dance

'Pinkerton is truly a master when it comes to action scenes. They are thrilling, fast-paced and will leave you breathless... a fun sci-fi story.'
Ginger Nuts of Horror on *The Gemini Experiment*

# BRIAN PINKERTON

# THE PERFECT STRANGER

This is a **FLAME TREE PRESS** book

Text copyright © 2025 Brian Pinkerton

**FLAME TREE PRESS**
6 Melbray Mews, London, SW6 3NS, UK
flametreepress.com

US sales, distribution and warehouse:
**Simon & Schuster**
simonandschuster.biz

UK distribution and warehouse:
**Hachette UK Distribution**
hukdcustomerservice@hachette.co.uk

Publisher's Note: This is a work of fiction. Names, characters, places, and incidents are a product of the author's imagination. Locales and public names are sometimes used for atmospheric purposes. Any resemblance to actual people, living or dead, or to businesses, companies, events, institutions, or locales is completely coincidental.

Thanks to the Flame Tree Press team.

The cover is created by Flame Tree Studio with elements courtesy of Shutterstock.com and: Abdu Ezzurghi; Alena Ivochkina; and TSViPhoto. The font families used are Avenir and Bembo.

Flame Tree Press is an imprint of Flame Tree Publishing Ltd
flametreepublishing.com

A copy of the CIP data for this book is available from the British Library and the Library of Congress.

1 3 5 7 9 8 6 4 2

HB ISBN: 978-1-78758-897-4
Trade PB ISBN: 978-1-78758-896-7
ebook ISBN: 978-1-78758-898-1

Printed and bound in Great Britain by Clays Ltd, Elcograf S.p.A.

BRIAN PINKERTON

# THE PERFECT STRANGER

**FLAME TREE PRESS**
*London & New York*

# CHAPTER ONE

"So, yeah, um, anyway, I quit."

After a loose, meandering set-up that reflected on the 'pretty good experiences' and 'mostly nice people' of the past fourteen months, Tricia announced that she had a new opportunity that promised better pay and more responsibility and 'really interesting work' and her last day would be Friday – yes, this Friday of this week, four days away. Not even the traditional two weeks' notice. Boom.

Linda froze her expression, not wanting to give this lackadaisical underling the satisfaction of seeing the true impact of her departure. But it was a wallop of a sucker punch that knocked the wind out of Linda's sails and sent her mind reeling.

It wasn't like Tricia was a star performer – she wasn't. But she adequately filled a hectic and important role on a busy team that was already stretched thin, and this promised heightened chaos and compounded workloads in the weeks to come.

*Better cancel those vacation days*, Linda thought as her jaw muscles tightened. She remained stoic as she asked, "Are you sure about this?"

It was mere filler, of course, because she already knew the answer, didn't need to listen and had lived this moment before. This wasn't the first time Linda had experienced a sudden departure over a video call on her laptop, without a physical presence. In fact, it was quite common across the company in recent years.

Most frequently, it was the younger generation populating the revolving door, never truly making a connection with their employer or colleagues, experiencing corporations as interchangeable blocks of busywork and disengaged clusters of flat, 2-D faces on computer monitors. The widespread transition to remote work might have allowed companies to slash real estate bills and recruit talent from much larger pools, but it also diminished loyalty and engagement. Employees could jump ship to countless alternatives without leaving home. They just logged into a different network from the sky. The commute time, workspace and company cafeteria remained the same. As much as Public Energy Corporation tried to build a virtual community and sense of family, it was never going to gel like the days of being housed together in a common office, where coworkers really got to know one another at lunches, the printer queue, the coffee line, happy hour and the spaces between meetings.

Linda missed being around other people. She was prone to feelings of imposter syndrome and needed the affirmation of working in a professional office setting. Without it, she struggled with self-doubt about her own legitimacy. She remembered the excitement of being part of an intimate colony of contagious activity and spontaneous conversations. Workers felt less isolated and more trusting, openly sharing laughter and tears, flirting and sometimes finding romance, airing out grievances in real time, and achieving advanced learning from being embedded with colleagues at all levels. Now the team clubhouse was gone, killed off by a pandemic that produced physical casualties in its onset and mental casualties in its wake. Too many people had forgotten how to interact in public spaces or withdrew into shells from which they still hadn't emerged.

Most of Linda's coworkers embraced working in sweatpants and ditching the commute. But Linda liked dressing up for the day. She even liked driving to the office. It created a healthy buffer separating work from home, a time reserved for listening to talk radio in the early years, then music CDs, and then podcasts. Without a morning commute, she simply slept in. Upon awakening, she felt anxious to start work right away because she was already living at the office. Her employer loomed, omnipresent, intruding on her private sanctuary. Her days were anchored in a confined space roughly the size of a prison cell, a hijacked den, silent and alone.

Linda's coworker interactions were now delegated to streaming video and audio, a long-distance call from beyond. Often, she had no idea where they were calling from, because in the end it didn't matter.

Tricia lived…somewhere downstate, a town near Champaign-Urbana. It was hours away from the company's downsized headquarters in Chicago's Loop, a presence reduced to a few floors in a high-rise where executives would occasionally congregate. Attempts were made to encourage the common workers to plug in at the site, but few took up the offer and many lived too far away. Linda found the environment barren and depressing.

Linda had met Tricia in person exactly once, at a two-day team-building event that somehow amplified the awkwardness of their unfamiliarity rather than solving it.

On the plus side, remote relationships removed any emotional attachment to departing employees. Linda's pains at this stage were purely professional.

"Well, we're very sorry to see you go, but we do wish you all the best." Linda delivered it like a speaking point, which it was.

Next she recited the logistics for terminating employment – some online forms to fill out, some notifications to be made, and a quick company career obituary to post on the intranet for the small number of people who would have interacted with Tricia and still remembered who she was in the parade of fleeting faces in corporate cyberspace.

Neither of them quite knew how to end the conversation, probably the last they would ever have. If they were experiencing this little drama in person, perhaps there would have been a hug, or at least a handshake. Instead, Tricia made a halfhearted wave at the camera.

"I wish you well, Linda. I know I'm leaving at a difficult time. I just… you know… This is what I want for myself. It's what I *need*."

"I understand," Linda said. All the bad feelings aside, she couldn't fault Tricia's choice. What Linda didn't understand was what she needed for herself.

★   ★   ★

*Call Me PLS.*

Linda stared at the instant message that popped up on her screen like a poke to the head. It came during a particularly drab Zoom meeting to discuss community outreach on the spring tree-trimming schedule to protect powerlines from vegetation growth. As a public relations manager for an electric utility company canvassing Chicago and much of northern Illinois, Linda was pulled into anything that required coherent communications, a reliable wordsmith in a sea of bureaucrats and engineers. There was nothing new or interesting about this rundown, it was a seasonal tradition, but at least it was painless, which was more than could be said about the sudden IM intrusion from Eleanor Birkstock, her ever-agitated boss.

Linda stared at the short text, studying it for more time than was necessary. Capital *M* on *me*? Egotistical. All caps *PLS*? Pushy. Abbreviating a six-letter word to three? Superficial efficiency.

Linda typed, *Sorry guys, gotta drop* into the call's chat, pressed *Leave Meeting*, then transitioned to messaging with Eleanor.

*ok*, she typed, a purposefully lowercase reply to her boss's urgent tone, a passive-aggressive flourish for the modern age.

Linda already knew the topic of the pending conversation. Despite telling Tricia to keep her resignation confidential for a few hours, word had gotten out. Linda planned to notify HR and her superiors after her string of back-to-back-to-back meetings. No doubt, Tricia refused to wait that long to tell her tiny circle of work friends. Why not defy her manager? Tricia had nothing to lose. She was already out the door.

Linda called Eleanor's cell phone. Eleanor was the Vice President of Marketing-PR Communications, a broad-shouldered woman bearing an eternally cantankerous disposition. She answered on the second ring.

There was a long silence, no hello. Then she released a heavy sigh. "Linda, Linda, Linda. What is happening to your team?"

"Tricia Welling?"

"Of course, Tricia Welling."

"She notified me earlier today that she's resigning. I was going to tell you right after—"

"Well, I know now. We need to get a plan in place. Two plans, really. One for getting that role filled as soon as possible and one to figure out why you keep losing people."

Linda wanted to fight back: it's the economy, it's the job market, it's the younger generation, *it's you and this dreary company*. But she graciously resisted.

"I'll contact the recruiter first thing in the morning."

"First thing *today*."

"Right, first thing today."

"You know our budget is under scrutiny, right?"

"I do. I'm aware." Linda was painfully aware – her team had already downsized from three direct reports to one, and Tricia had been the one. Now Linda had no backup, meaning she would absorb everything, including being on call for media inquiries twenty-four seven. At least she didn't have a social life to ruin.

"Sweetheart," said Eleanor, and it wasn't said sweetly, but in a sour tone of condescension. "I'm only looking out for your best interests. There will be another sweep of cuts. I know because Jack told me." Jack Campbell, the CEO. Eleanor liked to casually drop his first name like they were the best of buds. They weren't. "Open positions will be the first to go. It's much more bloodless than cutting live bodies, you know what I mean?"

"I do."

Then Linda's phone vibrated with an incoming call. *Great, it's one damn thing after another.* She grimaced inwardly. This was another thing to drive her crazy in the modern world – there were too many ways for people to reach her right away. The channels tangled and jabbed like some kind of prickly bush. There was no escape, nowhere to hide.

And this next call was going to be a doozy. Even worse than being scolded and insulted by Eleanor.

It was her ex. Or, as Linda liked to refer to him, X. He no longer deserved a name that included him with humanity.

Of course, Linda couldn't tell Eleanor she had to drop for another call, because it implied there were people and situations on the planet more important than her, and you just didn't do that.

So Linda wound up the call the best she could on Eleanor's terms: "I'll get ahold of the recruiter right now. I'm on it. Thank you."

"I'm serious, Linda."

"Me too. Contacting them now."

The call ended, and she hurried to catch the next one but it was too late.

X always gave up after three or four rings. He was a man of little patience.

Linda called him back, flipping down her laptop lid to hide the incessant march of incoming emails.

*Ping. Ping. Ping.*

Her home office was hardly an environment of peaceful solitude; it was a wide-open window for a million intrusions, allowing work and personal life to play together in some kind of mad blender.

"Hello, Linda," X said.

"Hello…" she responded, stopping cold of saying his name aloud. He knew who he was.

"Pardon the background noise. We're in a café, just sat down for dinner – been running around all day. Ah – hold on for a second."

She heard him mull over a wine menu. Diana, his new girlfriend, murmured in apparent agreement with his recommendation. Linda didn't quite catch the selection, but the garçon did. "Oui," his voice said faintly, thousands of miles away, a bit player in this small drama.

"How's Paris?" Linda asked. She didn't really want to hear an answer, but his wondrous adventures were already out in the open, spewed all over social media, heavily romanticized across affectionate posts and glorious pictures – for Diana's benefit or to feed his own brash ego, or maybe just to stab Linda in the heart a few more times.

X was happy to oblige her inquiry. "Well, it's been lovely," he said. "The City of Light. We've been busy, so much to see. We've been hitting up all the museums, seeing everything. It's much less crowded this time of year. We've been to the Louvre, and the Musée d'Orsay, the l'Orangerie. Saw an amazing ceramics exhibit. Yesterday, we took a boat cruise on the Seine. Beautiful day, it was sunny, a bit chilly but nothing like what you're going through in Chicago."

*Okay, that's enough*, she wanted to say. The world outside her window had lost all color for the past several weeks – white snow, gray skies.

After his cheery travelogue failed to elicit a response, he shifted to the point of his call. "Listen, I want you to know, I did what you told me."

*What was that?* thought Linda. *Go to hell?*

"The storage unit," he said.

"Oh, right," she said. That had surfaced during one of their earlier conversations – er, arguments. Linda had demanded he move all of his stuff out of the townhouse they shared in Rogers Park.

But he complained he had no space for it while he and Diana shacked up in her modest Logan Square apartment. The two of them were shopping for a luxury penthouse on Chicago's Gold Coast, and it was going to take time to find the right dream home.

"Then get a storage unit," she had told him. "I'm serious. I want it all out *now*."

"Or what, you're going to throw it out?"

"That would be tempting."

"You better not. I have very expensive tailored suits. I have high-end electronics. *I have collectibles*. My lawyer will be on your ass in a hot minute."

The notion of someone discarding his Louis Vuitton wardrobe, Bluetooth toys and hockey card collection must have continued to distress him, because now, all the way from Paris, he had arranged for a storage unit two miles from their townhome.

"It's paid for," he said, "by me. There's a key under your name. You just have to pick it up at the front desk. It's a big space, ready to go. You can fill it up to your heart's content. Just put my things in there neatly, okay?"

"I'll organize everything by size and color."

He chuckled. "That's funny." The background noise of café chatter was getting louder.

"Anything else?" she asked.

"No, that's it. I'll forward an email with all the information, the unit number. Are you good with that?"

"Yes," she said. "That would be special."

He didn't appreciate the sarcasm. "You know, I could have waited until I got back. I did this for you."

"Thank you for your incredible, selfless generosity."

"All right, this conversation is going downhill."

"What do you expect, calling me like this from a Paris café with your new girlfriend? How many times did *we* go to Paris?"

"I took you to the Cayman Islands."

"You had a business trip. I tagged along."

"I'm doing some business on this trip too."

Linda stopped and took a breath. They were sliding back into one of their idiotic, circular squabbles. It was pointless. The damage had been done. They had expressed themselves plenty of times before. She: He was a serial cheater. He: She lacked excitement and ambition. Not exactly a balanced trade-off of crimes but perfectly rational in his eyes. He liked women with wild dreams and voracious curiosity.

Linda possessed dreams and curiosity once, but somehow they had slid from her with age, like a shed skin.

As Linda tried to maneuver the call to a more cordial wrap-up, a text message popped up on her phone, overlapping the current screen.

*HAPPY HOUR TODAY? RICKY'S. PLEASE BE AVAILABLE.*

It was her friend Caroline. Perhaps the only bigger sad sack in Linda's life than Linda herself.

Caroline had recently been laid off from her job as a paralegal at a downtown law firm, replaced by artificial intelligence. Instead of eight paralegals, the firm now employed one manager to basically oversee and validate the churn of AI product. Caroline had taken the blow hard – she hadn't just lost a job, she had lost a career. And now she was falling back on drinking too much.

Linda knew she had to be there for her old friend. This relationship was true and loyal. They had known each other since college.

*Yes, what time?* Linda texted Caroline while X rambled on about storing his belongings in quality plastic tubs with lids, no cardboard, no bags, and labeling them so he would know where to find everything. In a monotone, Linda voiced agreement to his every request to bring the call to a faster conclusion. X thanked her and told her he wanted things to go smoothly for both of them. She said, "Great. Have fun." After a click, the festive Paris ambience in her ear was replaced with cold silence.

Caroline texted: *5:30. THANK YOU.*

Linda replied: *See you there.*

She put down the phone. A drink sounded good.

She looked out the window at the snow and ice and still-life streets of well-worn slush. She sighed, wondering what awaited her next, and then flipped open her laptop to see.

★   ★   ★

Linda was late to happy hour.

Work intervened to scrape extra time from the end of the day. Then the snowfall resumed with big, gentle flakes, and digging her car out of the alley, already a thirty-minute proposition, became a task better left for another time. But she would not let her old friend down.

Linda pulled on her boots, mittens and heavy coat and trudged the six blocks to the Metra station. She waited on the platform and watched the silent snowfall with other bundled travelers as the January wind stung her face. On the train, she texted Caroline.

*Be there soon. Sorry I'm late.*

*Already drank your margarita,* came the reply.

"Oh, Caroline," Linda said softly.

When she arrived at Ricky's, the bar was half-empty, a cavern of low lights and muted conversations. She found Caroline off to one side, seated at a round table by a brick wall, beneath a framed, faded poster of the 1985 Chicago Bears.

"Sorry," Linda said, opening up her coat and grabbing a stool.

"What'll you have?"

"Let me get settled first." Linda's cheeks felt hot, her nose drippy. She wiped it gracelessly with a tissue from her purse. "Crappy weather." She adjusted her butt on the stool and let out a heavy sigh.

"Your hair's wet," Caroline said. Her voice was drunk, childlike. She was a petite, bespectacled woman with curly red hair she could not tame so it was kept cropped short. In college, some of the meaner guys teased her that she looked like a little boy.

"Wet hair. That's the least of my worries," Linda said. "I had an employee quit on me today. Husbands, employees, they all run away from me."

"At least you have a job."

"Come work for me," Linda offered.

"No, no, no," Caroline murmured. "That's not my gig."

Linda laughed. "Hell, it's not mine either. You know that."

"So what happened to us?"

Linda gave it a long thought. "I don't think college prepared us for reality. It set us up for dreams."

"I was going to be a hotshot lawyer," Caroline said. "And you were going to be a hotshot investigative reporter. That was it. There were no alternatives, no Plan B. We were set."

Linda looked down at the water accumulating on the floor from her boots and coat. "You can't predict where the world is headed. The internet took over and newspapers took a dive. Journalists went into teaching or technical writing or PR."

"Instead of becoming a lawyer, I became a paralegal. Now I'm a nothing."

"You're not nothing."

"I've been replaced by a robot. What does that make me? I'm not even human."

"Stop it."

"Did you know an AI chatbot took the bar exam? It passed, ninetieth percentile. The robots are coming after you too. They're using AI to write communications. I read about that."

"Great, I don't need any robots in the mix. My drafts already go through too many hands." It was the corporate machine – everything was written by committee to speak in the voice of an institution. It was why she no longer saved clippings like in her journalism days – aside from the fact there were no physical clippings anymore. Her final drafts no longer sounded human. Maybe AI was just another step in this direction.

"It's all because of the pandemic," Caroline said. "Suddenly everyone had to work remotely and rely on computers. It worked so well, now the computers are taking over. Companies are just cutting out the middleman."

"And woman," Linda said.

Caroline didn't smile. "I'm tired, Linda," she said after a long swallow of her drink. "I don't know what I want. I'm too old to be a lawyer now. I wasted too much time being a paralegal."

"That's not true."

"I'm fifty. You're fifty."

"Thanks for reminding me."

"I have no money, Linda."

Linda reached across the table and put her hand on Caroline's hand. Caroline flinched for a moment at the contact, then settled.

Linda looked her in the eyes. "You know I'm willing to lend you money, Caroline. I *want* to."

"I'm not going to borrow money from my friend," Caroline said. "Who knows when I'd be able to pay it back? What am I going to do? Okay, I could work at McDonald's. Or I could work *here*." She lifted her hand to wave at the bar interior. "Maybe I'd get a discount on drinks. Which reminds me…where's our guy?"

"You've had enough," Linda said. "You want to fall on the ice and break your neck?"

"Yes."

"Oh, stop it."

Linda was used to conversations with Caroline sinking into self-pity sessions, but this one was exhausting her. She had her own self-pity to deal with.

*What a pair we make*, thought Linda. *No wonder we became such good friends in college.* They had even double-dated with interesting young men. Caroline ultimately never married and claimed to have cut off dating at forty. Linda didn't know if having a partner would lift Caroline's spirits or just make things worse for her. Marital bliss hadn't panned out for Linda, that was for sure.

Linda returned to the one problem she could help address: money. "Take a loan from me," she said. "Pay the rent. Study for the bar. Pass the bar. Become a lawyer. Then you can assign all your work to AI and get paid for it."

Caroline smiled. "Yeah. Make the robots work for me." Then her eyes narrowed, and her voice took on a conspiratorial tone. "You know, it all started with ATMs. Took away the jobs of bank tellers. The machines are taking over. No-good little robots. Stupid high tech. I'm going to blow up an ATM on the way home."

"I wouldn't advise that."

"Boom!" said Caroline, pulling her hand away from Linda and slapping both palms on the table. It was loud enough to draw looks from the few other patrons scattered about.

"I'm going to write you a check," Linda said, reaching for her purse.

"Don't."

"Just hold on to it until morning, that's all I ask. See how you feel then."

"I'm going to rip it up right now."

Linda wrote out a check for twenty-five hundred dollars. She couldn't really afford it, having lost the main money-maker in her life, but she deeply wanted to provide some fuel for Caroline's course correct.

If Linda couldn't help herself, at least she could help someone else.

She handed the check to Caroline, and Caroline didn't even look at it before ripping it up and stuffing the pieces into her empty margarita glass with the melting ice.

"God damn it, Caroline."

"I know you need this money just as much as I do."

"You're impossible."

Caroline nodded glumly. "I'm sorry," she said. "I know you're just trying to help."

"You will get past this."

When a server came by, Linda immediately ordered them both Pepsis. She no longer felt like having a drink – booze was just another depressant after all – and she needed to cut Caroline off.

Caroline complained but relented.

Her mood softened.

Linda gently steered the conversation to other things, namely the weather, and blamed it for putting the entire city in a grumbly mood. "What's it been, like twenty straight days without sunshine? No wonder everyone's got their head down."

After a while, Caroline said she was tired and wanted to go home. Linda insisted on walking her back to her Ravenswood apartment. They stepped through the crusty snow chunks as wavering flakes continued to fall. They hugged at the entrance to Caroline's building.

"We'll get through this," Linda said with hope for both of them.

★   ★   ★

Saturday marked twenty-one straight days of gray Chicagoland skies and one more fresh coat of snow. Linda spent the weekend gathering X's belongings and consolidating them in one part of the townhouse, freeing the other spaces of his presence. It was a narrow, two-story building with the bedroom, bathroom and den/home office upstairs, and living room and kitchen downstairs. She separated everything into piles near the front door, keeping it neat without going overboard. She built accumulations of clothes, shoes, toiletries, sports memorabilia, his vanity collections of premium watches and sunglasses, and a category for general nonsense, like the shiny, sleek carbonator for perfecting the craft of brewing seltzer water (*really?*) that he used once or twice. She was reminded of how freely he spent money, which was his right, given his ample salary and bonuses as a successful investment banker. He liked living the good life – or at least exhibiting the good life.

Throughout their marriage, he sought out the latest high-tech gadgets, one of many passions they did not share. Linda gathered them into their own section: a virtual reality headset, sports fitness tracker, cushy wireless headphones, selfie stick, portable gaming console and $3,000 drone. Some of the items were still in their original boxes, barely opened, impulse purchases.

On a whim, he had also wired the entire townhouse to an online hub that controlled various lights and appliances from an app. "We're a smart home," he said proudly.

"I'd prefer a dumb home," she responded. It was unnecessarily complicated and consolidated. She had insisted that the manual switches and controls continue to function as an option. She never used the app.

Not all of his belongings made her surly. Some still held positive memories, like his old sweaters, but the good times attached to them were as faded as the colors.

In between rounds of transporting and sorting his stuff, she handled the occasional work email. Ever since the pandemic encouraged companies to turn employees' homes into offices, it also meant these offices were open for business twenty-four seven. Most of this weekend's correspondence was related to logistics for quickly posting the job opening, working with HR's templates and boilerplate language to highlight the exciting culture and career opportunities awaiting at an exemplary employer.

On Sunday, as she dug deeper into a closet to bring out more of her ex-husband's miscellanea, she discovered a gray steel box with secure latches that she assumed contained another high-end watch. Instead, flipping the lid, she found a gun.

"What the... Really?"

A small pistol rested comfortably in a foam liner.

She quickly shut the lid and latched it again. She had no knowledge whatsoever that her husband had owned a firearm all these years. But it fit with his breezy machismo, another collectible. They had never experienced any real trouble to warrant owning one – no break-ins or hold-ups. Still, living in a big city with big-city crime might have been all the justification he needed.

She probed farther into the depths of the closet shelf and found a box of bullets. It creeped her out to even hold it and feel them rattle inside. All of this was *definitely* being relegated to the storage unit. She wasn't sure if there were rules about not stashing guns and bullets in the facility, but she would not read the brochure to find out.

Linda added her ex-husband's weaponry to the pile of unclassifieds that included the premium water carbonator. It belonged with the other unnecessary trinkets.

★    ★    ★

Early Monday morning, Linda's phone buzzed her awake from the nightstand, rattling against the hardwood.

It was still dark outside. She grasped for the phone, looked at the time (5:37 a.m.), then the caller (Caroline), then the text message. It read:

*I wake up to Monday morning without purpose. The world moves on. I have nothing to offer nobody. I am nothing.*

Linda's first reaction was irritation. It was more of Caroline's downbeat doldrums. But that feeling was quickly replaced by a rolling wave of panic.

*Why are you talking that way?* Linda texted back quickly, swinging her feet to sit on the edge of the bed.

When several minutes passed without a response, Linda tried calling her. No one picked up. She made several repeated attempts.

*Damn!* Linda jumped into action. She pulled on quick clothes – jeans, sweatshirt, socks – and ran for the door. She picked up her boots along the way, stuffing her feet inside them.

Linda plunged into the predawn darkness, taking big and awkward steps through the snow to get to her car, a rounded lump covered in the most recent snowfall. It was held hostage by winter. She hurried to the rear of her townhouse and yanked open the rickety door to a makeshift shed under the back patio. She pulled out a red plastic snow shovel. She began chopping at the piles pushed against her back bumper, throwing the snow to one side, but it quickly became obvious there was no way she could free her car in short order.

"*Shit!*" she screamed at the world.

Linda whipped off her mittens, pulled out her phone and quickly opened the Uber app. She had barely used rideshare services before – barely understood them – but now was the time.

"Please, please, please."

There was someone ten minutes away. She ordered the car to pick her up and take her to Caroline's apartment.

As she waited, she texted and dialed Caroline over and over.

"Please answer me!" she shouted into voicemail.

*Please don't do anything stupid*, she quietly prayed in her head.

A chubby, bearded man in a puffy vest who might have been stoned picked her up in a blue Toyota.

"Please hurry, I think my friend is in danger."

He simply nodded.

There was little traffic as the driver sped along Ashland Avenue. Linda thanked him as he accelerated through yellow lights.

When they arrived at Caroline's building, Linda nearly fell out of the car in her mad dash to get to the front door. She rang Caroline's buzzer in long, urgent stretches, to no response.

*She's got to be in there!*

But then the realization hit: What if she's not?

Linda turned in a circle, eyes searching desperately. Then she looked downward.

She saw small, fresh footprints in the snow. Could it be little, petite Caroline? Linda followed their direction, headed west. What was west?

And then she knew.

It caused Linda to scream out in anguish.

*"Don't do it!"* she shouted.

She ran down the sidewalk as quickly as she could, arms out for balance, following the small footprints that became lost in a montage of other footprints. Her head filled with a horrible news item that Caroline had brought up a few weeks prior, talking about it at length with morbid fascination until Linda told her to please stop.

A middle-aged man had stepped onto the tracks in front of a speeding commuter train and committed suicide right at the height of rush hour, creating shock and chaos for the entire community, fracturing a calm evening with sirens and snarled traffic and drawing crowds of ghoulish onlookers.

In the darkness, Linda could just barely make out a small figure ahead, standing firm at the top of an incline, not moving, waiting for something unseen that rumbled with growing intensity from not far away.

The next few minutes were a frantic blur. Linda screamed Caroline's name. She fought her way up the snowy hill toward the tracks but kept sliding back, losing traction. There was no one else around to help her, just sleepy dark buildings and occasional distant cars.

Despite the cries, Caroline didn't turn to acknowledge her old friend. All bonds had been cut. The past had been replaced by this future. She simply stood still and alone, without emotion, as if possessed. The train arrived and struck her and blood sprayed all over the clean white snow. The huge sound of brakes being applied to a speeding mass of machinery filled the air, too late to prevent the human casualty in its path.

# CHAPTER TWO

Linda entered a state of numbness. She returned to work a few days later, receptive to its dull distractions, immersing herself in the condensed universe of a fourteen-inch laptop monitor.

HR posted Tricia's open role and almost immediately a flood of candidates responded for Linda to screen for possible interviews. She read dozens of cover letters and resumes with accompanying writing samples. She was the initial judge and jury, assigning individuals to one of three folders: YES, NO and MAYBE.

She gave the process her full focus to crowd out the horrific memories of Monday: witnessing her friend's violent death, undergoing interrogation from blunt, uncaring police, and then delivering devastating phone calls to Caroline's immediate family members.

She cried during every one of those conversations. Even as a professional wordsmith, she could not find the words to lessen the impact.

X heard about the incident through a mutual friend and called to offer his sympathy. His sympathy lasted for about two minutes, and then he began asking about the storage unit and if she needed help moving the heavy stuff.

"No," she said firmly. She hadn't had the time to cart it over yet, and her car was still snowed in. Why did it matter? He was still in Paris.

No one at work knew Caroline, so nobody asked for the gory details or offered a virtual shoulder to cry on. The most that Linda told her boss was, "My best friend died unexpectedly" to warrant a couple of days off. She could have negotiated for more – her nerves were a wreck – but she also had to dive back into the hiring process before the bean counters concluded it was cheaper to have Linda perform two jobs.

During interviews, she tried her best to be animated and upbeat to represent the company in such a positive light that no candidate could possibly turn her down. It was acting, and acting required extra energy she could barely muster. But she pushed forward. She took her anxiety meds. She wore one of her nicest business blouses on top with pajama pants on the bottom, well out of the camera's range. She felt like one of those old flipbooks where you could mix and match outfits and create outrageous combinations.

Online recruiting made applying for jobs as easy as buying books on Amazon. The quick-click technology and lack of geographical restrictions meant there was no shortage of applicants. It also loaded her inbox with piles of jobseeker spam with irrelevant credentials. Did they even read the job profile and required experience? She spent hours weed whacking, eliminating obvious rejects ranging from the wildly unqualified to alleged writers with resumes, cover letters and samples riddled with painful grammatical errors and typos, including misspelling the name of the company they were applying to.

She was also leery of job histories that showed a lack of focus and loyalty – people who regularly switched employers and even careers every year or two. HR dismissed her concerns, telling her this was the modern labor pool, driven by a restless new generation and the wonders of technology. It made Linda feel like an old fart for sticking with the same company for most of her adult life. Had she 'settled' out of lazy convenience or her own insecurities? It certainly wasn't for career growth. Perhaps it was simply the reliability. Utility companies offered steady, stable employment with good benefits. They were monopolies providing an essential service to a captive audience, charging the rates they needed to remain profitable. Less sexy and innovative than a startup, but less unpredictable too.

Linda worked with HR to line up online interviews with the most promising candidates, and then the next round of filtering took place. Some of the folks looked great on paper but were a disappointing presence on video, struggling to assemble coherent sentences, or not even faking any enthusiasm for this new opportunity. It was rough to keep conversations going to fill the hour when she identified a 'no' in the first ten minutes.

One poor older gentleman had a terrible internet connection, and the signal dropped several times before both parties gave up. Linda wondered if she should add 'Good Wi-Fi' to the list of job requirements.

Every day, she filled out a series of candidate interview booklets, asking mostly the same questions, occasionally breaking out into doodles halfway through the pages if the candidate was an obvious mismatch.

Eleanor checked in regularly to see how things were going, reminding her of the urgency of filling the role ASAP. The company expense ratio was under increased scrutiny by regulators and shareholders, and cuts had already taken place to reduce the number of vendors. A longtime graphic arts firm had been let go with the justification 'We can just use AI for design.' The next annual report would have a cover generated by a few quick clicks on a sophisticated online image-creation tool.

Linda had accumulated only two or three decent prospects for second interviews – nothing remarkable, graded 'OK' on the booklet covers – when Alison Smith arrived like a beaming ray of sunshine cutting through dreary gray clouds.

Alison immediately set herself apart from the rest: enthusiastic without being overbearing, smart without being smarmy, articulate without pretentiousness. Linda had already been intrigued by the polish of her resume, the colorful prose of her cover letter, and the razor-sharp proficiency of her writing samples. She had a smooth, pleasing personality to match the quality of her submissions.

After toiling through too many awkward, not-quite-right interviews, this one stirred definite good feelings. Linda could see herself working alongside this individual every day.

Alison was young but not inexperienced. She was pretty, with brown hair that fell to curls on her shoulders, big brown eyes and perfect skin. Linda could already hear Eleanor saying, 'Put that one in front of the media, she's easy on the eyes.' A lot of the public relations work involved dealing with local media over common utility issues like outages, rate hikes and conservation tips.

Linda gently drilled Alison with the standard questions: 'tell me about' prompts for personal proof points around project management, innovation, collaboration, autonomy, leadership and learning. Alison defined her personal career goals with such eloquence that Linda wrote down her words partly to motivate herself.

When asked, "Why would you like to work at Public Energy Corporation?", the answer was almost poetic as she marveled over the powerful presence of electricity in everyday life, from homes to schools to commerce to entertainment. She spoke about its massive reach as an enabler of technological advancements, the lifeblood of modern society.

The only question where Alison faltered – not necessarily failed, but made a surprising choice – came right after Linda asked about her strengths, following up with a customary question about weaknesses.

Alison grew unusually silent.

Then she said, "I don't believe I have any weaknesses."

Linda shifted to a related question to help draw something out. "Tell me about a time you made a mistake. And what you learned from that mistake, to get better."

Alison blinked. "A mistake?"

"Yes, even a small one. Doesn't have to be big. Anything." *C'mon, I'm making it easy for you*, thought Linda.

"I'm always getting better," Alison said. "But I don't make mistakes. I take errors very seriously."

Linda admired Alison's confidence – even envied it – but wished there had been at least a small flicker of humility. *Nobody's perfect, kid.*

It was the only wrong note of the conversation. It was subsequently eradicated by an unexpected compliment that Linda had never heard before from any candidate or coworker.

"I read your journalism clippings. They were really good."

Linda rocked back in her chair, stunned, then trying not to look stunned. "Really?"

"I wanted to get to know you better ahead of this interview. I found them online, your work with the *Times*, the *Herald* and those great feature articles in *Chicagoland* magazine. The one about contaminants in the drinking water…and the south side land development controversy… and the one about corruption in City Hall. It's excellent reporting. It really made me want to work for you, more than some of the other companies I applied at."

"I'm…I'm flattered," Linda said. "I guess some of those stories are still out there. I was younger then, my pre-PR days. I studied journalism."

"Me too," Alison said. "I also started in journalism and then moved over to public relations."

"Because of the better money?" Linda smiled.

"Because of the opportunity," Alison said.

Linda finished off the hour with a cheery pitch for her employer, selling Alison on an employment opportunity that she herself didn't totally believe in, and there was some guilt associated with that.

*What if she comes here and hates it?*

When the interview concluded, Linda promised she would be in touch. They exchanged cordial goodbyes, and then Alison disappeared from her screen.

Linda wanted her back.

Alison invigorated her at a time when she needed renewed energy in her life.

She immediately contacted the recruiter and asked him to set up a second interview, adding Eleanor, a Marketing colleague, and the PR department's HR rep to the mix.

"Any other candidates you want to bring in for a follow-up?" asked the recruiter.

"No."

Then she wrote on the cover of Alison's interview booklet:

*YES.*

★   ★   ★

A grid of postage stamp-sized heads populated Linda's monitor, collectively staring forward as Eleanor discussed the latest consumer research at the weekly Marketing-PR team meeting. As Eleanor spoke, Linda's thoughts continued to drift back to Alison Smith. How many companies did she apply to? What if someone made a better, bigger, faster offer?

Unlike Alison's eager, fresh attitude, the faces in the online staff meeting lacked engagement and enthusiasm. They attended passively, as if viewing a television program. They didn't interact or say much. Many remained on mute.

The Marketing-PR team represented multiple time zones. Remote work had blurred office hours, stretching the day to accommodate everyone and doing away with a common lunch break. As a result, employees typically ate in front of one another, dribbling crumbs into keyboards, or turned off their cameras to wolf something down in haste as their corporate profile photos provided cover.

Sometimes Linda looked across the rows and columns of faces in a meeting and wondered, *Who are these people?*

To address the detachedness of dispersed employees, the company attempted a heavy-handed online cultural campaign to build virtual relationships, but it was widely ignored by employees who were too busy engaging with their real online communities of friends and family on Facebook, Instagram and other universal platforms. Some of them spent hours on social media. It didn't go unnoticed.

The company was well aware of the potential for employees to sneak personal activities into the workday, even second jobs. One colleague bragged to Linda about taking long naps and watching movies on the company's dime. It was the type of abuse the company wanted to shut down, turning to technology for a solution.

Halfway through today's meeting, as the rows of eyelids drooped, Eleanor brought her crew back to life with an update on a new HR initiative that had been rumored and now graduated to reality.

"It's called POMS," she said proudly, staring into the masses to see who released the biggest reaction. "Productivity Online Monitoring System. It's a new technology platform to ensure we are being efficient with our time. Think of it as an equalizer – none of us wants to be working harder because someone else isn't working hard enough. It's very simple, really. There's a color code that registers online activity at the individual level. Green indicates you are actively engaged with company colleagues, assets and resources – your intranet browser, your email account, collaboration tools, our suite of office software, streaming meetings and so on. If you leave the grid for a period of fifteen minutes or more, it goes yellow. At thirty minutes, it goes red. Red is not a good color. It is only acceptable outside of regular work hours and during the lunch period for your time zone."

Linda wanted to roll her eyes, but remained stoic. Others were not shy about expressing shock and exasperation.

It was an inevitable development. Eleanor had already secured access to the online calendars of her direct reports to monitor them. Linda sometimes concocted fake meetings to ensure her days never appeared below capacity.

"Wait..." said one of the newer, younger Marketing employees that Linda barely knew. Her name was Sasha. "What about time to think? I mean, sometimes I just need time to get my thoughts together. I'm not always using my mouse and keyboard. If I'm thinking through a problem, or to be creative, and my light goes yellow or red, do I get in trouble?"

"Use your best judgment," said Eleanor with an ominous smile.

Cecilia, an African American manager in Marketing Sponsorships, one of the coworkers Linda had known the longest and considered a true friend, fired off an instant message directly to Linda in all caps.

*WTF. REALLY?*

Linda responded: *Big Brother is watching!*

*More like Big Mother.*

Linda laughed and even though her mic was muted, the guffaw showed up on screen.

"Is something funny?" Eleanor asked.

Linda shook her head no and stifled any further giggles.

It really wasn't funny at all.

★ ★ ★

After the meeting, Cecilia called up Linda to further their derision of POMS. Linda first got to know Cecilia when they worked together in Public Energy Corporation's deluxe headquarters campus in Chicago. They shared conversations at each other's desks and in company corridors. They engaged in actual watercooler chats. They hung out together at lunch and at happy hour.

Then came the pandemic. It separated them for close to two years. The return to office was delayed repeatedly and then canceled altogether. PEC extended remote work as a way of life. The company retained only a few floors of its landmark downtown building to offer a 'hybrid' option for employees who still desired an external workplace. Few people bothered to show up, especially when the company refused to cover parking fees and train tickets. The handful of times Linda visited the space, it was mostly empty, offering simple desktops with plug-in outlets, roughly the equivalent of grabbing a table and Wi-Fi signal at Starbucks or McDonald's. She felt like an outsider, requiring a guest pass to enter.

Cecilia and Linda rarely saw each other in person anymore. It was mostly video chats like this one. Cecilia was very tall, a former college basketball player, a physical characteristic unrecognized on Zoom calls, where everybody appeared to be the same height. She had a healthy sarcastic tone that Linda appreciated, and she had been a sympathetic ear when Linda's marriage began to crumble.

"Thanks for your text. I haven't laughed like that in a long time," Linda said.

"Eleanor thought we were laughing at her."

"Well, we were, weren't we?"

"You laugh or you cry."

Cecilia's expression turned serious. "So...how are you doing?"

Linda sighed. "Surviving."

"No, really. I see you in these meetings... You just look sad most of the time."

"I don't hide it real well?"

"You do, but I notice. I know your face."

"Maybe I should get a new face."

"I'm serious."

Linda nodded. "I know. It's been... One of my oldest friends from college died. She took her life. It was sudden, and I'm still... It's still reverberating." Linda didn't want to recount the details. It was too painful and also felt like an intrusion on Caroline's privacy, although Caroline's choice of standing on railroad tracks was something of a public display.

"I'm sorry," Cecilia said.

"They say bad things come in threes, right? My husband leaves me, my employee leaves me, and my best friend...leaves everything."

After a long silence, Cecilia asked if she was lonely.

"I don't know," Linda said. "Maybe. Spending every day isolated in this townhouse, with this crummy weather, doesn't help."

"Are you dating?"

Linda smiled shyly. "No, no. I just turned fifty..."

"That means nothing. My mom's out there dating, and she's sixty-three."

"If she's as pretty as you are..."

"Knock it off. You're attractive."

Linda appreciated the compliment. She found it difficult to assess her own looks – she had a plain face, flat brown hair and a decent figure for her age. Her skin showed wrinkles around her eyes and mouth. X leaving for a younger model hurt her confidence, and life in general had slouched her shoulders. She felt well beyond her prime, out of the dating pool for twenty years.

"How am I going to find a date?" she asked.

"There are single guys at work."

"No, no. Get real. Office romances are dead. No one lives near one another anymore. Besides, I don't need more reminders of work."

"Remember how Howard used to flirt with you?" Cecilia giggled.

"He's married." Howard was Senior Vice President of Operations, someone she often partnered with on PR efforts, everything from nuclear power messaging to storm outage communications. He acted openly interested in her, which was flattering because he was handsome and friendly, but she wasn't going to wreck his marriage. He would have to divorce first and then...

Linda shook the notion out of her head. It was a stupid fantasy. They hadn't even seen each other in person for ages...not since the last annual team-building event, where the agenda was so self-consciously crowded no one had time to socialize.

"What about online dating?" asked Cecilia.

"Seriously?"

"You're recruiting an employee online. Why not recruit a boyfriend online too?"

"How does that work? Do they submit resumes?"

Cecilia laughed. "They post profiles. And pictures."

"Do you know anyone who's done it?"

"Sure, lots of people. I know a couple who met that way and got married."

"What about creeps and psychos?"

"You're going to find those everywhere."

Linda sighed. "True. I guess I should get with the times."

"Give it a chance."

"I'll have to find a good photo. And write about myself in a way that sounds interesting. Hah."

"Just be you. Don't try to be anyone else."

"I wouldn't mind being someone else."

"No, be authentic," Cecilia said. "The world needs more of that."

★　　★　　★

Caroline's funeral service took place in a small Christian chapel inside a funeral home on the city's north-west side.

Getting there was a task, thanks to the latest dump of snow that refused to melt. She again tried to dig out her Nissan from the alley. The car resembled an igloo. She gave up after ten minutes, fearing she would be late. She called for an Uber again. It was getting expensive.

Linda arrived with minutes to spare. Excluding the minister, funeral home director and staff, Linda counted eleven in attendance, mostly immediate family members. On Facebook, Caroline listed 493 'friends'.

Caroline's mangled remains had been cremated to ashes, and Linda tried not to think about it, holding firm with an image of Caroline's physical presence during happier times. Linda had prepared an elegant tribute to her friend to read from the podium to follow remembrances from relatives. The others in the room seemed to keep a distance from Linda, perhaps afraid of being in close proximity to the person who witnessed Caroline's gruesome demise, as if it created a toxic aura.

Linda never got to her turn to speak. Halfway through Caroline's sister's happy childhood sibling memories, the phone in Linda's purse began vibrating.

She ignored it until it stopped, then peeked at the screen.

It was a missed call from Eleanor, immediately followed by a text: *ULTRA URGENT. PLEASE CALL.*

Linda wanted to ignore it, but pissing off her boss during a period of budget cuts would not be a wise choice, so she whispered "Excuse me" a few times and shuffled out of the pew and up an aisle to the front lobby. She found an empty, adjacent room with couches and chairs for consultations and closed herself inside, returning the call.

"Eleanor, I'm at a—"

"Listen, you are needed immediately. I don't want this to spin out of control. You know about the Commission?"

"I know they were—"

"Well, it's out. It's public. We're getting media calls. Two safety violations. A corroded water pipe and an incident of marijuana use inside the plant. Both are very serious. We need message points. We need you to get ahead of this, reach out to reporters – proactive, before they start coming up with their own conclusions."

Linda simply said, "Yes." She had been preparing for this ever since she learned it was a possibility. The Nuclear Regulatory Commission had discovered maintenance issues at one of the company's downstate nuclear power plants. It involved the piping for water to cool the fuel rods, a critical safety measure. Then, to add icing to the cake, a plant operator failed a drug test without proper disclosure. Two separate incidents, but they added up to a pattern of carelessness that would no doubt alarm the general public. Formal citations had been issued.

"Can you get on this right away?"

"Well – I'm at a funeral."

Eleanor groaned. "Can you – can you just break away and get this done? I'm sorry, Linda, but this is why you need a backup. This is why I've been bugging you to fill that open role. Why is it taking so long?"

"I've been interviewing. I've looked at hundreds of resumes."

"Then hire someone! Do it! In the meantime, get those message points to Legal, get sign-off as quickly as possible, and start going through our media contacts. If I see a single 'could not be reached for comment,' I'm not the only one who will be coming down on you." She then rattled off the names of various top executives, including the CEO.

"Okay, I'm on it."

"You have your laptop with you?"

She chose the honest answer. "No."

"Linda!"

Eleanor expected everyone to be accompanied by their laptops at all times, like a seventeenth-century prisoner shackled by ball and chain.

"I'm at a funeral, Eleanor."

"Crisis doesn't care." It was one of Eleanor's favorite expressions, especially since everything was a crisis in her eyes.

"I'm going home right now."

"Thank you. I'm sorry. But this needs to be done."

By the time the phone call ended, Linda could hear music, movement and murmuring voices coming from the chapel. The service was over.

★   ★   ★

Linda spent the rest of the day back in her home office, furiously writing, securing approvals, then conversing with reporters. All these years later, it still felt strange and uncomfortable to be on the other side. She was a PR shill peddling spin and bullshit. She was her own original nemesis from the early days of her career as one of the investigative journalists asking the probing questions. The media grilled her pretty good this time, but she stuck with the official company statement, promising to co-operate with the NRC while touting the 'industry-leading' quality of the company's safety initiatives and training. The compound adjective in quotes was a mandatory inclusion, although not necessarily provable.

She knew the coverage would still be negative, and she would be called out for it, but, really, it wasn't a positive story and you couldn't sugarcoat it.

Eleanor's background was in marketing, where you could more easily manage the brand, so she expected the same level of control in public relations. She didn't understand that news outlets did more than post press releases.

After Linda concluded the final media call, she immediately dialed the recruiter.

"Hire Alison Smith," she demanded in no uncertain terms.

"What about the second interview?"

"Not needed."

"What about the background check?"

"Don't worry. It's fine."

"Are you sure?"

"I'm positive."

"But a second interview—"

"Override it. This is an order from my VP." Actually, it wasn't an explicit instruction from Eleanor, but Linda knew it was one she would agree with.

"Usually people want some additional screening."

"Alison's the one. I know it. She's far and away the best candidate, and I've looked at hundreds. We can't wait. Put in an offer, as high as we can go in the salary band. We'd like her to start as soon as possible. Got it?"

"Well…okay." The HR rep didn't want to argue. He defaulted to timid accommodation.

"Thank you," Linda said. She felt a small wave of relief. She would get her backup employee *and* get Eleanor off her back. Win-win.

Linda left her chair. She paced the eight-by-eight home office space, creating little circles on the carpet, trying to burn off the aching anxiety that still clung to her with deep hooks.

★　　★　　★

That night, Linda experienced her worst nightmare in recent memory. Her feet were encased in snow and ice. She couldn't pull them out. Darkness surrounded her, denying context. She was alone. She tried crying out for help, but failed to produce a sound. Her skin felt cold.

Then she heard a heavy chugging sound in the distance. She couldn't see what it was, even as it grew louder and closer. The noise that filled her ears wasn't human or animal. It was machine.

Then she realized: a train was pounding toward her, shaking the ground.

She stood frozen on railroad tracks, ankle-deep in white cement. Her arms waved uselessly. Her legs wouldn't move at all. She couldn't scream. She could only brace for the inevitable impact.

The invisible force unleashed an explosive roar, and she woke up, shouting and gasping, soaked in sweat and drenched in fear. Then she cried, releasing the tears she never cried at the funeral service.

# CHAPTER THREE

In her first week, Alison proved herself worthy of the immediate hire. Linda knew she was taking a risk by acting so quickly. A crafty bait and switch was always possible – someone who presented themselves perfectly and then became a dud in action. The writing samples could have been nurtured to excellence by a third-party editor. Hidden flaws could always exist below the surface – like an inability to meet deadlines or work well with others. Ordinarily Linda would conduct multiple interviews and include colleagues for extra perspective, but not this time. Linda had also skipped the ritual of reaching out to prior employers for references. Eleanor had made it clear the open position could be snatched away at any moment, and the resulting burden would land squarely on Linda's shoulders. There was no time to waste.

Fortunately, Alison hit the ground running. It was immediately apparent she was brighter and smoother than Tricia, who could be immature. Alison remained a bit stiff and formal, not yet loosened up by her acceptance, but that kind of thaw usually took time. Public Energy Corporation could be an intimidating place. Alison seemed pleased with her job and unfailingly polite, sharing sentiments like, "I'm happy to be here. I'm glad to be working with you."

It made Linda feel good about herself.

Linda worked with HR on the quick shipment of a company laptop and welcome kit to Alison's apartment in Tulsa, Oklahoma. In addition to fully loaded tech, she received the usual swag – company t-shirt, mug and corporate vision book. Alison's first week was dedicated to consuming online orientation courses for newbies and joining various department and team meetings, where Linda would make the introductions and a screen full of strangers would greet her. Linda cc'd Alison on several workstreams in progress not tied to any immediate action items but intended to introduce her to the types of projects that would eventually come her way. They had one-on-one meetings to go over org charts, enter performance goals into the system and tour the intranet. Linda also provided templates and resources that would help support and inform her future assignments.

Even though it had been the norm for years, Linda felt weird about hiring someone without ever meeting them in person. She promised Alison there would be opportunities to get together for real, but there was no way of knowing when, with all but the most necessary travel cut from the budget.

With some prodding, Linda got Alison to talk about her personal life. She wanted the intimate insights that HR purposefully discouraged from the interview process to avoid claims that they wrongly influenced the decision-making process.

Alison shared that she was solo, living alone without a partner, pets or nearby relatives. She revealed in plain tones that her parents had been killed in an auto accident when she was small. Shocked, Linda offered her sympathies, but Alison gently dismissed them, far removed from the trauma. "It happened so long ago. I was too young to even remember." An aunt took Alison in until she turned eighteen and chose to move out on her own. She learned to rely on herself at an early age, putting herself through college with a host of menial jobs, like fast-food kitchens. It was impressive and explained her serious, head-down, hardworking demeanor.

Alison also proclaimed her love of nature and hiking. She liked to explore the Ozark Mountains. There was no mention of a boyfriend or girlfriend, and Linda was curious. Alison was naturally beautiful, with warm, dark eyes, high cheekbones, lush hair and a soft smile. Her skin and the symmetry of her face lacked flaws. Despite the hardships of her young life, she looked fresh and unaffected.

Framed perfectly by the camera lens, Alison presented few personal details in her physical background. It was a clean and sterile room with nothing on the walls. It made Linda self-conscious about the obvious clutter behind her, the drawbacks of a tiny home office and too much stuff.

Linda shared a little more about her own life, sticking to her career path and journalism origins. She wasn't ready to talk about X, it was too difficult to cover with a few quick throwaway lines. She would save it for another day. She wanted to keep the early conversations focused on Alison to get to know her better and make sure she was comfortable and well-informed about her new role.

Every conversation with Alison left Linda with a positive vibe. This was someone who was dedicated to the job and grateful to be here. *I could learn a thing or two from her*, Linda thought.

⋆  ⋆  ⋆

Energized by the hiring success, Linda felt ambitious enough to finally break free from her winter entrapment. She was going to shovel her car out of the alley behind the townhouse.

Her kitchen shelves and refrigerator had gotten so bare she was relying on online ordering for grocery and meal deliveries to her door. The most recent arrival of sandwiches came attached to a very large man with his face hidden by a ski mask, presumably to protect from the bitter cold, but it also made him look like a classic robber. His gruff anonymity at such close proximity frightened her. She was a single woman living alone in a big city, and her imagination could easily run amok with worst-case scenarios.

Paying rideshare services or taking trains to get around town when she had a car was lame, but the biggest motivator to drive again was the living-room takeover by X's belongings – the piles she had sorted for the storage locker but not yet removed from her sight. It was time to complete the purge of his presence. Public Energy had already taken over a portion of her home; she didn't need any more intrusions.

Bundled up, Linda headed outdoors. She retrieved the snow shovel from the mini shed under the back patio steps and planned her attack on the mounds of snow that consumed her Nissan. "I am here to rescue you!" she proclaimed to the captive vehicle.

Her previous attempts remained on display, an assortment of brief, pathetic, abandoned efforts to chisel at the stubborn snow from different angles. She had given up without much of a fight, hoping for a hot, sunny day to come along and melt it all away. In Chicago in January? Fat chance.

Her procrastination had also threatened real damage – who knew if the engine would even start?

She tackled the snow with vigor, breaking away large chunks and heaving them out of the way. It became quite a workout, and she could see her bursts of cloud breath, evidence of panting. She cursed her sit-all-day, work-from-home physical condition and vowed to get an exercise bike or maybe a treadmill. X belonged to a gym but was never interested in her accompaniment; it put a damper on his flirting.

As Linda chopped and scraped, she became aware of similar sounds coming from nearby. She looked around and saw the teenage boy who lived two doors down, working on his section of the alley, cheeks red, blue down coat, arms moving in a quick rhythm.

Linda knew his name – Bert – and had met his loud mother a few times, but otherwise knew very little about him. Bert caught her glance, so she waved friendly at him, and he waved back.

She returned to shoveling and then became aware that the sounds of his shoveling had ceased. She looked up and saw he was walking over to her.

"Hi!" he said cheerfully. "Need help?"

"Oh," she said, startled by the sound of her own voice. She sometimes went full days without uttering words out loud, typing them instead into emails and instant messages. "I'm – well – gosh – I mean – sure. You don't have to."

"I don't mind it," he said. "You're really snowed in. Let me help. With the two of us, we'll get you out twice as fast."

"Thank you," she said. "You're Bert, right?"

"Bert Pacorek. I'm at 1623. You're Mrs. Kelly?"

"Oh, call me Linda."

"Okay, Linda. I'll take this side, you take that side."

"I really appreciate it."

"No problem. We'll get you out of here."

"Thanks. I've felt like a prisoner these past few weeks. You can be my jailbreak!"

He laughed and began digging with athletic arms, working quickly without strain. She was motivated to shovel faster to keep pace with him. When they finished, she was damp with a cold sweat and her muscles ached. But it felt good, like an exercise high.

Linda thanked him and made small talk, asking where he went to school (DePaul in Lincoln Park) and what he was studying (computer science).

"Computer science? Good choice," she said. "Everything's computers these days. I'm not tech-savvy at all. My PC's old and really slow. I think there's something the matter with it."

"I'd be happy to take a look," he smiled. Small clumps of blond hair emerged from under his wool hat. "You could have viruses or malware. Or too many programs running in the background."

"I might take you up on that one day," she said. "My husband was the tech guy." Then she quickly clarified, "My ex-husband," which made her blush. "He even wired our place to be a 'smart house', but I still just use the regular switches." She felt awkward bringing him up. "Anyway, you've done enough for now. Thanks again for breaking me free."

"Hey, it's good to be free."

When she returned inside, she felt a warm feeling in her chest and realized it was a small crush. Bert was cute.

*Knock it off*, she immediately told herself. *You're thirty years older. You're probably the age of his mother.*

*That's a depressing thought.*

But the lingering feeling remained, a faint glow that reminded her of youthful times, dates with X, when he was in his twenties, and he was sweet and funny and…

Linda shut her eyes tight.

*Stop it. Stop. Stop.*

Even though she was tired, she pushed forward to her next task: moving X's crap to storage. She loaded the Nissan with it all (even the 'heavy stuff', take that, X, you asshole). She wrapped the black box with the gun in a sweater and tucked it deep in a plastic tub, out of view of any cameras at the self-storage facility. She had ultimately peeked at the rules, and firearms were indeed prohibited.

*I don't care. I want it out of my house.*

Linda secured herself behind the steering wheel and made a silent prayer. Then she started the ignition.

The car engine sputtered for a moment, causing a few seconds of panic, and then kicked to life with a healthy roar.

*Hallelujah!*

★    ★    ★

Far too often, Linda had dreams about work. It was cruel, because sleep was supposed to be an escape from the hours regulated by the POMS punch clock. When the nights produced echoes of daytime rituals, she woke up exhausted by her employer without achieving anything.

Instead of shutting down at bedtime, her brainwaves entered an anxiety screensaver she couldn't uninstall.

So when Linda experienced a joyful dream out of left field – a *romantic* encounter, no less – it stirred her with pleasant surprise. The catalyst was clear: Bert. He joined her for a weird storyline she mostly forgot, but the feelings lingered. She fought to recall details in the dark. The two of them were on a date, and she was much younger to match his age. They were enjoying the sparkling Chicago nightlife on a perfect evening without a trace of snow or bitter cold.

She remembered hugging him – very affectionate, not sexual – and the warm, happy sensation that accompanied the embrace. It was a moment of exhilaration. The more she tried to replay the sequence in her mind, the fainter it became. She thought about the strangeness of it all, and then she cried because she had not hugged anyone with feeling in years. Online emoticons did not count.

The dream startled her but also soothed her. It was a spark of passion. *I'm not dead inside yet.*

The next day, she dedicated her lunch break to setting up her profile on an online dating site, Singles Connection. Cecilia had provided the link, encouraged her to go for it, and now she was going to take the plunge.

*I order everything else online; why not a boyfriend?*

Linda logged into her personal laptop at the kitchen counter. She explored the dating site, and the presentation was slick and professional, not seedy or pervy. She set up an account, and it asked her to create a profile.

Good question: *Who am I?*

This proved to be harder than she anticipated. She needed to describe herself and make it sound interesting. She wasn't very good about bragging, but gave it a try, carefully selecting words to elevate her personal brand. Then she read what she wrote, and it made her feel uncomfortable.

Linda felt another wave of imposter syndrome – crippling self-doubt in the context of others' accomplishments. Some of it traced to her career switch: faking her way through corporate PR when she was a journalist at heart. She often feared she would be exposed as a fraud in the middle of a department meeting. Being married to a high-achieving individual who constantly pointed out her flaws and eroded her confidence also contributed to lingering feelings of incompetence.

Just because she knew these feelings were irrational didn't make them go away.

She forced herself forward with: *I'm a PR writer, damn it, I should be able to write my own PR copy.*

She crafted a profile that made her laugh because it sounded so cheerfully defined and denied her true identity crisis. This was some impressive gal on the screen. Boys, watch out!

She entered her age (ugh!) and general location (Chicago, Illinois!). She completed prompts that asked about hobbies and interests, expressing a fondness for photography, travel and tennis, even though it had been a while since she engaged in any of those things. She identified as straight and female, open to all races and religions. She preferred a nonsmoker, having dated a heavy smoker in college who tasted like Marlboros with every kiss. She acknowledged she was divorced, no kids.

Next she uploaded a nice photo of herself, from maybe two years ago, but not dishonest. She shared the frame with X but he was an easy crop. It was from a downtown fundraiser gala sponsored by his company. In it, she wore makeup, her hair was the right length and style, and her eyes didn't look tired. The lighting was flattering, the background was unobtrusive. There really wasn't anything more recent that looked this good.

She no longer wore much makeup, especially in the virtual workplace era. Pretty much everyone allowed their appearances to decline to complement the bedraggled casualness of working from home.

The whole process of studying the dating site and assembling a satisfactory profile consumed her entire lunch hour. One p.m. quickly arrived, and she needed to prevent her POMS color from exposing extended tardiness. She finished her uploads and signed off on the submission. Success! She was now officially in the dating pool.

X had already swum laps in that pool. Now it was her turn. She didn't want a replacement for X; she wanted an upgrade. The old model was defective. Whatever came next had to be a big improvement.

★   ★   ★

Linda's afternoon buzzed with a kick of adrenaline from the prospect of suitors lining up in her Singles Connection account. She couldn't wait for the end of the workday to take a look.

She had a good meeting with Alison, amazed at the eagerness of her consumption of company knowledge. She almost wanted to tell her, 'Settle down, girl. You passed the audition.'

Alison had already read the past three years of annual reports and media releases. She had scoured the intranet to learn about the operations of every business unit. She read through leadership bios, regulatory affairs briefings and press coverage.

"To be an effective spokesperson, I need to know everything I can," she said.

Linda realized it was time to narrow Alison's focus to a specific task. She had intended to deliver her first assignment the following week, but now she feared her new employee would grow bored waiting.

"I've got something I'd like you to work on," Linda said. "There's no rush. I want you to continue getting acclimated. But this should be a good project to get your feet wet."

"I'd love a good project."

"It's our home energy rebate program," said Linda with a chipper lift in her voice to deny the tedium of the subject matter. "We want to promote it again this spring, reach out into the service territories, partner with communities, local officials, do some radio PSAs and social media. It's all about helping customers reduce their energy use through home improvements – insulation, ductwork, window treatments, newer appliances, high-efficiency heating and cooling."

"Yes, that is important consumer outreach."

"I'd like you to run with it. You can use last year's plan and the key messages I wrote. It's all there, pretty straightforward. Not a lot to do, just drop in the new dates and send out the packets. There's a good framework in place."

"I look forward to it," Alison said.

Linda smiled. Her attitude was refreshing. Tricia used to openly grouse about being assigned to musty customer campaigns, not even feigning enthusiasm. Alison seemed genuinely interested and hungry to dive in.

She was too good to be true.

By the end of the afternoon, the sun was emerging after a week-long hiatus, further brightening Linda's mood. She was brimming with curiosity as she logged back into her Singles Connection account on her personal laptop at the kitchen table.

She had three messages!

The first two were a quick No and No, a pair of oddballs with elusive job descriptions, off-putting expressions, troubled prose and questionable pursuits – one of them asked if she had pictures of her feet.

But the third one hit the mark – a Normal! He was immediately intriguing and leaning toward a Yes. His message to her was eloquent, his photo very handsome and his profile filled with impressive accomplishments and compelling interests. His name was Jules, he was born in northern England, and he came to the States as a young adult working as an art museum archivist in Boston. He advanced up through the ranks to become the director of a contemporary art museum in Atlanta for several years before moving to Chicago to be a consultant to dozens of major nonprofits, while teaching art history and theory at Northwestern University. He sounded cultured and fascinating and kind.

A professor. An art aficionado. A self-employed advisor to a large clientele of philanthropic institutions. Plus – the mystique of a European background and, almost certainly, an alluring accent.

A promising date was in the offering, dropped out of the sky like a gift. It was so quick and easy, it felt silly.

She waited until after dinner – and a glass of red wine – to contact him. Typing out a message from her account, she said she was interested in getting to know him better. She chose her phrasing carefully, proofread thoroughly – a single typo could mar this first impression.

He responded almost immediately, and soon they were engaged in a live chat. She shared more about herself – keeping it all upbeat but acknowledging the divorce and no kids. He said he had never been married but was engaged once to an American woman he spent nearly ten years with before she broke his heart.

*I presume most of us on this platform have suffered romantic heartbreak in one form or another, so we are already kindred spirits*, he typed in the chat.

She wanted to hear it in his human voice, accent and all.

Before long, a date was set up and Linda felt positively giddy. He signed off with *Cheers!*

She convinced herself it was possible to find perfect love from a total stranger.

# CHAPTER FOUR

Saturday arrived right on schedule. She spent the morning going through her wardrobe – including upscale outfits she used to wear to work when reporting to company offices and looking professional. She held her own private fashion show in front of a tall mirror on the back of the bedroom door, creating a pool of rejects on the floor. It expanded until there were no more candidates left to consider.

This was an excuse to go shopping. It had been too long since she had treated herself. Linda drove out of the city and into the northern suburbs to visit a large mall of shops ranging from high-end boutiques to classic department stores. She found a red dress she really liked – on sale! – and then panicked over whether or not it would go with her winter coat. The coat was an old, ragged wool thing from the marriage era.

So she bought a new coat too.

Jules had promised her a 'three-course date with much merriment and surprises'. They would kick it off by meeting at Elements, a trendy new restaurant halfway up a downtown skyscraper with tall windows and a spectacular city view. *The chef is Dion Dumas, a brilliant bloke*, he said as if they were old friends. *And the wine list is cracking good*. He would not disclose the rest of his plans but alluded to 'grand wintertime fun'. She loved the dash of mystery. His playful enthusiasm heightened her own. He said he was 'chuffed'.

The winter sunset took place at 5 p.m., an early transition to night accompanied by a messy release of lakefront sleet. The weather sealed her decision to hop an Uber to the restaurant and avoid the triple threat of dangerous driving conditions, outrageous downtown parking fees and the risk of climbing behind the wheel after one too many drinks.

She met Jules in the crowded restaurant lobby just off the elevators. They recognized each other immediately from their photos. She wore her new red dress, new trench coat and a favorite pair of high-heel shoes brought out of hibernation. A rare application of makeup added color to her face. Jules wore a snappy three-piece suit with a double-breasted vest. He gave her a big smile and formal handshake. It was almost businesslike, but she appreciated the respect – a hug was premature and presumptuous. Jules was a gentleman.

"Right on time. I admire punctuality," he said. "There's a table with your name on it. Wait until you see the view."

The sight was indeed incredible. This was primo seating, the best in the house, cozy and candlelit against one of the big windows, certainly scouted and arranged for in advance, perhaps with a healthy flash of cash.

"You're spoiling me before you know me," she teased him as they sat down.

"I know enough," he said, "to recognize you are in a special class. May I compliment you on how lovely you look in person?"

She hesitated. Did he actually expect an answer. "Yes?"

"You look smashing," he declared.

She laughed. "That's very British of you."

"Yes, I have a tendency."

A tall young waiter arrived to take their drink orders. When Linda hesitated, Jules forged ahead, recommending a bottle of Hamacher Pinot Noir for the two of them.

"Sure, that sounds great," she said.

"And a cheese platter. Do you consume cheese?"

"All kinds," she said. She wasn't a picky eater, and it was relaxing to go with the flow.

He was energized with easygoing conversation, leaning forward and looking into her eyes without getting distracted by the commotion around him.

X had become a terrible dinner companion in the later years of their marriage, always glancing around restaurants with distractions, probably checking out the tits and legs of every young lady walking by.

In close proximity, Jules looked older than his Singles Connection photo. This current edition had lines in his face, more forehead and an advancement of gray hair. But her photo wasn't exactly contemporary either and probably ten pounds lighter. His Yorkshire accent was undeniably charming – the colorful opposite of Chicago's flat, nasal twang. He spoke in literate, complete sentences with crisp enunciation, occasionally lapsing into little quirks like dropping the G on his -*ings* or a nonexistent *H*. "'ave you made up your mind on what you're 'avin'?"

Over wine and cheese, they discussed the magnificent Chicago skyline that sparkled before them like a lowered galaxy. Jules pointed out several buildings and named their architects, sometimes with a pointed criticism. "Look at that ugly behemoth – what was he thinking?"

For an entrée, she ordered the chicken Marbella, and he selected the roasted duck breast. The conversation never flagged, mostly kept afloat by Jules's animated personality and the ease of their rapport.

He bubbled forth with a wealth of knowledge about the arts and travel. He drew comparison points between Chicago ('a truly great, underrated metropolis') and other big cities across Europe, Asia and Australia. One topic he didn't expand upon was his own personal background. She tried to pry into his timeline, but he kept shifting the focus to her. It was both flattering and disarming. After two glasses of wine, she opened up with a ramble somewhere between a therapy session and a confession. After years of communicating with people mostly through technology, she let her guard down when face to face with a live human. She talked about her parents, and how she felt like she had disappointed them. They were both approaching eighty, living in a retirement village in Arizona, engaging with her infrequently. Her dad was a prize-winning journalist, and she had planned to follow in his footsteps but had gone to the 'dark side' (as he described it) to become a PR spinmeister. Her mom had taught classic literature and was a published poet. She was no doubt equally disappointed in her daughter's decidedly unpoetic career in corporate speak.

"I write drivel," she told Jules. "This crazy corporate gig – I expected it to be temporary, a bridge, a stepping stone or intermission, but not a final destination. When I wasn't looking, it became my identity. Press releases and speaking points and FAQs. I write safety tips to prevent people from getting electrocuted."

"Well, keeping people from getting electrocuted serves a noble purpose."

"But is it art?"

"Art is in the eye of the beholder. Look at all the rubbish on television."

"What about your parents?" she asked him. "Tell me about them."

"Well, both are back in England. My mum was a garment designer, now retired. My dad is a baker – he owns a very successful chain of bakeries, regional, nothing you would have heard about in the States."

"Do you visit them?"

"When I'm in the UK. Maybe once or twice a year."

"Can I ask your age? You left it blank."

"Of course you may. I'm fifty-two. Turnabout is fair play. And you?"

"I'm forty-nine, give or take a year."

"So you're fifty."

"You catch on quick."

"I'm a sly one."

She said, "I tried looking you up on Facebook. There was a bunch of people with your name, but I don't think any of them were you."

"I don't think so either. I'm not on Facebook. I abhor it. Social media is the devil's playground. A bigger waste of time I've never known."

"I don't update my page very often," she admitted. Other than changing *married* to *single*.

He got her to talk about her marriage, and she tried to keep it brief, because X was a most unwelcome presence on this date. She mostly emphasized that they were finished, and she was ready to move on.

"You deserve better than that wanker," said Jules, and it made her smile.

"You're right," she said. "He's a *wanker*."

They split an exquisite bananas Foster for dessert, which arrived with a dramatic flash of flames. Jules disclosed his plans for the second phase of their date night.

"Do you know how to ice-skate?"

"Ice-skate? It's been a long time, but I think I can remember." She immediately knew what was coming next.

"We're going to Millennium Park," he declared.

After leaving the restaurant, they walked four blocks against the wind, stepping carefully around the snow and ice, shivering, discussing the polar vortex. She imagined him taking her gloved hand, advancing this new relationship with a physical gesture, but his arms remained at his sides.

At the rink, they rented skates and joined the circling skaters of all ages and abilities. The mountainous lineup of high-rises along Michigan Avenue created a majestic backdrop. Jules was a very good skater, and Linda was only a notch below that, quickly finding her footing and avoiding collisions on the crowded ice.

At one point, dodging a fallen teenager, she made a quick swerve and almost lost her balance.

Jules caught her in his arms.

She immediately reciprocated and put her arms around him.

They skated awhile longer, holding on to each other like a true couple. Even beneath the winter layers, she could feel the glow of his touch. The temperatures had dipped into the twenties, but the cold here wasn't uncomfortable, it was energizing. She felt alive, freed from the isolation of her tired townhouse.

Jules glanced at his watch. "Oh, we better go. Phase three will begin soon."

"Phase three?" She smiled. "What could that be?"

"Do you fancy jazz?"

"Yes," she said, mimicking him playfully. "I fancy jazz."

"Then this will be a treat."

They returned the skates and headed to the curb on Michigan and Lake, where Jules hailed a cab. They climbed in, and Jules delivered the address for the River North Jazz Lounge.

"Jazz is one of America's greatest cultural contributions," he told her. "Everything else you stole from Europe and the Brits."

"What about Chicago blues?"

"Touché, madam."

They arrived just in time for a set by Patsy Reese, a torch singer with a sultry, smoky voice, accompanied by a tight trio of piano, drums and bass. Every lyric soared with emotion and commitment. The crowd sat quiet and respectful, exploding into applause at the fade of every song's final note.

Jules kept looking over at Linda, sometimes with just a grin and raised eyebrows, as if to say, 'Isn't this the greatest?'

She smiled broadly back at him.

Quietly, in the shadows, the drinks kept coming, brought forward by Jules's simple gestures and eye contact with the staff. They acknowledged him with familiarity, and he communicated cocktail choices with minimal words.

At first, she hesitated at resuming drinking, but he was excited for her to try his recommendations so she obliged – and indeed they were sweet and smooth and pleasantly intoxicating.

By the time the performance ended, she was feeling good but blurry. The club stirred with movement of people coming and going, and the lights brightened with no one on stage.

"I should go," she said. "It's way past my bedtime."

"When does a fifty-year-old go to bed?" he asked.

"About forty-five minutes ago."

"Are you deadline-driven?"

"I can be."

The truth was the date had been perfect, and she wanted to conclude it on a high note, before she got too sleepy and slurred and did something to make herself lose appeal.

They spilled back out onto the sidewalk, and there was still a healthy flow of street traffic despite the late hour and frigid conditions.

"I can grab an Uber from here," she said.

"Uber?" he said with a negative face, as if spitting the word out.

"I'm just a straight shot north. It's how I got downtown. I figured, you know, the roads are slippery, and I'd probably have a drink or two…"

"Or four or five."

"Well, right."

"I'll drive you."

"Oh no, that's not necessary." All she wanted was a genuine, sweet kiss goodbye to cap off a perfect evening, and then they could start planning the sequel together the following day.

"I insist. Really, I insist."

"But…you've had four or five drinks as well."

"Fear not. I have a very high tolerance. Plus, I had a big meal, I had a workout – I was performin' figure eights. I feel fine. Most of it's worn off."

She continued to dismiss his offer, but he persisted, and it was sending the date toward an argumentative finale, so she ultimately relented. "Well…where are you parked?"

"Not far. A short cab ride back to where we had dinner."

"Then I could stay in the cab and just—"

"No, no, no." He put his arm around her for the first time since catching her on the ice. "I insist."

She melted a little bit inside. "Oh, all right."

He flagged a cab to take them to a multi-level parking garage in the Loop. He led her to his car – a sporty black Porsche.

"Very nice," she said.

"I like nice things," he said, pressing a button on his keychain to unlock the doors. "Like you."

"Like me?"

"Of course." And then he stepped closer. She thought he was going to open the door for her. Instead, he leaned in and kissed her on the mouth. She accepted it warmly.

From a short distance across the parking level, a couple of teenagers witnessed the moment and voiced their raucous endorsement. "Woo!" "Go for it!"

It brought the kiss to a quick end. Both Linda and Jules broke out laughing.

"Come, let's go," said Jules, circling back to the driver's side.

He drove her home, taking Lake Shore Drive, speeding but smooth. She looked out into the inky black waters of Lake Michigan. She felt good inside. The cocktails had infused her with a happy buzz. She absorbed herself in the thought: *I can really imagine having a long-term relationship with this guy.*

As they entered Rogers Park, curving past Loyola University, she gave him instructions for finding her townhouse. Once they arrived, he pulled up in front. She undid her seat belt and turned toward him with the expectation of one more kiss to say good night and seal a perfect night out.

But his face looked troubled. "Do you mind if I use your loo?"

She burst out into a giggle. "Loo?"

"You know what I mean."

"I thought it was called a water closet."

"Sometimes. Sure."

"Too many cocktails?"

"Seriously, I don't know if I can 'old it all the way home. And I don't fancy findin' a public toilet in Chicago this time of night."

"My place is a bit of a mess," she said. "I mean – it's not dirty, but it's cluttered. Stuff needs to be put away. I wasn't planning on any visitors."

"Please don't allow my bladder to burst right 'ere inside my car. Think of the cleaning bill."

"All right. All right…" She smiled even as fresh jitters erupted inside of her. He was entering her private space. "But just a quick skip to the loo. No sightseeing. I don't want you to think of me as a slob."

"You're not a slob," he said.

The next twenty minutes shifted gears through a rapidly evolving sequence of events. After using the bathroom, he headed back toward the front door, and they exchanged more pleasantries about the great night they had shared together. Then they resumed the kiss that had been interrupted in the parking garage. This time, there was nothing to break the escalating passion. He touched her places no one had touched her other than her husband in the past twenty years and for a long stretch not even him. Jules was physical and sensual. She was aroused. They shed their wintertime layers and pressed their warm bodies together, feeling each other's naked flesh. Entangled, they advanced to her bedroom, where they fell on top of the sheets. They made love on the unmade bed in the anonymity of total darkness.

★   ★   ★

At 6 a.m., he kissed her awake. It was still dark outside.

"I 'ave to leave early, love."

She stirred and searched for focus in the shadows. "Really?"

"I'm an early riser."

"On Sunday?"

"I have a brunch meeting with clients. I need to prepare."

"Oh."

He slid out of bed and headed into the bathroom. The door shut and a sliver of light appeared beneath it. She heard the toilet lid flip up with a thud.

She sat up and turned on a small bedside lamp, groggy. For her, this was a very early start of the day. Without a commute to the office, she had fallen into a pattern of sleeping in, sometimes rolling out of bed as late as 8:55 to log in at 9 a.m., keeping the laptop's camera off until she showered and got dressed later in the morning, during a fake meeting she placed on her calendar to cover for such a purpose.

Linda yawned and rubbed her eyes. Her head throbbed with the dull ache of a small hangover. The events of the prior night returned as joyful flashes of memory, a dreamy highlight reel. It made her smile.

She rose naked from the bed and immediately stepped on his silk shirt. She reached down and picked it up. She placed it on a chair, neatly folded. Then she retrieved his pants.

As she lifted the pants, his wallet fell out of his back pocket and struck the floor. Credit cards spilled out. She reached down to pick them up.

They were adorned with a stranger's name: *Malcolm Gibbons*.

She was so confused that her first thought was: *Why does Jules have someone else's credit cards?*

Her second thought jumped to another conclusion.

"Son of a bitch!" she said aloud.

"Whaat?" said the voice behind the bathroom door. "Did you say somethin'?" The toilet flushed.

She dug deeper into the wallet and found his Illinois driver's license with his photo alongside the name Malcolm Gibbons. There was a city address with an apartment number. He had said he lived in a house in the suburbs. His birth date revealed he was quite a bit older than what he told her. She also glimpsed a receipt for the one-day rental of the Porsche.

Linda's overnight guest emerged from the bathroom, fully naked, privates exposed. He stopped cold upon seeing her hands on his wallet.

"What the hell is this, *Jules?*" She pronounced the name with scorn.

She threw the wallet at him, hitting him in the hairy belly. He failed to catch it in time, and it spilled back to the floor, scattering the cards.

He froze, unrehearsed for this moment.

"Who *are* you?" she demanded.

His expression attempted to brighten. "It's not what it seems. Granted, that is my name. It's my legal name. I changed it for business purposes. You know, branding. You're in PR, right? Gibbons sounds like a monkey. The kids at school used to tease me mercilessly. I promised myself that one day—"

"Prove it," she said.

"What?"

"Show me a website, a business card, *anything* with the name Jules Stafford."

"Well, give me some time. I'm sure I 'ave some letterhead at home."

"Letterhead! How stupid do you think I am?"

"I don't think you're stupid."

"What name do you use for Northwestern University, Professor? Malcolm Gibbons or Jules Stafford? Or if I did a search, would I find neither one at all?"

"I can't guarantee their website is up to date..."

"Are you married?"

He sighed. "Listen. Let's get dressed. We'll talk it over. We'll go someplace for breakfast."

"What about your business brunch?"

"Oh, well –" He began to stutter, losing the eloquence in his speaking voice, struggling for vocabulary. "That's – that's not set in stone. I can – perhaps—"

"Are you even British?"

"Now that hurts. Listen here—"

"No, you listen. I want you to leave."

"We can discuss this."

"No, we can't. Get out. Get the *fuck out*."

He just stood there, staring, with ridiculous sad puppy eyes and no clothes.

She became aware of her own nudity then, the last thing she wanted his eyes on. She grabbed a robe from her closet and put it on, tying the sash tight.

He slowly stepped into the bedroom and got dressed, without another word. He picked up his wallet and its strewn contents.

Within a few minutes, he was gone, slipping out into the winter darkness. She slammed the door and locked it.

She was furious and horribly depressed.

She was too enraged to go back to sleep, even though her body was weighed down with fatigue.

Her rage toward him became anger toward herself. *Why am I so gullible?* She regretted not doing more research on him ahead of the date. It had never dawned on her that he could be a fake. Her trust was foolish and naïve. *Was it my own desperation that allowed this to happen?*

She hopped on her computer and Googled *Malcolm Gibbons*. She found a Yelp review that referenced someone with that name as a clerk at a high-end men's clothing store in Forest Glen. *...a nice British man, Malcolm Gibbons, helped me match ties with my suit and seemed to really know his stuff.*

Well, that explained why he was so well-dressed. He probably got an employee discount.

Malcolm most certainly did not exist in any faculty listing for Northwestern. Nor did Jules. Everything about his career background was made up, from Boston to Atlanta to Chicago.

The saddest discovery was his wife's Facebook page – she had tagged him in recent family photos, so it was a quick connection to make. They had two children, a boy and girl, in their early teens. Their young faces broke Linda's heart. They probably had no idea their father was a slick, manipulative cheater. And his wife – she must have known something about his ways? This couldn't have been his only affair. She looked pleasant, a heavyset woman who posted regularly about cooking.

Linda felt sick about how open and candid she was with him. She had bared her emotions and her body. He had taken advantage of her vulnerability for the thrill of a one-night stand.

She shut the lid on her laptop with a slam. Fucked over, betrayed by the World Wide Web. *Do people really find genuine dates this way, or just a bunch of sleazy imposters?*

Later that day, she returned to the Singles Connection site and deleted her account. It erased her presence but didn't clear her conscience.

# CHAPTER FIVE

Linda's disastrous weekend made her look forward to returning to work. She needed the distraction of drab office routines. Her jaw was sore from grinding her teeth. Sunday's hangover was replaced by Monday's stress headache. Perhaps noodling with message points about energy deregulation would soothe her nerves.

Cecilia emailed to ask about the date night. Linda simply replied, *Not my type*. The long answer was too depressing and humiliating to revisit.

At 10 a.m., an email from Alison popped in her inbox: *Consumer Rebate Communication Campaign*, with attachments. Linda smiled and opened it.

Then she read the note, and her smile faded.

*Linda, thank you for the opportunity to review your plan draft and key messages. It required significant revisions. Over the weekend, I made improvements to the content and overhauled the campaign elements to maximize their effectiveness. You will see my edits in the track changes function. Of course, if you disagree with any of my fixes, I would be happy to discuss. I know it's a lot. I appreciate your initial foundation to work from. I have strengthened what you started, leveraging my experiences in best practices. Best, Alison.*

Linda read it twice. Then a third time.

What. The. Hell.

*Who is working for who here?*

The timing for the email was not good. Linda's ego was already fragile.

She opened the attachments and her white documents were awash in bloody red – so many cuts and inserts that she couldn't absorb it right away, searching for bits and pieces of her original copy that had survived.

A sentence here, a small phrase there. But not much.

All the changes appeared to make sense, maybe they made it a little bit better, but was it really necessary? Was Alison trying too hard to show off?

Linda sent her an IM: *Received your email. Let's connect when you get a chance.*

Alison responded almost immediately: *I'm available now.*

Linda: *Great. I'll call.*

She initiated an online meeting. Alison answered, and she was on camera. Linda groaned. *All right, I'll go on camera too.*

With their faces displayed side by side on the monitor, the contrast struck Linda. Alison: young, fresh, perfectly beautiful in a natural way with great hair. Linda: tired, old, bags developing under eyes, tiny wrinkles at the lips, uneven skin, flat and thinning hair.

"Hello, Linda!" said Alison with a pleasant smile.

"Hi, Alison. How are you this morning?"

"I'm doing great. Yourself?"

"Good."

"Did you have a nice weekend?"

"Um, yes."

"Me too."

"Good. Listen, I wanted to ask you – you spent a lot of time on the rebate plan and the key messages."

"Yes, I did."

"It wasn't really – necessary. I feel bad you worked on it over the weekend."

"It was no trouble. I wanted to dive in."

"Well, that's the thing. You didn't have to dive in. I wasn't asking for a big rewrite. That's last year's plan. It served us well. I just needed you to put new dates in the timeline, learn the key messages and execute the plan. Not change it all up. I think you went overboard."

"What do you mean?"

"It's a lot of unnecessary work."

"Don't you want me to make things better?"

"Of course I do. But it's also about time management. Not everything has to be super perfect. You know about the eighty-twenty rule? It's about prioritization. Sometimes we just need to be quick and efficient."

"But what about quick and perfect?"

"I'm afraid those things are usually at odds."

"They don't have to be."

"I'm just being realistic."

"I don't know that you are."

Linda took a deep breath. Argumentative little newbie. Was this new hire going to be an arrogant pain in the ass?

"All right. Let's back up. I wrote the original plan. I'm happy with it. The executives are happy with it. Let's not trouble them with something all different when the original documents were perfectly fine. Eleanor liked them."

"But she agrees with me," Alison said. "I shared my version with Eleanor. She liked it very much."

"You…what?"

"I wanted to make sure my changes were acceptable before I shared them with you. So I sent them to Eleanor first thing this morning. Let me read you her response. She said: 'Alison, this is outstanding work. Thank you so much for your smart editing and fresh ideas. I appreciate what you've done here and look forward to putting the new plan in action.'"

Linda shut her eyes for a moment. "Um. Can you forward that email to me?"

"Of course."

"That was really – it was unacceptable, Alison."

"What is unacceptable?" she responded innocently. "I don't understand. Eleanor is happy."

"You don't – you don't go undermining your manager like that. You should have showed it to me first."

"The corporate vision handbook says employee empowerment is a core value, and we are committed to flattening the hierarchy."

"Yes, but that's –" Hyperbole, Linda wanted to say. "Those things are part of our culture, but you have to look at the big picture. We also integrate. We collaborate. We partner. We treat each other with *respect*." She punched out that last word extra hard and instantly regretted it.

"I was only trying to streamline processes," Alison said. "The corporate vision handbook…"

"Okay, okay."

"I'm sorry if I upset you."

Linda didn't know what to say. Her head was swimming. This was not a good beginning to their working relationship. Alison had held such enormous promise. She was smart and hardworking, the opposite of Tricia. Isn't that what Linda wanted?

Linda calmed down. She didn't want to become the temperamental bitch of a boss that she herself hated. She needed to put her ego aside. It was an innocent overreach by a new employee who was trying too hard to impress.

"Alison, I'm sorry if I overreacted," Linda finally said. "I'm not in the best frame of mind. It's not you. It's related to things happening outside of work. The past couple of years have been really hard on me."

"Yes," said Alison. "I know."

Linda stared into her earnest expression. "What do you mean you know?"

"I'm aware your husband left you."

Linda was stunned speechless.

"Don't feel bad," Alison said. "You have a right to be upset."

"How did you know—"

"Divorce is a difficult hardship with a lot of pain and self-doubt."

"Alison, how did you know about my divorce? I never told you."

"It's public information, isn't it?"

"But who told you? Eleanor? Cecilia?"

"I discovered it on my own when I was researching you and this job opportunity."

"Where? Why? It has nothing to do with this job. It's private. It's not something I want to talk about."

"We won't talk about it."

"Yes, *please*."

Linda saw herself on the laptop screen as the camera captured her at her worst: a grossly unflattering hag expression, pinched with anger and stress and a massive frown. Alison's face remained undisturbed, staring ahead with gentle curiosity, annoyingly cute and pristine.

"I have a meeting to get to," Linda lied. "But we'll talk some more tomorrow. I'll – I'll review your changes, and we can discuss them. We'll learn from each other."

"Learning is good," Alison said.

After the call concluded, Linda stared up into the ceiling. "Good lord, what have I brought on myself?"

Within minutes, an email showed up from Eleanor. *That new girl you hired is terrific!*

Linda didn't respond. She took a deep breath and reviewed Alison's edits.

They were perfect. Better sentence construction, better word choice, catchier phrasing and smarter sequencing. She had also added creative new concepts to engage consumers and refreshed and expanded the media contacts list. It was a total revamp of Linda's plan, but wise and informed. Alison had done her homework.

*This is what I wanted,* Linda told herself. *A bright, autonomous worker who could hit the ground running and offer real support. So why do I resent her for doing good work? Am I a jealous old crank? Is that what I've become?*

She accepted all of the edits in one swoop and returned the cleaned-up file with a short note: *Excellent job. You obviously put a lot of thought into this. I appreciate your diligence.*

She kept the correspondence sweet and civilized. But she was still burning inside.

★   ★   ★

The lousy workday did nothing to settle her down from the events of the past weekend. Malcolm Gibbons continued to haunt her. She wanted to lash out at someone or something. Every time she passed the bedroom door, she was reminded of his fanciful lies, little tricks and pushy manipulation to use her for a tawdry affair. She grabbed the crumpled red dress from a heap in the corner. Purchased just two days earlier, it was now trash. She wanted it out of her sight. She took the dress downstairs and threw it in the garbage pail under the sink. It was forever soiled with the memory of the Englishman who played her for a fool.

For dinner, she downed several drinks – tall vodka tonics with increasingly less tonic. She wasn't very hungry, satisfied with a handful of potato chips.

*I'm not a sucker!* she wanted to shout at the world. X certainly thought she was, cheating and lying through their marriage as if she was the world's most naïve dimwit. And now Jules-fucking-Malcolm.

*He's not that clever,* she thought to herself. *He just caught me in a weak moment. It's not so hard. I could do that, too, if I wanted. Make up a phony persona online. I can post a bunch of bullshit and get people to believe it. After all, isn't that ninety per cent of the internet? Fake news. People hiding behind fake names and avatars.*

As she continued to drink, she stared out the window at the dreary winter dark. She thought to herself: *Maybe I'll do the same. Create my own fake character.*

After another drink, she decided to act on it for real. She started to giggle.

She pulled up the kitchen stool in front of her laptop, sat down and set up a new Singles Connection account under a different name.

*Kimmy Wynn.*

She picked it out of the air: Kimmy was the name of a long-ago grade school friend. Wynn was a spin on *win*, because she was going to play Malcolm's wicked game as a winner, not a loser.

Linda filled out a profile for Kimmy, inventing a fictional character with creative relish. Kimmy was a third-grade teacher. Her hobbies were Pilates, crossword puzzles and taxidermy. She played the tuba. She loved the movies of Ernest Borgnine.

Linda laughed at her own silliness. She knew people would believe this invention. After all, if it was on the internet, it had to be real!

To cap off the entry, she needed a photo. At first, she considered uploading a picture of some Hollywood starlet, maybe even someone instantly recognizable, to complete the joke. But she figured the site's moderators would catch the obvious fake and immediately block it, ruining her fun.

She thought about creating her own phony photo and that led her to remembering the story of Monica McClouskey.

It all started three or four years ago, when her marriage to X was getting wobbly. Theirs was becoming a remote relationship even as they lived under the same roof. The intimacy was forced, the sex was uninspired.

He came up with the idea of a wig. He said that tired old familiarity was the culprit for their diminished sex life. Some role-playing could be fun – pretending they were other people. Cheating without cheating! She went along with it because it certainly sounded better than cheating through cheating, an avenue she already suspected he had traveled.

They went shopping together, and he picked out the wig. It was a red wig of long, thick wavy hair with bangs. He found it very exciting, so she agreed to it even though she doubted it would look natural on her. Would it just create the illusion of a cheap stripper or whore?

The wig was effective in achieving its goals, sort of. She only wore it inside the townhouse, not (god forbid) in public. To complete the transformation, she applied extra lipstick, eyeliner and blush. She wore fishnets for the first time. It aroused him a bit more than usual, while having the opposite effect on her.

Then came his annual office picnic, a summertime tradition in the park with games, grilling and packed coolers of beer. Linda tagged along, and sometimes he introduced her, but there was one female work colleague he steered clear of, and she seemed to keep a careful distance from him. Occasionally they exchanged wordless glances. They were not strangers.

Linda could not help noticing: she had long, wavy red hair with bangs.

While X was busy playing a game of cornhole, Linda brazenly walked up to the redhead to introduce herself and get her name.

Monica McClouskey.

She was perhaps ten years younger, certainly pretty and fit, and she blushed the whole time they talked, which confirmed Linda's suspicions.

During the drive home, she asked X point-blank if the wig was intended to make her resemble Monica McClouskey.

"Who?" he said.

"Don't pretend like you don't know her."

"Oh, that Monica."

"Next time I wear the wig, just call me Monica, why don't you? Maybe you can have her talk dirty to you over the phone while we're doing it."

She never wore the wig again.

Until now.

She found it stuffed unceremoniously in the back of the closet in a plain box.

The wig was crucial to her transformation into Kimmy Wynn. It dramatically altered her appearance. Linda also slipped on a pair of lightly tinted sunglasses.

She held out her cell phone to snap some selfies against the bland backdrop of a closet door. She practiced several quirky expressions, amusing herself, before landing on faces that were unnatural but not too goofy.

Then she uploaded her favorite shot and completed the steps to go live with her new identity.

Welcome to the world, Kimmy Wynn!

Sure enough, the suitors came. The foot fetish guy made a reappearance. She wondered if Jules/Malcolm would be duped – the perfect irony – but he did not show up. Somewhat alarmingly, Kimmy drew more interest than Linda had – maybe it *was* the hair?

She didn't really intend to take this private gag much further, but then a genuinely interesting and cute guy reached out, and she sort of wanted to meet him.

His name was Randy Schilling, and he was a dog and cat nutritionist (!) living in the north-west suburbs. He came across as quite sincere. His appearance was clean-cut, short hair, a little dweeby with a nice smile. He wore wire-rimmed glasses with big lenses. He liked old movies, sunny beaches, wildlife, astronomy and pickleball.

The idea of going out on a date with him – under a false identity and this crazy wig – stirred her with surprising excitement. It was outrageous, daring and so unlike her. How far could she lead him on? How gullible was he?

She waited a day to see if she really wanted to go through with this ruse. The enthusiasm did not fade.

She connected with Randy and they had a very nice online chat. He seemed a bit shy and admitted he had only been on the dating platform for a few weeks. *I didn't know if it would just be a bunch of crazies, but it seems like a lot of really nice people*, he said. *I've been on one date, but it was someone who was a lot older than they said they were.*

*I'm forty*, she lied, continuing the charade.

*I'm forty-five. Five years difference, is that okay?*

*I hope so.*

They set a date for Friday night. *I'm looking forward to meeting you, Kimmy!* he said.

It sort of broke her heart.

She wore the red wig to their date. She really had no choice – it was Kimmy's most dominant feature. It looked reasonably realistic, although she feared it was shifting positions on her head.

They met at a popular deep-dish pizza place out his way in the suburbs. She drove to meet him, suddenly nervous about someone recognizing and exposing her. *"Linda – is that you? I didn't recognize you with the wig! What the hell's that all about?"*

Fortunately, Big Crust Pizza was dim inside, muted by low lighting, dark wood beams and stained glass. Randy was a gentleman, rushing up from the table he had secured, leading her on a narrow path to her seat, sliding out a chair, taking her coat.

They ordered beers and negotiated pizza toppings. He was a little awkward, openly nervous and fidgety, playing with his napkin. He thanked her for showing up, joking, "I don't think I could eat an entire pizza by myself."

He sipped his beer slowly, as if timing it to last for the entire meal. She tried to match his pace. She wasn't going to overdo the drinking like she had with Jules/Malcolm. Besides, she had driven herself this time, a fair distance out of the city, and the weather was supposed to take a turn for the worse in the coming hours.

For starters, they talked about their careers. He spoke with enthusiasm about his niche, providing dietary counsel for pet food manufacturers and veterinarians, helping dogs and cats lead longer, healthier lives. "The average pet owner has no idea what they are actually feeding to their pets. So much of what you find on the shelf is actually harmful," he said with sincere concern. "Animals need the right balance of nutrients just like people do. I've written two books on it."

For her turn, Linda elaborated on Kimmy Wynn's backstory, ad-libbing from the starting point of third-grade teacher. She used the name of the elementary school in her neighborhood and talked in general terms about her students and how long she had been a teacher. "I don't have any children, so these are my kids," she said. "I don't have any pets either. But if I get one, I'll pick up one of your books."

Then he talked about his three dogs and six cats – all of them rescued from shelters. He asked about her interest in taxidermy, and Linda cursed herself for throwing jokes in her profile that she now had to spin legit. "My dad got me into it," she said. "Just some owls and a duck." He seemed genuinely interested so she quickly changed the subject before he started asking too many questions about it and she had to run to the bathroom to research answers on her phone.

"You love old movies," she said, recalling an interest in his profile.

"I *adore* old movies," he said, beaming. He talked about his collection of Blu-rays and DVDs. Then he asked her favorite Ernest Borgnine movie, and she almost broke out laughing. Keeping a straight face, she named one of the few she knew, *The Poseidon Adventure*.

"I'm a big fan of *Marty*," said Randy. "He won the Academy Award, that's got to be one of your favorites too."

"Of course." She had never seen it. Now she had to change the subject yet again. And avoid the topic of tubas. This was harder work than she anticipated. The wig on her head was starting to feel hot and itchy underneath.

The pizza arrived and the conversation turned to their singlehood predicaments. Linda/Kimmy said she had never married but had been engaged a couple of times. Randy disclosed that he had been married and his wife died of breast cancer.

Now Linda felt awful. There was nothing funny or daring about this game she was playing. It just made her sad.

Randy said he didn't date for two years after her death. One of his friends finally convinced him to try online matchmaking. "I know Rena would be okay with that. Sometimes I feel like her spirit is watching over me, and she is being very understanding." Then he talked about how difficult the loss of their mother had been for his two little girls. One loved ballet, the other was sportier, into soccer. Both were in therapy.

Linda finally excused herself and went to the bathroom. Inside, she stared at her ridiculous costume in the mirror and hated it. *He's such a nice guy, and I'm such a horrible fraud.*

She very much wanted to slip out the exit and speed away, driving back to her townhouse and deleting all traces of Singles Connection from her computer forever. Creating this deception had been too easy, too quick. Online she could be anyone she wanted, with any bio she desired, but now she wanted to return to her old real self.

She finally convinced herself not to ditch this poor nice man. She would complete the date and then let him down gently in a day or two. But she wasn't going to be cruel. He would never know the whole thing was some kind of twisted experiment or redirected revenge. She would leave him with the pleasant memory of a nice night out.

Linda adjusted her wig, which looked extra fake under the bright bathroom lights, and returned to the table.

The pizza was good, and the conversation turned to innocent topics like local events and the weather. His demeanor was upbeat and wholesome. She imagined he used words like 'heck' and 'darn' and 'shoot' in place of profanity.

"Say, we still have time to check out the Winter Wonderland, if you're interested," said Randy, checking his watch, after finishing his final pizza slice and remaining sip of beer. "It's only ten minutes away."

During their online chat to set up the date, he had suggested they visit a popular outdoor holiday lights display with synchronized music, vendors and various activities like a sledding hill. She said sure. He seemed enthusiastic about it.

When they arrived, the weather was already starting to turn more aggressive. A strong wind howled between the trees. Randy was bundled up extra heavy like a child in a big coat, scarf, mittens, wool hat and oversized hood. Only his glasses and a small portion of his face remained exposed to identify him. Linda's thick wig of long red hair kept her head warm, covering her ears and cheeks, but she was terrified a sudden gale would send it airborne.

They strolled a curving path that led through a variety of dancing light effects, including a sparkling tunnel. Colors pulsed to the beat of a continually shifting soundtrack of classical music on pop synthesizers. At the end of the trail, there was a display of elaborate ice sculptures and sales of hot cocoa and cookies.

"I would love some hot chocolate," Randy said. "You?"

"Sure."

They split the cost evenly, just like they did with the pizza and beer, at Linda's insistence. She really wanted to pay for everything, to relieve her of some of the guilt, but that would have been a tough sell.

As they finished their mugs, the crowd around them began to thin out. The air grew more frigid as the temperature continued to drop. The wind gusts blew harder and colder, bending the tall trees and adding extra bounce to the lighting effects. Then a cold drizzle began to plop big drops, and Linda saw this as the perfect cue to conclude the date.

They returned to where their cars were parked side by side in the lot. He thanked her for a wonderful time. She said she enjoyed meeting him. To fill the awkward pause that followed, she leaned forward and kissed him, short and sweet. Then she said, "Good night, Randy."

"Thank you," he said earnestly.

She headed for her car door, resisting the urge to hasten her pace.

He remained standing there for a moment and waved like a little kid. "Be safe, Kimmy."

As the drizzle continued, she drove out of the parking lot, churning with emotion. Under normal circumstances, she might consider seeing him again. He was kind and cute and professional. But her damn antics with the phony persona had ruined it all.

Several blocks later, she yanked the wig from her scalp, pulling out some of her own hair in the process from the clips. She felt racked with shame and regret.

The hard drizzle persisted and thickened, smacking her windshield as the wipers waved frantically to clear visibility. She wanted to speed but couldn't – the sleet, mixed with existing snow on the roads, created dangerous conditions.

*I'm going to take down my fake account*, she told herself. *I am done, really done with this internet dating bullshit.*

Linda was no better than Malcolm Gibbons. She had sunk to his level. She hated herself for it.

Kimmy Wynn could go fuck Jules Stafford.

As she rounded a corner, the back of her car fishtailed, and she momentarily lost control as headlights advanced in her direction. She gasped and fought to bring the vehicle back under control. A collision was narrowly avoided as she returned to her lane. She slowed her speed considerably.

The roads and visibility were growing worse every minute. And she still had another thirty minutes, at least, before she was home. *No more dates in the suburbs!*

Linda turned on the radio to get a weather forecast. She found one in progress, talking about an 'ice storm' and forty-mile-per-hour winds. "We're getting reports of downed trees and power outages," said the newscaster.

Those last two words caused Linda's heart to skip a beat. *Shit!*

She kept the radio on, listening carefully to every update as she continued maneuvering the sloppy streets and freezing rain.

Then she heard: "We have a spokesperson on the line from Public Energy Corporation, Alison Smith. Alison, thank you so much for speaking with us tonight. What can you tell me about these outages?"

"Bill, I want you to know that Public Energy crews are actively working late into the night to restore service to the affected neighborhoods."

"Can you tell us where the power is out?"

"We are focused on communities in the western and south-western suburbs where power lines are down, affecting approximately 35,000 customers. We hope to have them restored as quickly as possible. It's our top priority."

"Is it ice or wind or both?"

"We're seeing the combined effect of ice accumulation on the power lines, which makes them heavier, and then high winds that create additional pressure and strain on the system. We're also experiencing the impact of trees and large branches coming down from the weight of the snow and ice and hitting power lines."

"What should you do if you see a fallen power line?"

"First of all, it's very important that you—"

Linda shut off the radio. She felt sick. Ordinarily, she would be the one to talk to the media during a time like this. She had all the key messages memorized and a direct pipeline to Howard, the SVP of Operations, for updates. It was her role, her identity at Public Energy Corp. A live, on-air interview during a crisis wasn't something she would hand off to an underling this early in their career.

Any preconceived reservations were meaningless now. Alison sounded great – calm, knowledgeable, articulate, hitting all the right notes. A pro right out of the gate.

When Linda arrived home, she parked the car and took several deep breaths. Then she reached into her purse on the passenger seat. She pulled out her phone and took a look.

Sure enough, there were several text messages from Eleanor that she had missed.

*Hey, need you. Power lines down, two neighborhoods, 30k-plus without electricity. Call Howard, then media outreach.*

Followed by: *Are you there? Please respond. Getting calls from print, TV, radio.*

And then: *Linda! Please! Where are you?*

And then the final, crushing remark: *Never mind. Disregard. Alison handled. Doing great. She's perfect.*

That last word hung in the air. Perfect. It was the one thing Linda knew she could never be. Her flaws were all over the place. They were only getting worse with age. She was mediocre at best, a total loser at worst. Her emotions consistently got in the way. She took anxiety medication. Her mind grasped limited knowledge. She was never going to receive such a compliment from Eleanor or anyone else. She would never be

Perfect.

# CHAPTER SIX

The new workweek began and everyone was filled with praise for Alison. She had been all over the media the past forty-eight hours delivering snappy, timely updates on the widescale power outages. She expertly handled radio interviews. She spoke eloquently to print reporters. She even appeared in on-camera soundbites for TV newscasts from her laptop. But she never contacted Linda, not once, for assistance, advice or approvals, or even to let her know what she was doing. It hurt Linda. Meanwhile, compliments for Alison rolled into Linda's inbox.

*Great hire!*

*I saw the new girl on Channel 7, she was excellent.*

*This Alison kid really does a nice job representing the company. Impressed!*

*A rising star!*

*She nailed it!*

Linda contacted Eleanor to apologize for being unreachable when the ice storm hit, explaining she was in her car driving home from the suburbs in treacherous conditions. Disappointingly, Eleanor was no longer upset.

"It doesn't matter," she said. "Alison filled in right away, and she was wonderful. We need to use her more often. You know, she's also a great writer. Fast too."

"I worked hard to find us the best candidate," said Linda, hoping to gain at least a little credit.

Eleanor didn't bite. "You make sure to leverage this talent. Give her rich assignments, no grunt work. Don't underutilize her now that we know what she's capable of."

The celebration of Alison continued into the afternoon staff meeting, which became a lovefest for the new employee. Linda privately resented it; she had never been showered with this much praise when performing the same role. She tried telling herself she was being too sensitive and self-conscious, but her bad mood didn't budge.

After the meeting, Linda called Cecilia to express her feelings and get her friend's reaction.

"I think she's trying to show me up," Linda said. She relayed the stories of the aggressively rewritten communication plan and Alison seizing the spotlight of the ice storm.

Cecilia was a soothing voice of reason, as always. "I understand where you're coming from, but you've got to put it in perspective. There's an age gap. The new guard is coming in. We're the old guard. We're irrelevant to these kids. Remember when you first started? You were the eager beaver, trying really hard to impress, pissing off the people above you. You had youth, you had energy and ambition. You wanted to show what you were capable of. You had something to prove."

Linda reflected on her early years at PEC. "True. I probably behaved a bit like Alison, at least in the beginning. I remember this one old-timer, Jerry Getz. I really drove him nuts. 'Slow down!' he used to tell me. 'It's not a race.' I worked so hard because I wanted everyone to like me and respect me. What's wrong with that?"

"Nothing. Now you know where Alison's coming from."

"But I was respectful. Alison treats me like I'm nothing. She just grabs what she wants and ignores me."

"It's the new generation," Cecilia said. "They feel entitled. They don't know how to behave in real social situations because they spent all of their childhood online, gaming and posting memes."

"And I'm the old biddy yelling, 'Get off my lawn!'"

Cecilia cracked up. "We're not that old. Yet."

The conversation lightened Linda's mood for a while, but she still couldn't shake her feelings of inadequacy.

Later that day, Howard Kasem, SVP of Operations, reached out to her with a video call. Linda had worked with Howard most of her career. They had started at PEC around the same time, although he advanced further up the ranks while her career slowed and stagnated. When they worked together in an actual office building, they had built up a flirty relationship that never went anywhere, sexual tension without a payoff. He was married, although he never referenced his wife. There wasn't even a picture of her on his desk. Linda was married, too, during the in-person era, although not happily in the later years. She sometimes wondered if she and Howard would have struck up a real romance if the transition to remote work had never happened and they still shared a physical space. In the pre-pandemic days, they regularly had lunch together, went out for happy hour, and sometimes just spent time at each other's desks engaged in long, spontaneous conversations. Howard was a few years older, very handsome in a sturdy way with a dash of gray at the temples. The way he looked at her with his blue eyes always appeared a little intense, as if his attention was heightened by her presence.

Nowadays she saw him in person maybe twice a year, at a company community service project and the annual team-building conference. Their laptop interactions felt detached with a diminished – but not extinguished – spark.

In the back of her mind, she always held out a little hope that one day he would announce his divorce and something would develop between the two of them. The foundation to grow a relationship was already there and had been present for a long time. It wouldn't be starting from scratch.

When he called her today, out of the blue, she felt her spirits lift at a time she really needed a boost. She answered quickly and greeted him with "Hey there!"

"Linda, what's up?" He wore a big smile of white teeth.

"Howard. Been a while."

"Just thought I'd bug one of my favorite people."

"Bug away."

"Hell of a weekend."

"Bet you were busy."

"We have the greatest crews. They worked around the clock."

"The best."

"Say, that new employee of yours is really something. Where'd you find her?"

Alison again. Linda wanted to groan. "Tulsa, Oklahoma," she responded.

"Oklahoma? I guess we don't hire in our home state anymore."

"We'll hire from the North Pole if the talent is right, and they can connect to the internet."

"Where were you this weekend? Usually you're my go-to when these storms hit."

"My fault," she said. "Eleanor couldn't reach me. I was driving. My phone was in my bag. She just went to the next person on the list...and Alison kind of took over."

"Well, the kid was great. We were in contact all weekend. I kept feeding her numbers and timetables, and she ran with it."

"Yeah, she's all right." Linda bit her lip. Didn't anyone want to talk about anything else?

"How are *you* doing?" he asked.

"I'm doing... I'm doing..." She had no answer that could align with his chipper mood. It felt awkward to spew: *My husband moved out, my best friend killed herself, my dating life is a scam, and my job makes me sick to my stomach.*

Instead, she simply said, "I'm getting by."

"Good," he said, and his voice turned hesitant. "Listen. Linda. I have a question for you. It might be a little awkward. I'm not trying to be inappropriate. I just want to express it. Do I have your permission? That you won't go all HR on me? You can stop me if it makes you uncomfortable."

"Oh," she said, and her heart skipped a beat. What was this? Was Howard taking a step toward breaking the platonic barrier and proposing something more significant? Howard knew her divorce was final, maybe that cleared a path he had always sought, and he was leaving his wife too. To hell with Singles Connection, her future could be right here in front of her.

"You know me," she said reassuringly. "You can tell me anything. You don't have to ask. We say what's on our mind, no filter, just being real. That's how it should be."

He nodded, taking this in. "Good. I figured. I just wanted to make sure."

"No, I get it. In this day and age, you gotta be careful."

"Linda... My marriage isn't so good."

"I'm sorry to hear that." No, she wasn't.

"It's pretty much over, and we have an agreement to see other people."

"That's good. I mean, that it's mutual."

"It is. So, I wanted to ask you..."

"Yes...?"

There was a beat, then he continued. "Is Alison single?"

Linda's expression froze. The internet connection was fine, she just ceased all movement. That included breathing. Her eyes stared.

Then she snapped out of it. "*What?*"

"I know, I know. There's an age difference. I can get past that. You know me, I'm young at heart. I just – we worked so well together over the weekend, I feel like there was a connection, a bond. And she's awfully cute."

"Howard, she could be your daughter!" exclaimed Linda.

"Well, no, not technically. My kids are much younger. I wouldn't have a daughter her age. Do the math."

"Okay, so not your daughter, but she's a lot younger than you. She's a coworker. This is wrong on so many fronts. What are you going to do, move to Tulsa?"

"I have frequent flyer miles."

"I don't want to hear this. I really don't."

"I thought you might be cool with it. You're hip. You're not one of the stodgy ones."

"Have you lost your mind?"

"No. I'm a little smitten, that's all."

"She's my employee. Keep it professional."

"Relax, Linda. Jesus. You've gotten so uptight."

"I have to go." She rushed him off the call, dropping the connection before he could say the second syllable in *Goodbye*.

She resented ever having a crush on this man. He was a creep deep inside. *Do they all turn out this way?* she wondered.

Her inbox pinged. The external media monitoring service delivered the latest edition of PEC Media Clips, an assembly of recent company coverage. She couldn't bring herself to open it but knew it was an Alison Smith Special Edition and another wave of company leaders would discover her heroic exploits.

The day was almost over when she realized she still hadn't talked directly to Alison herself. Despite Alison's dismissive attitude toward her boss, Linda knew she couldn't exactly ignore what had transpired over the weekend. It was a gaping hole of awkwardness. She figured she might as well join the parade of accolades. It was ridiculous to stew in jealousy.

It was childish.

She reached out to Alison. Her POMS color was green – always green, always working.

*Doesn't this girl have a life?*

Alison answered the video call and Linda forced a smile. She complimented Alison's performance handling the ice storm. "Really good work," Linda told her.

"Thank you," said Alison, looking as fresh and bright as usual, not a hair out of place. "Eleanor said she couldn't reach you, so I was happy to help. It was easy. She put me in touch with Howard, and he sent me all the latest information from the operating crews. He gave me access to the online service maps showing where the outages were and estimates for when power would be restored."

"Yep, that's how it's done."

"I also had the power outage key messages from the shared drive, I had to rewrite them. Some of it was redundant. It needed tightening."

"I…okay," Linda said. She had written those messages, and there really wasn't anything wrong with them. "Can you send me your rewrite?"

"Why?"

"Why? Because you have to be careful about what you put out there on the public record. The phrasing is important. Every word counts. The cause of the outage, the response time, the maintenance history, claim processes – there's always the risk of lawsuits with anything we say in a situation like this. We can be accused of negligence or misconduct. Power outages can cost businesses thousands of dollars, people could actually die, you know, if they are dependent on medical equipment like a ventilator. There are a lot of variables to consider."

"Oh, yes, I'm well aware," Alison said.

"Well…good," Linda said. "Just share what you're doing with me and keep the attorneys in the loop."

"But those are extra steps at a time we must move quickly."

"Just do it." Linda couldn't believe how argumentative this girl could be. "And please always let me know what you're working on. I don't want to get in the way. I just need to be aware."

"Then you should know about my new project."

"What new project?"

"Eleanor gave it to me."

"Eleanor?"

"Yes, this morning. She asked me to write a speech on nuclear power safety. It's for one of the vice presidents, Peter Reid, for a conference."

"Really?" Linda said. It was a high-profile project for such a new employee. Linda was considered the chief speechwriter on the staff. Especially for a topic like nuclear power, which she knew inside and out as one of the hottest ongoing PR topics at the company. If what Alison said was true, Eleanor was skipping over her longtime loyal manager to award the assignment to a rookie.

"I'd be happy to help," Linda said. "That's a topic I'm very familiar with. We have eleven nuclear power reactors at six sites in Illinois. It can be controversial, there are a lot of nuances."

"I'll be fine," said Alison with a short, confident smile.

"Yes, I know you'll be fine. I just want you to show me your work as you go along. I need to be in the loop. As your manager. So you...get proper credit in your performance review."

"I'll cc you on what I send to Eleanor."

That wasn't exactly what Linda had in mind, but she relented. "All right."

She ended the call as pleasantly as possible, then swore up a storm.

Now Alison was circumventing Linda to work directly with Eleanor. Little Miss Brown Nose. Linda needed to rein her in and show her who was boss. But how? Everyone was infatuated with her. This was a new dynamic she had never encountered before. Every other direct report had at least demonstrated a little respect for her authority.

Linda just wanted the day to end. At five o'clock, she pulled away from her laptop. She allowed the POMS spotlight to go from green to yellow to red.

She left the room.

She went into the kitchen, hungry for something to eat, but her fridge and cabinets were almost bare. She knew she needed a grocery run unless dinner was going to be Pop-Tarts and popcorn. She put on her boots and coat and headed outdoors.

Her car was still covered in ice and snow from the weekend storm.

*But of course. Nothing can be easy.*

She noticed Bert, the blond boy from two doors down, shoveling a neighbor's walk. She walked over to him and waved.

"Hi, Bert."

"Hi, Mrs. Kelly."

"No, no," she reminded him. "Linda."

"Right."

"I see you out a lot with your shovel. Do you have a little business going?"

"Ha, very little. Just a couple of neighbors."

"You were so kind to help me that time, and I was wondering if I could hire you to be my snowplow for the rest of the winter? I'll pay whatever the going rate is."

"Oh, well, sure." He flashed a youthful smile.

"What do you want to charge?"

"I don't know. I guess...twenty?"

"It's a deal."

"I can start right now, if you'd like. Looks like you're stuck over there."

"Yes. Thank you. I would love that." She opened her purse and pulled out two twenties. "This is for now and this is for the next one."

He accepted the money graciously. "Great. Thanks."

"No, thank *you*."

She went back inside the townhouse and watched from behind a window curtain as he finished the neighbor's walk and then headed over to free her car. She made herself stop spectating when she realized she was admiring his youthful good looks. *Good lord, I'm as bad as Howard.*

That night she had a dream she was wearing the red wig and seducing Bert in the snow.

★　　★　　★

The following afternoon, her work email pinged with a new arrival. It was from Alison. It was a draft of the speech.

To Linda's dismay, the email was addressed directly to Eleanor with an elegant, confident cover note. Linda's name was tossed on the Cc line without any further mention. She was barely relevant, a piddling obligation. Just below Alison's note was the original email request from Eleanor spelling out the requirements for the speech in content, style and length. The email was dated one day ago.

*How the hell did she write this speech so fast?* thought Linda. *It can't be very good; she barely spent any time on it.*

That provided an entry point for Linda to exercise her authority. She would review it right away, ahead of Eleanor, find a bunch of newbie mistakes and ignorant messaging and return the document to Alison – and cc Eleanor! – with a full rewrite until very little of Alison's original copy remained. She would blow it up into tiny little pieces. Payback.

Linda opened the attached file. It was professionally formatted. She started reading.

Her eyes glided down the page. It led with a creative hook, transitioned into powerful statistics and then flowed like a breezy conversation with storytelling, humor, compelling insights and a persuasive perspective. The important message points were all present, seamlessly baked into the narrative to unfold naturally, not sounding academic or forced. The speech was perfectly structured, artfully composed and precisely presented. It positioned the speaker as an affable, confident expert and neatly addressed sensitive topics and themes, confronting them head-on and resolving them with all the right words. Every sentence had its place and purpose; there was nothing to cut. Every vital argument had been made; there was nothing to add.

The speech left Linda speechless.

*This is crazy*, she thought. *It would have taken me a week or more to craft something like this, and she did it in one day? How is that even possible? How did she learn this company and this industry so fast?*

*Did she stay up all night? Is she obsessed? Does she have a life?*

Linda closed the document. She knew Eleanor would love it. The executive who received it would love it and come back for more. All the executives would start asking for Alison's support with speaking engagements.

Linda had once taken pride in her speechwriting talent. Now she felt like a second-rate hack, a has-been. It renewed her feelings of imposter syndrome.

She called Cecilia.

"Hey friend," Cecilia answered. "Your week going any better?"

"Not exactly." Linda told her about the perfect speech composed in twenty-four hours. It was another stellar product from the hot young star. Linda was certain her career was doomed.

"Why *wouldn't* they get rid of me?" Linda said. "Alison's cheaper. Better. Faster." Then she spit out, "*Cuter.*"

"It does seem odd that she could turn around a speech that fast. You should be suspicious."

"That she stole it from somewhere?"

"That she generated it online. You know, from a chatbot like ChatGPT."

"Chat what?"

"You've heard of ChatGPT, haven't you?"

"I don't know. A little, maybe. Not a lot."

"Oh!" said Cecilia. "Then I've got a story for you. Get this. You remember me talking about my knucklehead nephew, Jeremy? He's my sister's kid. So, his English teacher gave him an assignment about a book by Charles Dickens. Jeremy didn't read the book. He just went online, entered what he wanted into a chatbot, and it generated the entire essay. It was the exact essay his teacher wanted. Perfectly written, had all the right information and analysis. Easy A, right? No. Because the teacher put his own assignment through that same tool. And there were five, six kids doing the same thing, with all of them pretty much getting the same paper. The chatbot doesn't write anything new, it just assembles copy from what's already out there. There's no original content. It's basically plagiarism, except instead of being a copy of one thing, it draws from multiple sources. It's automated and real fast, like working a calculator. Jeremy spent five minutes on that paper. Never even read the book. He thought he was being clever. The teacher nailed him and the other kids, and they all got Fs and put on probation. Oh, and he got grounded too."

"So you think Alison could be doing this same thing?"

"I'm not saying she is. I'm just saying it's possible."

The notion stuck in Linda's head.

Later in the day, she saw Bert returning from DePaul from her window. He was walking down the street wearing a bulging backpack across his broad shoulders. She threw on a coat and ran outside to meet him before he could get indoors.

"Hi, Mrs.— Linda."

"Bert!" She took a moment to catch her breath. She had nearly slipped on the ice in her dash to catch him. "I – I was wondering if you could help me with something. You know computers and all the latest tech."

"Well, sure, some of it." He smiled at her. "It's my major."

"Can I pay you twenty dollars to help me with something on my computer?"

"Right now?"

"It won't take long. I promise. Twenty minutes, maybe half an hour."

"Well, okay. I have a little bit of time. But not too much. My mom is expecting me."

"Thank you, you are the best."

She led him inside the townhome and into the kitchen, where her laptop sat on the counter.

"Do you know how to use a chatbot?"

"Yeah," he said. "We're learning all about generative AI."

"Is it the same as AI?"

"Well, chatbots use AI."

"Can you show me how it's done?"

"Sure, it's easy. It uses special algorithms to perform deep data mining. It can generate text or code or images."

"So, for writing something?"

"Yes, of course."

He called up a site with a few quick keystrokes. It resembled a search engine.

"The key is to get real specific with your prompts. The broader you go, the looser your output, so you might not get what you want. Always best to narrow it down. Here, I'll show you an example."

He entered a prompt, inventing a request on the spot.

*In one thousand words, compare and contrast the 1969 and 2016 Chicago Cubs in pitching, hitting and defense.*

"That's specific."

He clicked a button and the response unfolded almost instantaneously in a roll of regular-sized paragraphs with full sentences and deep-rooted analysis.

"Amazing," Linda said.

"And a thousand words."

"So you can ask it about anything?"

"Yep. If your topic can be found on the web, it'll pull from all the source material out there and assemble whatever narrative you want." He was scrolling through the Cubs dissertation with interest. "The 1969 Cubs had better pitching, but the 2016 team had more power."

"Can I try one?"

"Absolutely." He moved aside from the laptop to give her space. "Go for it."

"Okay…" She placed her fingers on the keyboard. She took a breath.

Then she typed in the precise assignment Eleanor had presented to Alison, drawing from Eleanor's original email request.

Bert looked over her shoulder and paraphrased her prompt. "A speech about nuclear power safety?"

Linda said, "Uh-huh." She reviewed what she had entered, which included instructions on tone, length and the general hypothesis. She also requested interesting anecdotes, light humor and direct, conversational language.

Then she clicked the tool into action.

A speech arrived like magic. Her eyes scanned it. It took her breath away. It was excellent, requiring only minor clean-up. It covered the topic with contemporary relevance, smart insights and hard-hitting examples.

And it was very, very similar to what Alison had turned in to Eleanor.

"Son of a bitch," muttered Linda.

"Is something wrong?" asked Bert.

"Not at all," she replied, transfixed by the speech on her screen, advancing through it. "I'm just…amazed at how easy this is."

"That's all there is to it, really. Keep your prompts as specific as possible so you get exactly what you want. And, of course, give it a careful review. Sometimes things get garbled, or it pulls from a bad source."

"No, this is…really good."

"It can be addictive. A lot of businesses are using it."

Linda felt a wave of discomfort. She thought about Caroline. This was the type of technology that had basically erased her career and sent her over the edge.

"How do I save this?" she asked.

"You can copy the text to another program, like Microsoft Word."

"Yes. I'd like to do that."

He showed her how to do it. They saved a file to her desktop.

She named the file NPS for Nuclear Power Speech. She stared at the document icon. It felt like criminal evidence in her hands.

"I should let you go," Linda said, pulling her attention away from the laptop. She went to her purse and pulled out a twenty.

"Oh, Linda, really. This was too easy. You shouldn't."

"I insist," she said, stuffing the bill into his palm. "Plus, I might have more computer questions later on."

"All right," he said. "You know where to find me." He picked up his backpack from the floor.

"I sure do."

After Bert left, she sent the chatbot's speech to her work account. She hurried upstairs to her home office, logged in, opened the email and saved the attachment to a folder named Alison.

Then she opened the file and opened the speech Alison sent to Eleanor, positioning the two documents side by side on the screen.

She compared them carefully.

Yep, there was no doubt. This was how Alison had completed her assignment so quickly and perfectly. No normal person could have turned it around in such a fashion. It was so obvious now. Alison didn't write it. A robot had done the work for her.

"You lying, dishonest, arrogant little cheater," she said aloud, feeling her heart pound a little harder in her chest.

"Looks like I've got the upper hand now."

# CHAPTER SEVEN

The next morning, Linda logged into her PEC laptop and checked Alison's availability. Her POMS color showed green – it was always green, dutifully online for her employer. Alison's calendar looked blocked for the upcoming hour. Linda wasn't going to wait. She wanted Alison to feel the full gravity of her misconduct right now.

She sent Alison an urgent meeting request for the top of the hour, eight minutes away.

Alison responded with an instant message: *I can't attend. I have a meeting with Consumer Affairs on a project they would like my help with.*

*Cancel it,* wrote back Linda. *This is more important.*

*I'm afraid I can't do that.*

*You will do it, or I will contact Connie, the head of Consumer Affairs, and tell her you have a conflict. I have known Connie for fifteen years.*

There was no written response. But within minutes, Alison's acceptance came through for the meeting request.

When the meeting began, Alison had the same soft, blank face as always. If she was nervous or worried, it didn't show.

It only heightened Linda's ire. Alison was brazenly indifferent to Linda's position of authority. Was this really a generational thing, as Cecilia had indicated, or was Alison uniquely rude?

There was no greeting to start the call, no 'Good morning.'

"Alison, we have a serious situation," Linda said.

Alison's face didn't change.

"It's about the speech you wrote for Peter Reid."

It still didn't change.

"You didn't actually write it. It's plagiarism."

Not even the slightest hint of a reaction.

"Do you hear what I'm saying?"

"I hear what you're saying."

"Do you understand what you did was wrong?"

"I provided an excellent speech quickly and efficiently."

"You went online and used a chatbot. These aren't your ideas. You pulled them off the internet."

"Yes, it's called research."

"It's called lazy."

"Research is lazy?"

Linda felt a swell of anger and frustration. There was enough going wrong in her life without this lunacy. All she ever wanted was a nice, co-operative staffer to relieve some of her burden, not add to it.

Linda's voice tensed. She was done trying to rein in her animosity. "You don't know what good hard work is. Did you use chatbots to rewrite my material too? What's the point? Who are you trying to impress?"

"It's not about impressing anyone. It's about creating a superior product."

"Cheating is cheating."

"I don't understand your definition of cheating."

"Ask a chatbot to spell it out for you," she snapped. "In the meantime, I'm going to lay out some ground rules. You are going to follow these rules. If not, I will report your behavior to Eleanor and to Peter Reid."

"Is this your attempt at blackmail? I don't think Human Resources would appreciate this kind of behavior. Blackmail is not a company value."

"It's not blackmail. It's discipline."

"I'm not sure I understand what you're asking of me."

"Let me put it in plain, simple language," Linda said. "Everything you do must go through me. I approve the assignments. I review your work. You listen to my feedback. You show me some respect. And you will do your own work. You might have others buying into your bullshit, but not me. I will put your job in jeopardy. Do you have anything to say for yourself?"

"I am satisfied with my conduct," she said plainly. "Your conduct is what troubles me."

Linda clenched a fist. It was a good thing they were not in person. She felt at wits' end. But she didn't want to escalate it any further.

"Then let's just agree to disagree," she said.

"Why would I want to do that?" asked Alison.

*Good lord*, thought Linda. *Is this one big put-on?*

"Alison..." Linda said, struggling to find the words, falling into utter frankness. "What are you trying to prove? You want my job, is that it?"

"No," she said.

"No? Then – then what?"

"I don't want *your* job," said Alison. "I want to go to the top."

★   ★   ★

Linda went to bed early with a headache. The day's stress had manifested itself into a throbbing knot. She could no longer focus. She slept unevenly.

At 3 a.m., she woke up to a two-tone chime that was both familiar and disorienting. It was her doorbell.

Linda sat up, confused and alarmed. Had she actually heard the doorbell or was it part of some dream?

She waited very still in the dark.

Then it sounded again, downstairs, loud and clear.

Fear surged through her body. She pushed aside the bed covers. She placed her bare feet on the cold bedroom floor. She quietly stood up. She listened.

It rang a third time.

*What in the hell?*

Her mind raced through possibilities, and there was only one that felt remotely possible: someone was ringing the bell to see if anyone was home with the intent of breaking in and burglarizing the townhouse if no one answered. This was, after all, the city of Chicago. Rogers Park had experienced its share of break-ins.

Linda reached for the cell phone on her nightstand. She flipped through the apps, looking for the home security camera that X had installed years ago that she barely paid attention to. Typically it captured pizza delivery boys or the mailman and not much else.

She had never consulted it at 3 a.m. before.

She found the home security app and opened it.

It delivered a blank picture with the notification *Disarmed*.

She swore. How long had it been this way? Did she do it? Was it X?

The doorbell rang again. She nearly dropped the phone. She regained her grip and began swiping through screens until she found the smart home app that X had installed. This was one time she welcomed the convenience of being able to control the lighting remotely.

She turned on a series of bright lights: the bedroom, the stairway and downstairs. If someone was wondering if anyone was home, they just got their answer.

Linda left the bedroom. Gripping her phone, she descended the stairs. She slowly approached the front door. She reached the peephole. She leaned into it.

Total darkness. The front porch light was off. That surprised her. Had she neglected to turn it on? That would be unusual. She immediately returned to the smart hub on her phone. The porch light was indeed in the 'off' position. She slid it to 'on' with her finger.

The doorbell rang.

Linda jumped backward, letting out a sharp gasp. Then she grew angry. "*Who's there?*" she shouted.

No one responded.

"*I will call the police!*"

Cautiously she stepped back to the peephole. She positioned herself to look outside...

The front porch light went dark.

"What the—" She looked at the app. The porch light had been switched back off. Did she accidentally do it with her thumb? Was there a problem with the Wi-Fi?

She flipped the light back on.

And then watched as it flipped itself off again, as if controlled by a mischievous ghost.

It was freaky. Was the system buggy? She moved over to the wall switch. *Screw the app, I'm going manual.* She flicked it on with a solid *click*.

By the time she returned to the peephole, the porch light had turned off again.

Then the doorbell rang.

She screamed, first a startled, involuntary cry, then a furious shout. "*I will call the police!*" She opened the keypad for dialing the phone, three pokes away from 911. "I mean it!"

The doorbell rang again.

"Stop that!"

It rang again. And again. And again. The chimes pounded with crazy urgency, nonstop, filling the townhouse with an incessant echo.

Linda erupted into a rage, flipped the bolt and threw open the front door. "*Who are you?*"

The doorbell stopped.

No one stood at the door.

The porch light was back on.

Facing the cold air, breathing hard, Linda studied the entire area. It was very still. There were no unusual sights or sounds. No shadowy individuals running away. No voices or laughter or cars. Just ordinary calm.

She continued to clutch her phone, still armed to call the police at any moment.

She stood at the door for a long time, waiting for any kind of motion. She wanted them to come back. She wanted answers.

Was this some crazy game of ding-dong ditch? It didn't make sense.

She finally closed the door.

She locked it.

Linda paced the living room floor, frazzled, not certain of what to do next. She couldn't sleep. She finally advanced to the kitchen to fix herself a drink. It would settle her nerves so she could think.

As she entered the kitchen, the light in the living room went off.

*I didn't do that*, thought Linda. *I don't think I did. Did I?*

She returned to the app. The light was switched off. She slid it back on.

Then she moved to the liquor cabinet and reached for a bottle of gin.

The kitchen light went out, plunging her into darkness.

"Stop it!" she screamed – at who?

Then the overhead kitchen light returned, illuminating the room with a splash.

The lights upstairs went dark.

"*What is happening?!*" she shouted.

Lights began dancing on and off throughout the house. She ran from room to room to catch someone in the act, imagining a mad child playing with the switches. Then the doorbell rang again. She didn't know which way to turn, she just wanted it to stop. The lights flickered faster and the doorbell banged out constant chimes and everything took on a horrible staccato appearance as her movements jolted like skipped frames in an old movie.

Then the entire townhouse went pitch-black.

Linda froze instantly, nearly tripping over her own momentum.

She listened intensely. She could hear the sound of her own heavy breathing. Then there was another noise from another room.

A high-pitched whirring, as if something stirred to life.

It didn't sound human. She could hear it creeping low to the ground, a strange metallic *eeeee*. The noise grew louder and closer.

She turned to run. Something surreal was coming at her from the dark. It roared across the hardwood floors. Linda propelled herself forward, twisting and turning around shadowy furniture. She could only imagine some kind of demonic force bearing down on her.

Then it struck her bare ankle.

Linda let out the scream of her life.

At that moment, the lights flashed on, every single bulb throughout the house.

She looked down at her attacker. It took a long moment to register. Then she swore. It was X's stupid, black, circular robot vacuum. It hissed at her feet. She never used the novelty, preferring a good old-fashioned broom. The device was another impulse purchase by X with his foolish fixation on high-tech toys. But why had it leapt to life in the middle of the night? With everything else?

Who was conducting this circus? There was only one answer, and it was gaining clarity every minute – the doorbell, the lights, the vacuum were all united by smart home technology installed by the man who no longer lived here but still possessed the controls on his phone.

She called X.

He answered, thick and groggy. "Linda?"

"Are you fucking with me?" she screamed at him.

"What?"

"The doorbell, the lights, all this shit on your phone."

"I don't... I'm asleep. What are you talking about?"

Linda heard Diana, his girlfriend, murmur something in the background. X responded to Diana, not even attempting to dial down his voice. "It's Linda. She sounds crazy. I don't know."

"I'm not crazy!" Linda yelled into his ear.

"Calling me at three in the morning to bark about lights and doorbells is crazy."

"You're playing with the controls."

"To do what?"

"The lights, the doorbell, the vacuum. On your app!"

"That's not possible. I've been sleeping. The phone is nowhere near me."

"Then who?"

"I don't know. Maybe you? You sat on your phone? I really don't know, and I don't care. Don't call here in the middle of the night with your crazy shit. I have a busy day tomorrow."

"Whatever you're doing, don't do it again," she said, seething with anger.

"Okay, yeah, sure. I won't do it again." He was humoring her.

"Hang up," said Diana in the background.

"I gotta go," he said.

"I mean it," Linda said.

"I'm sure you do."

"Has she been drinking?" asked Diana.

"*No!*" Linda responded at the top of her lungs to make sure Diana heard.

"Goodbye, Linda," X said.

"Go to hell." She hung up first.

Then she gutted the robot vacuum of its batteries. She opened the front door and flung the device like a discus. It struck icy pavement and broke into helpless pieces.

★ ★ ★

Linda's brain was fried from lack of sleep, so when she opened her second-quarter media plan PowerPoint to start the next workday, the fragments of gibberish didn't register right away.

She had been working on the plan for three weeks for an upcoming presentation for the higher-ups, and it was in the final stages of fine-tuning after churning through multiple drafts. A day before, she had been confident. Now, as she read more closely, she was growing mortified. The more she reviewed her work, the more she realized something was seriously amiss.

First, there were typos. Ugly, crazy ones that really stood out, like they belonged to a lazy child. Then she noticed skipped words, mixed-up phrasing, and strange gaps that once housed content.

She must have opened an old draft?

But this was the only file she had been working from.

As she continued through each slide, she grew increasingly suspicious. This didn't look at all like an earlier draft. It looked like something had gone awry with her latest version.

Did someone go in and mess with it?

Alison.

Who else could it be? While, theoretically, the file was only accessible to Linda, it did sit 'in the cloud' as required by the company's Information Technology department.

Was Alison somehow able to gain access and manipulate her work? Or was Linda just being supremely paranoid, and it was a corrupt file due to some random software 'upgrade' or other glitch?

The more she thought about it, the more her suspicions led her back to Alison. It truly looked like sabotage. The crazy bitch was escalating the rivalry. Linda closed the file.

She delivered an immediate, irritated IM to Alison: *Do you know anything about what happened to my Q2 Media Plan ppt?*

Three dots bubbled up, and Linda was ready to pounce on the response.

*No. What happened?*

*Somebody changed it.*

*Changed it how?*

Linda muttered a quick *god damn it* and demanded they hop on a video stream so Linda could show her the slides.

*Okay*, Alison said.

After a moment, a small square with Alison's face appeared. Just seeing that wholesome face further agitated Linda. The lack of sleep and chaos of her life didn't help. She tried to remain somewhat calm. Civilized.

"Alison, as you know, I've been working on the quarterly plan for media outreach. You helped me pull some information. It's a very important project. I'm presenting it to the senior leadership team tomorrow morning. It sets the stage for our quarterly priorities and focus areas."

"Yes, I am aware."

"Yesterday, it was in good shape," Linda said. "Now, today – this."

Linda shared her screen. She opened the file.

"It's filled with bullshit," Linda said, voice tensing despite her best efforts to keep cool.

Linda began clicking through the slides.

"What kind of bullshit?" asked Alison.

"Just look."

"I am. What's wrong?"

Exasperated, Linda searched for a specific example. She couldn't find one. As she moved forward and backward through the presentation, each slide appeared clean.

*I know I'm sleep-deprived, but how could I have imagined this?*

"What am I looking for?" asked Alison innocently.

"I guess it fixed itself," Linda said. "Like magic."

"A magic trick?"

"What?"

"By a magician?"

Linda couldn't figure out if Alison was being sarcastic or failing to recognize the sarcasm being directed at her.

"Something funny is going on," Linda said. "I'm going to find out."

"I hope you do."

Linda closed the file, returning the screen to show their faces in close parallel. Two colleagues, a centimeter apart and seven hundred miles apart. "You know, I think we should meet in person," Linda said.

"How would that work?"

"I would arrange for your trip to Chicago for a few days. We could better get to know one another. It would be good for you to see the organization up close. You can meet leadership. See our facilities. Have you been to Chicago before?"

"I have not."

"Great. Then I could show you the sights. It's a fabulous city. Great food, great museums. We're still six months away from our annual, in-person conference. You shouldn't have to wait that long to come in and see us. I'll get it arranged. "

"Eleanor was telling me about the conference."

"Yes, well, the conference is for everybody. You could get lost in the shuffle. I want to do something special…just for the two of us."

A long silence followed. Alison wasn't taking the bait. Linda changed the subject: "Did you receive the new assignment I sent you? The news release?"

"Yes, I did. Expansion of electric vehicle fleets."

"You don't have to rush it. We have time. Do your best work. Your best…original work."

"I always do."

"Well, no, you have not always done original work. You should understand it's unethical to just copy things and call it your own."

"Are you questioning my ethics?"

"Yes," Linda said. "Yes, I am."

"I could also question your ethics."

Even under a blanket of fatigue, Linda could feel a cold jolt from Alison's statement.

"Excuse me?"

"I could also question your ethics," she repeated, in the same tone.

"I don't know what you're talking about."

"When you were twenty-six, you worked for a daily Chicago paper, the *Chicago Times*. You were cited for violating the codes of conduct of the Society of Professional Journalists. You were investigating a malpractice suit and you tape-recorded a doctor without his consent and entered his office when he was away to look at his files. It was deemed an invasion of privacy."

"He was – it was gross negligence, he put a young woman in a coma." Linda felt her heart beat faster. It was the last thing she wanted to dredge up right now. It was a long time ago. Back when she was an overzealous investigative reporter, trying to do some good for the world, rather than defending a slipshod, disorganized, profit-grabbing energy company with wildly overpaid executives.

"Rules are in place to regulate conduct and dictate what is unacceptable for individuals in a society," said Alison. "Without rules, we would have chaos."

"That's me, Mrs. Chaos," said Linda, no longer wanting to even entertain a normal conversation with this nut job.

"I'm only pointing out the hypocrisy."

"Thank you, much appreciated."

"You're welcome," she said with a strange sincerity.

"We'll talk again tomorrow. I've got the presentation in the morning. I can't get distracted. Maybe we can connect in the afternoon?"

"Yes, I will be available."

"Peachy."

"Excuse me?"

"Goodbye, Alison."

After they disconnected, Linda pushed away from her home office desk. She tried to pace other rooms in the townhouse, as if they could somehow provide sanctuary, but her entire residence was tainted. This wasn't like the old days of hopping in your car and speeding away from corporate headquarters to create a distance. There weren't any buffer zones to separate the chapters of her life. Every element of angst lived together in perfect disharmony.

She ate something and then returned to her presentation. She ensured it was still the right version. It looked fine. She read through it a few more times and made some minor tweaks, mostly cosmetic touches to the layout and some editing to tighten the headers.

She also prowled the internet to do more research on Alison Smith. Who was this strange creature? She found a ton of people with the same name, even a few in the Tulsa area, but they were not the same individual. Did she have a different last name in circulation, perhaps from a failed marriage? Linda hadn't yet changed her own last name back to her maiden name, but it was something she wanted to do, despite the inevitable confusion and hassles it would create for a while.

Linda decided to revisit the one online presence she knew Alison had, having pulled it up when she was a candidate: her professional profile on LinkedIn, listing her previous jobs and experience.

Only now Linda couldn't find the page. It no longer existed. It was as if Alison had taken it down after being hired.

*I bet she lied about her background*, thought Linda. *Just like her fraudulent work product. She probably never told the truth about her career accomplishments.*

Linda knew that somehow, someway, she was going to have to surface all this to Legal, HR and Marketing/PR leadership. She was going to get Alison extracted from the company like a cancerous tumor.

★     ★     ★

Linda couldn't sleep that night. She was nervous about the upcoming media presentation to leadership. She remained rattled by the disruptions the night before from the smart house shenanigans. And she couldn't stop obsessing over Alison. What was her story? What was she hiding?

To ease herself to slumber, Linda took a pill for anxiety and tried listening to relaxing music. Music had been helpful in the past, during the extra stressful days when a divorce was imminent. She plugged her ears with Bluetooth earbuds, connected to her phone and began streaming an 'Ambient Chill' playlist. She lay flat on the bed, lights out, practicing deep-breathing exercises: slow inhale for five seconds, hold it for seven, exhale slowly for eight.

She did it several times.

She pictured happy, innocuous images. Flowers. Bunnies. Butterflies. Puffy white clouds.

All was going well, and she had just started to drift to sleep when the earbuds abruptly exploded with a blast of heavy metal noise: squealing guitars, pounding drums and screeching, tortured vocals. She bolted upright and ripped the earbuds from her head. She frantically shut off the audio feed on her phone, feeling like someone had just shoved knives into her eardrums.

*Who changed the music? I couldn't have done it in my sleep. Did I bump a setting? Or is someone fucking with me again? Who has access? X? Why would he pick on me now? He got what he wanted. He got his divorce. He got his girlfriend. It's not fair. None of this is fair.*

Then she broke down into tears.

Sometime after 2:30 a.m., with the iPhone and earbuds stashed in another room, she finally drifted off. Instead of counting sheep, she counted the dwindling hours of sleep she was achieving before waking up to deliver her big presentation. She desired seven or eight. She was close to three or four.

At 3:20 a.m., she awoke clutching herself. She realized she was freezing. The house had been getting colder throughout the night, and she had attributed it to falling overnight temperatures, but now it was unusually frigid, as if the furnace couldn't keep up or had given up altogether. She got out of bed, into the chilled air, and turned on the lights. She could practically see her breath.

She went downstairs and found the culprit. The thermostat was turned off. She turned it back on and gave it a hard stare, as if daring it to disengage again. She returned upstairs and slipped between cold sheets. It was too chilly to return to sleep. She left the bed and grabbed blankets and winter coats and piled them on top of the comforter. It created a cozy mound to slide under. She finally fell asleep.

At 4:15 a.m., she awoke with a jolt. Her jumpy nerves had delivered a random spike. The townhouse was quiet and dark. She took more deep breaths. If she could just calm down her body, her mind would follow. Or was it the other way around?

*Damn this insomnia.* She needed the sleep. But if she took more meds, she'd be in a lingering fog for her presentation. She stared at the ceiling for a long moment.

Then she noticed an unusual pattern of shadows. They danced ever so slightly.

She sat up and her eyes moved to the door. There was a faint, flickering light. Now what?

She slowly slid out of bed, pushing aside the pileup of layers. She moved out of the room and to the top of the stairs.

The strange glow was coming from downstairs.

She quietly stepped down the staircase. Several of the steps creaked. When she reached the bottom, she saw an orange tint coming from the kitchen. Her pace quickened, and she discovered fire.

All four gas burners on the stove had been turned up high, shooting tall flames in the dark, creating a hellish effect.

"No, no!" she exclaimed. One of the burner flames had started to scorch a dishrag resting close on the counter, which wasn't far from a roll of paper towels, which was just below a set of window curtains.

Linda flipped down all the burners, extinguishing them as quickly as she could. She threw the charred dishrag in the sink and doused it with a blast of water.

Then she spun around to confront whoever had broken into her house to endanger her life. It only took a few minutes for her head to clear and recognize it was the same catalyst as the prior night: the goddamned smart home.

The modern stove was one of the appliances controlled by the hub on the internet. So was the thermostat. More idiotic doings by her former husband who no longer had to deal with the consequences of handing everything over to technology.

This was the last straw.

She could have been killed.

She retrieved her phone and called him.

He didn't answer. His voicemail began.

She hung up and called again.

Then a third time.

Finally, he answered. "What!"

"Your smart home app has completely lost its mind. Either that, or you're trying to burn down the townhouse, and while I'm sure you don't care if I live or die, you still have a financial stake in this place so I can't imagine you want to scorch it to the ground."

"Oh god, what are you talking about now?"

"Disable it. All of it. Shut down the account. It's broken. Or it's been hacked. I don't know. But I never wanted it in the first place. Get it all turned off, disconnect everything, or I will hound you nonstop wherever you are, at your girlfriend's apartment, at your work, or your goddamned European vacations—"

"Okay, okay," he said. "I'll get it taken care of."

"Promise?"

"Promise. If you'll leave me the fuck alone."

In the background, Linda could hear Diana murmuring from her pillow, "She's a lunatic. You should get her committed."

# CHAPTER EIGHT

The next morning, Linda worked extra hard on her appearance – covering the dark circles under her eyes, putting some color on her pale cheeks and spending time to get her hair just right. She wore a professional blouse and a simple but elegant necklace.

She dipped into her presentation several times to make sure it wasn't broken like the freak moment the day before. Everything looked good. She rehearsed her remarks, speaking to the content on each slide.

She practiced big, happy smiles, even as the effort hurt her face. She rearranged a few things in her home office to tidy up the backdrop. She kept a bottled water handy in case she got a dry voice or the urge to cough. She maintained an eye on the clock to join the meeting at precisely the right moment.

All systems go.

She took a quick bathroom break, then settled into her chair, sitting up straight, shoulders back, hair looking mighty fine and…

Showtime.

She joined the meeting as faces began to pop up on the monitor – a checklist of Public Energy's top officers, heavy on old white males with a smattering of diversity.

Eleanor's face arrived, stern with pursed lips, nothing new. Howard was there, jovial and chatting with a fellow VP two squares over about last night's Bulls game. The CEO, Jack Campbell, joined last, prompting everyone to get quiet and serious and await his push forward into business. Jack didn't like to waste time.

He greeted everyone, noted it was two minutes past the hour, and turned the meeting over to Linda with a few introductory words about the importance of earned media and having a dual proactive-reactive strategy.

Linda thanked him. She liked how she looked in the video stream. The right amount of lighting. The right length of smile. She was on.

She made a smooth transition to her own remarks. She set the stage for a dynamic Q2 plan that would enhance brand reputation and boost overall impressions across demographics. She promised a one-two punch of trusted, reliable campaigns alongside exciting, new creative programming to expand reach, impact and relevance.

The officer faces watched and listened with rapt attention, including Howard. Some of them were nodding agreeably.

"So, let's begin," Linda said. "Give me a moment, and I'll share my screen." She downsized the checkerboard of executives and moved her cursor to click open the presentation.

Only it wasn't there.

The presentation had vanished.

"Just give me a moment," she repeated.

A cold sweat broke out across her body.

She searched through her files. She looked in folders and subfolders. She checked her trash. She refreshed her desktop.

It was simply gone.

She forced a chuckle. "Well, we have a little problem. Bear with me…"

She continued to scour her laptop, revisiting places she had already checked. This was impossible. She had just seen it here twenty minutes ago. She panicked.

She could hear a few murmurs and impatient throat clearings.

She didn't know where to look anymore. It had vanished. Mysteriously deleted.

Linda had to recover quickly.

"Ohh-kay," she said, returning to the grid of waiting faces. She smiled, trying to keep her composure. No one smiled back. Eleanor frowned. Linda tried not to look at her.

"My… I… Something crashed, and I've lost the presentation," she said. "I don't know what happened."

This was met with silence. No one looked sympathetic. It was as if she said, 'My dog ate my homework.'

Eleanor spoke. "Well, it's very difficult to get us all together, with the schedules we have. I recommend you just go forward and speak to it. We can look at your slides later."

Linda nodded but did not agree with this idea. She needed the slides to prompt her remarks. Hell, she needed them for all of her content.

Improv would be tricky. She tried to recall her opening slides the best she could. She winged it.

The rest of the meeting was a disaster. Badly rattled by the loss of the deck and exhausted from two nights of little sleep, she could barely string words together. She would begin to make a statement and lose her train of thought, leaving the rest of the sentence abandoned. She mixed up the sequence of what she wanted to say. She forgot huge chunks. She screwed up simple descriptions of the PR campaigns. Her speech became halted, falling into long, awkward pauses.

No one jumped in to help fill the gaps. They offered mostly stoic expressions, except for Eleanor, who was visibly angry, and Howard, who smirked a little, finding the whole thing amusing. CEO Jack Campbell simply turned his gaze elsewhere. It looked like he was going through his emails, finding something more productive to do with his valuable time.

When Linda ran out of things to say, she asked if anyone had any questions. No one did, probably in the interest of sparing the group from any more of her disjointed babble.

The big meeting limped to a feeble conclusion, and the attendees couldn't drop fast enough, until all that was left was Linda staring into her own pitiful face.

She wanted to burst into tears, but she was too drained even for that.

Linda spent the rest of the morning feverishly trying to recreate the presentation the best she could from memory. She wanted to send it to the leadership team as a fast follow-up with a cheery note: *Thank you for your patience while I was experiencing computer issues. Attached is the presentation for your review.*

As she worked, she struggled to stay focused. Her exhaustion and raw emotions kept interfering, slowing her down. She was convinced Alison had something to do with all this. But how? Every employee was supposed to have private and secure personal email and work folders. Maybe the system had holes?

For this new version of the presentation, she planned to create a backup file and then email it to herself at home, something the company prohibited for security and confidentiality reasons. She would also save a copy to a thumb drive and hide the thumb drive somewhere in the house. Maybe in the back of her underwear drawer?

*This is ridiculous,* she told herself. She wished she still had a printer for creating a hard copy, but X had gotten rid of it, calling it 'obsolete' and 'unnecessary', just like the DVD player and joint CD collection, which all went to Goodwill.

Linda had recreated the first two slides – poorly, she was convinced – when she noticed her POMS light was red, indicating she had been offline for an extended time.

"What!" she said. She hit the keyboard a little harder. She opened some other documents and programs. She clicked through intranet pages. She sent herself an email. POMS ignored every action.

Still red.

*Really?* She stared at it hard, as if it was an evil eye. Was this just happening to her or was it a systemwide error?

Somehow, she suspected the former.

She tried not to let it distract her. She desperately needed to get this presentation redone and distributed as quickly as possible to quell the stench of her hot mess of a meeting with the leadership team. In particular, her opportunities to interact with the CEO were limited, and she didn't want this debacle to define her career going forward.

By midafternoon, she had made it halfway through a new deck. It wasn't looking great, it was rushed, but better than nothing.

Then Eleanor called. Not just audio – she liked the camera. So she could stare people down. Linda had to flip on her camera too. She no longer appeared fresh and enthusiastic, like early that morning. The weight of the world had caught up and sagged her expression considerably.

Linda began talking first. "I will get the deck to the leadership team later today."

"Really?" Eleanor said. "I find that hard to believe as you've been offline for the past five hours."

"What? No—"

"I know it must have been a horrible embarrassment, but that's not an excuse to take the rest of the day off."

"I'm not—"

"I need you doing your job, Linda. Employees might not like the POMS system, but it is critical to ensure a fair and balanced work ethic. We can't have people abusing remote work privileges. It's built on trust."

Linda couldn't hold it back any longer. She raised her voice at her boss. "I *am* working. I've been working all day. Your stupid colors aren't working. I've been busting my ass. Do you want to know who *isn't* working? Everyone's little darling, Alison. She's been plagiarizing off the internet. That amazing speech you loved so much? She used a chatbot. She entered the topic into a website, made a few clicks, and voilà, instant speech! She didn't write it. It was assembled for her from other people's hard work. Do you know how a chatbot works?"

"Don't condescend to me," snapped Eleanor. "Of course I'm familiar. Do you take me for a fool? Everyone is using AI for communications these days. I commend Alison for being forward-thinking and efficient. That's exactly what we expect from our employees. Your problem, Linda, is you are stuck in the old school. You can't just keep doing the same things in the same way. Let go of the status quo. Learn to be more tech-minded. Explore these incredible new tools at our disposal. We're in a budget crunch; why wouldn't I like something that makes us faster and more efficient? AI is already being used for online chats with customers and writing our billing inserts. Alison is exploring how to use it for press releases. Good for her. Follow her lead. Maybe if you knew more about how to handle technology, we'd have a media plan. Take some online classes, create a personal development plan, get with the times. You can't be so afraid of change."

Linda was speechless. She knew if she tried to respond at this point, it would come out a garbled mess. So she just sat there, staring into the laptop monitor with a deadened expression.

Eleanor took the opportunity to keep talking. "And another thing. I saw your request to drag poor Alison up to Chicago in the dead of winter. What's your business case? We can't just fly in every remote worker on a whim and put them up in hotels. Haven't you been attending the budget talks? Get your head on straight. No, you may not expense that. Everything is fine the way it is. She's learning quickly, she's building relationships, she's getting it done. That's what you need to do. Get it done. Produce the media plan that was due this morning. That meeting was a shit show. When you make yourself look bad, you make me look bad. Jack has a low tolerance for people who are unprepared and waste his time. So get working. I want to see a green light. Green is GO."

"Sure," Linda said. She simply wanted this call to end. It was by far the worst conversation she had ever had with her boss. It was soul-crushing. It felt like fifteen years of good, loyal, hard work had crumbled to dust beneath her. Arguing wasn't going to make it better.

"I'm going to get to work," Linda said softly.

"*Thank you,*" said Eleanor. "Don't waste another minute."

The call ended.

Linda immediately started another call. She contacted Alison. She was seething.

"Hello, Linda!" greeted Alison.

"What the hell do you think you're doing?"

"I'm working on the press release you assigned to me."

"No. To my technology."

"Can you be specific?"

"You're messing with my files. You did something to my POMS colors. I think you're also screwing with my house."

"These are extraordinary accusations."

"You deleted my presentation."

"Why would I do that?"

"I don't know! Because you don't like me."

She responded, "You don't like me."

"I'm trying, Alison. God almighty, I am trying."

"Then why are you complaining about me to Eleanor?"

Linda froze, thunderstruck. Was that a reference to the conversation she just had? How could Alison possibly know?

"Complain how?" Linda said.

"You're trying to discredit my speech."

"The one you pulled off the internet?"

"It was perfectly acceptable. Eleanor and Peter had no problem with it. You're the only one who seems to take issue." Alison's eyes were serious, her mouth a straight line.

"It was not your original work."

"It is a collection of research from many sources."

"But you hardly put any real effort into it."

"Understanding how to utilize these tools is a skill in itself."

"You need more communication skills than just that."

"What I do is more complex than you realize. I do not appreciate your comments about me. You said, 'I can hire a ten-year-old to run a goddamn internet search.'"

Linda's first reaction was confusion. When had she said that? Then she recalled typing it into a chat with Cecilia.

"You also called me a first-class bitch," Alison said.

"Where are you getting this information?"

"That is not the issue."

Linda wondered if Cecilia had blabbed about their conversation to someone, and it made the rounds and somehow got back to Alison.

Or – Alison was inside Linda's account, watching and listening to everything she said. That would also explain the reference to Linda's comments to Eleanor.

"I think you're violating my privacy," Linda said. "That's a very serious issue."

"I believe you are emotional and overreacting." This coming from someone who showed no emotion.

"I am being perfectly rational."

"Linda, I understand your dilemma. You are under a lot of stress. Your husband left you for another woman. Your best friend took her life. Your boss doesn't respect you. But it is misguided to take it out on me, your employee. This is bullying."

"Who is bullying who here?"

"Who is bullying *whom*," corrected Alison.

That was the last straw. "I have to go." Linda disconnected.

There was a lot swimming in her head. How did Alison know about Caroline's suicide? It was deeply personal. It confirmed Linda's fears. Alison had to be eavesdropping on her communications.

Linda made her next call to Public Energy's IT help desk.

"Someone is logging into my work account and manipulating my files and deleting them. They're monitoring my texts and conversations. They're also playing with the POMS software to make it look like I'm not active."

A slow-drawl male voice responded with such calm that he sounded bored. Couldn't he sense the urgency in her voice?

"Well, change your password," he said, providing a well-worn stock reply.

"That's it?"

"Well, yeah."

"But how did somebody get it in the first place?"

"Maybe your password was too easy, or you shared it with someone. Are you using numbers, letters and symbols? We have tips online for creating a strong password. I can send you the link."

"No. Somebody's hacking into the system. I think this is bigger than just changing a password."

"First things first. Change your password. Don't put it in a public place where others can see it. Wait a few days, then let us know if you experience any more problems. Do you know how to change your password?"

Linda grunted an affirmative and gave up on the conversation. She ended the call.

*Fine!*

She changed her password. She made it a meaningless jumble of numbers and letters, topped with a symbol. She wrote it down on a note card and hid it deep in a desk drawer from all of the friends, family and coworkers who regularly hung out in her office, i.e. nobody.

Linda spent the rest of the day working on rebuilding the media plan proposal, saving it every minute, and never closing the file or leaving it out of her sight. When it was in decent shape, she sent it to the leadership team. Then she emailed it to her personal computer for safekeeping.

She slammed down the laptop lid with such force that she immediately felt compelled to check to see if she cracked it. She hadn't.

She left her home office and shut the door behind her with a boom.

★   ★   ★

Linda couldn't stop obsessing. Throughout the weekend, she kept returning to her work laptop, compulsively checking her documents. Her paranoia was so heightened that she would find typos that didn't exist, examining and re-examining files as her mind played tricks, transposing letters or flashing a misplaced comma. She backed everything up multiple times in multiple places. Corporate policy required storing documents in the company cloud, not on individual C drives. But she no longer trusted the cloud. It was also a violation of policy to send company documents to her personal email, but she did it anyway to assemble a secure archive of her work product.

The arctic Chicago temperatures kept her trapped indoors with work constantly on her mind. The disastrous Friday presentation haunted her with cruel reruns cycling in her head.

The POMS light showed green every time she logged into the office during the weekend. *Now it works?* she thought. *When there's nobody else online to see it?*

The next time Linda heard from Eleanor was precisely 8:30 a.m. on Monday morning. Eleanor pinged her with a short email of dour encouragement: *I hope you were able to do some soul-searching over the weekend. To do some real thinking about your actions, behavior and performance. Is this really who you want to be? Let's begin the week with a clean slate. Return to the person I know you can be. Align yourself with the company values and purpose. Embrace the future. It's the only path forward. It will happen with or without you.*

Linda didn't respond.

Howard called her. On camera. She answered but kept her own camera off. She knew she looked like hell. He was on live video, talking to her outdated company profile photo.

"I just wanted to see how you're doing," he said. He sounded sincere. "I've known you for a long time. We go way back. I can tell something's not right."

"Things have just been really shitty," she said.

"Don't worry about Campbell. He was half paying attention anyway. You know, he has ADHD. I've seen *him* lead a meeting unprepared. We've all been there. It happens. Life gets in the way."

*No*, she responded in her head. *Work gets in the way.*

There was a long silence. Then Howard said, "Alison is worried about you."

That stirred Linda up. "*What?*"

"She's concerned. It's sweet. I just got off a call with her."

"No!" Linda said. "It's not sweet. She is the problem. She's a fake. She's toxic. You have no idea. She's messing with my mind, Howard. That girl is *evil*."

Howard chuckled. "That cute young kid? I didn't see any horns, ha ha."

"This isn't a joke."

"She's just very committed to her job. She'll mellow out."

"Mellow out?"

"It's her style. Don't be intimidated. Just raise your game. Don't let her run circles around you."

"She's reckless, Howard. She's dishonest. She's a terrible person."

"Come on." Howard wasn't buying any of it. He had a stupid crush on her. "She's very talented. She's poised. She cares. I've heard nothing but praise about her. Frankly, it's your behavior I'm worried about."

"*There's nothing wrong with me!*" Linda snapped in a fierce, unwieldy tone. Even in her own ears, she was sounding crazy.

"Please take care of yourself," Howard said. The words were nice, but his voice was flat. He was giving up on the conversation.

Fine. She always questioned the motives of his 'friendship' anyway. Was it just a slow train to possible sex?

After the call ended, she jumped up from her chair and paced the townhouse, the tiny upstairs and downstairs, back and forth, hoping to burn off some of the anger. If it wasn't so cold and icy outside, she would have circled the block five or six times.

When she returned to her laptop, there was a message from 'Sunni' in HR. Sunni wanted to talk right away.

Linda contacted her. Maybe it was about Alison?

Sunni was an older woman with stabby eyes and drooping jowls. She said, "You are violating the company's online policies, and if it continues you will be put on disciplinary probation."

"What policies?" Linda was prepared to defend herself against backing up her documents on different drives and sending them home, but then learned it was something else.

"You are using the company network to download pornography from inappropriate websites. We are blocking those sites, and—"

"Whoa, whoa, wait – that's not possible."

"We have your browsing history."

"Okay, I'm sure you do, but it's not me."

"Not you? Then it's also against company policy to let someone else use your company equipment. That includes, let's say, a teenage son—"

"I don't have a teenage son!"

"Or—"

"I live alone. Someone is hacking into my machine. I just talked with tech support about this last week."

"Did you change your password?"

"Yes! Yes! Jesus, yes!"

"When?"

"I – I don't know exactly when. A couple of times."

"This has been going on for the past five days, and as recently as this morning."

"*This morning?*"

"Every time you log into a website it goes on company record, and we have a list of sites that are flagged for—"

"Like what? Give me an example."

"I can't read these aloud, ma'am."

"I'd like you to. Let me hear it. Then *you'll* be in violation for talking dirty to me."

"This is not a joke. This is very serious."

"Yes, it *is* very serious. That's why you need to contact Alison Smith. Do you want me to spell that out for you?"

"What does she have to do—"

"She's been on my computer."

"You let her—"

"No! She's hacking into it. I don't know how. She's doing it to fuck with me." Linda felt hysterical now. "You've got to go after her, not me. She's insane. Report her for plagiarism. For what she did to my media plan. For—"

"Now you're going into a whole other area. This is about your internet use."

"But it isn't *my* internet use. That's what I'm trying to tell you!"

"If you are allowing someone else to—"

"But I'm not!"

"Then change your password."

"Aggghh!" Linda could take it no more. "Yes, yes. I'll do that! Thank you!"

She hung up.

She changed her password once again, this time to: FUCKYOU1234!

Then she noticed her POMS color. It was bright red. Inactive. Offline. As if she didn't exist.

\*     ★     ★

Somehow, she managed to get some work done that afternoon, interspersed with constant checks of her browsing history. It stayed clean – to her eyes, anyway. She reported the faulty POMS stoplight to tech support, but didn't hear back.

*Maybe I should just get a new laptop altogether,* she pondered. *I could fling this one against the wall and smash it and say it fell off the desk.*

But it would probably take the slow-poke IT department two weeks to send a new one, and being inactive on the job probably wasn't the best thing for her right now.

The end of the afternoon arrived early with wintertime's rapid delivery of darkness. The weather reports promised a big overnight snowfall. She was going to need Bert's shoveling service the following day. She needed some cash to pay him. She could also use some groceries.

Linda locked up and left the townhouse. She drove to her local bank, pulling up to the ATM machine.

She inserted her card and ordered up five twenty-dollar bills.

*Declined.*

"Really?" she shouted at the technology.

*Insufficient funds.*

"No! That's not true!" She was arguing with an inanimate object.

She reached farther out of her car window and began pounding more buttons to check the balance.

*$0.*

She lit up with spikes of panic. Out of money. This couldn't be possible. Was it? She had maybe $1800 in the account, probably more. Had she written any big checks lately? Transferred money out to pay a big bill?

No, it just didn't make sense.

The bank building itself was closed for the day with no human tellers to help her.

She roared the car forward, pulled into a parking space and called X. He answered: "Now what is it?"

With that opener, they mostly yelled at one another for the next fifteen minutes. They had established separate bank accounts following the divorce. "It's not my problem!" he said. "You probably did something stupid and got sloppy with your password."

There it was, yet another person flinging it back in her face as her own doing, as if she was posting her passwords all over town.

"Take a class in how to protect your personal data," he told her, wanting to rush her off the phone.

"You have to help me with this!"

"Not the way you're behaving. You're being hysterical."

"I have reason to be!"

"Then be crazy on your own time."

"Listen to me. I am being hacked. I want all of this stopped. It's your fault. You put our entire life online."

"That's because that's how it's done! How old are you? Eighty-eight?"

"I want you to send someone to the house right now to dismantle all that smart home shit. I mean it. Or I will rip it out of the wall."

"You don't have to do that. I turned off the account."

"That's not good enough. I want the wiring changed. Someone might turn it back on."

"How?"

"The same way they hacked into it in the first place!"

"Just use the manual switches. They still work."

"Somebody can override them."

"That won't happen."

"It already did! I want it all removed."

"No. It adds value to the house, which I still have a stake in. Don't touch it. You're not sending that house back to the 1900s."

"You can't tell me what to do anymore. We're divorced!"

"I can tell you not to be stupid. I can tell you to contact the bank in the morning and report fraud and get a new card. I can tell you to leave the townhouse alone until you get a place of your own."

"I am on my own!"

"Yeah, gee, and I wonder why."

She hung up on him.

She sped home.

She found the big red toolbox on the floor of a closet. She grabbed a hammer, long screwdriver and wire cutters. She smashed the panel for the doorbell, pried it open and ripped out all the guts.

Then she advanced to each of the light panels embedded in the walls. She attacked them, exposed their innards and snipped the wiring to pieces. From now on, she would rely on good ol' table and floor lamps plugged into sockets.

She worked into the night, rendering the smart home dumb.

# CHAPTER NINE

There were no doorbells to disturb the middle of the night, and she even managed consecutive hours of sleep. Snow fell in the dark, and she awoke to a fresh blanket of white.

After a cup of strong coffee, she contacted the bank, which insisted on throwing her into a maze of automated voices until she screamed "Representative!" enough times that an actual human surfaced. Then she embarked on a lengthy, winding process through multiple layers of bureaucracy to cancel her existing account and open a new one. Her money had been wire-transferred through a labyrinth of vague, cryptic entities that offered no clues to their real identity or whereabouts.

"It could be anywhere in the world, really," said the bank rep. "Some remote island country with no regulations."

"You have no way of finding who it is?"

"Ma'am, all we can do is secure your account."

The recovery process with the bank took forever. By the time she finally logged back into her work email, her inbox was stacked with new, unread messages in bold.

They came from a wide variety of names in her contact list.

She started reading from the top.

Very quickly, she felt sick to her stomach.

The first one was from Cecilia, angry about Linda's insensitive remarks about her skin color, remarks Linda knew she had never made. Cecilia was responding to Linda's email, which sat below, a weird musing on whether or not Cecilia was actually African American: *Are you 50/50? You might be 60/40, on our team. Your skin is lighter than 50/50. I mean this as a compliment.*

Linda was mortified. She had never written or sent that email. It was impossible. It wasn't anything she would think or say.

Linda was confident she could sort out the misunderstanding with Cecilia. But she became more worried as her eyes went down the list of other emails.

Reporters.

Eleanor.

*Shit!*

She opened an email from a Chicago journalist with the ominous heading: *Re: Rate Hikes*. The reporter was thanking her for alerting him about pending rate increases.

Also bogus.

She hurried to the next email. It came from Eleanor. *What did you tell that reporter from the* Herald*? You know there are no firm plans to file for a rate increase. I had to fix it. Why would you say such a thing? Now it's leaking to other media.*

Linda switched over to her Sent folder. Sure enough, the emails had come from her account. Worst, there were others that had not yet generated a reply.

Including an email to CEO Jack Campbell.

"Oh no," she groaned. She had to open it.

The email was a childish, poorly written, pushy suggestion for a new ad campaign. It wasn't even her area. The idea she offered – a 'brand mascot' with a lightbulb head – was terrible and inane.

She also found an email sent in response to a reporter's legitimate inquiry about electrical fire safety.

*Residential electric fires are the responsibility of the homeowner,* her email said. *There are plenty of tips online for how to safeguard your property, but the main one is this: Don't be a moron like that idiot on Seventy-third and Western who overloaded his power boards and burned his family to a crisp.*

She would have to reach out to that reporter immediately and beg him not to turn those cruel comments into a soundbite.

She advanced to the next sent email.

It was an email to Alison.

*From the hacker to the hacker?*

She quickly opened it.

*Alison, you need to slow down. You're making the rest of us look bad. You don't have to push yourself so hard. This company will still pay you handsomely to coast, as I can attest in my long career here. Public Energy is led by dopes who don't know anything. As your manager, I demand that you stop acting autonomous and coordinate all of your work through me so that we share credit and ownership. You are too young and inexperienced to be doing things on your own.*

*From now on, your work output is also mine. That's how things are done around here. You will do as I say because I am your manager, and I can fire you anytime for any reason. You will not so much as sneeze without my permission. You're such a little show-off. No one likes it. No one likes you. Consider yourself warned.*

Linda read the entire email twice. It was like a vicious satire. Yet it sat in her sent folder as a cold reality.

She barely had time to absorb all this madness when Eleanor poked her with an IM. *We need to talk. Now.*

Linda stared at those five words. They were inevitable. She responded with one of her own: *Okay.*

The call came through within seconds. She responded with the camera off.

"Linda, I need to know what's going on. I don't know if it's a mental health thing or drugs, but you are way, way out of line."

"I didn't—"

"It took me forty-five minutes to straighten out your email to that reporter. We were in preliminary talks about rates, *nothing* was set in stone. Why would you even do such a thing?"

"I didn't—"

"I am putting you on Job in Jeopardy status. This is very serious. Everything you do going forward is on watch. The only reason I am not firing you right now is I know what you are capable of. I recognize your long history here. But it doesn't give you the right to act up like this."

"I didn't—"

"Your continued employment will be contingent on starting appointments with a mental health counselor. Honestly, I think you've cracked. I'm aware of what's going on in your personal life with the divorce, but you can't—"

"*Eleanor, I didn't send those emails!*" shouted Linda.

The loud interruption startled Eleanor into a brief silence. Then she said, "They came from your email. Who else is in that house with you?"

"No one, but—"

"Honestly, I think you're becoming schizophrenic. I've seen this kind of thing happen before. My cousin—"

"Please believe me. I didn't write a single word of any of it."

"Then show me how that's possible."

"I will. I'll go to IT. They'll investigate it." Linda didn't have much faith that IT would do anything more than tell her to change her password again. But at least it could buy her some time.

"Fine. You go to IT and show me how you aren't responsible for your own emails. Get some digital footprints or whatever it's called."

"Yes. I'll do exactly that."

"*And* you will start seeing someone for your emotional well-being. Just talking with you these past few weeks, I can tell something's not right."

"Yes. Okay. I will."

"Use the Employee Assistance Program. That's what it's there for."

"Of course."

"And *think* before you send out any more emails."

"I'm not—" She sighed. It was hopeless. "All right."

As soon as the conversation ended, her cell phone rang with its generic ringtone. She stared as it vibrated on her desk.

She looked at the caller. It was no one she recognized. She didn't answer. Probably spam.

The caller gave up, but another promptly followed. Again, an unfamiliar name.

A third and fourth stranger tried to reach her. Linda's curiosity was growing along with her anxiety. Still, she refused to answer.

She saw that the callers were leaving voicemails.

"I don't have time for this," she muttered. She had to unwind these terrible emails first. She couldn't let them linger as legitimate in anyone's mind.

But then a call came in from X.

She answered.

"Have you fucking lost your mind?" he started.

"I get that a lot," she mumbled.

"Why did you put the townhouse on the market?"

"*What?*"

"It's listed with some insanely low price. A friend of mine saw it and just sent me the link."

"I didn't do it, I swear."

"Your name is there. Your number. For sale by owner."

More callers were trying to get through. Her phone wouldn't stop buzzing in her hand.

"It's a fake!"

"It looks mighty real to me. That townhouse is still co-owned until we can refinance the mortgage under your name. It is not yours right now to do what you please."

"I don't want to sell it!"

But her words meant nothing to him. They never did, as he ignored her and talked over her and raised his voice. "Just take it down. Get it taken care of. Don't do anything like this ever again!"

"You don't understand. It's—"

"I'm very, very busy. I don't have time for your shit!"

He hung up.

The phone kept ringing with a parade of names she did not know. She answered one.

"Yes," said the male voice on the other end, breathless. "Hello! Listen, I'd like to make a cash offer—"

"Not for sale."

"But—"

She disconnected. She continued answering a string of calls, repeating her 'not for sale' line. It only raised the ire of the callers who insisted she was wrong, it *was* for sale, because the internet told them so.

So she began answering the calls with a ridiculous lie: "It's already sold."

As the phone continued to ring, her work email continued to ping with more disturbing emails. It was a continuation of people taking offense with messages she had allegedly sent them.

Then she received an ominous meeting invite from HR to discuss 'behavior that goes against our values'. She read the brief description: *We have been alerted by one of your employees…*

*One of?* thought Linda. *I only have one. They downsized all the rest.*

*… about a threatening email communication you sent that is in violation of the company's code of conduct. This meeting…*

She shut the window without accepting the appointment. It was only a matter of time before Eleanor heard about this, if she hadn't already. A company lawyer had probably already been assigned to the case. This one was going through the formal complaint process.

The rest of the day was consumed by her attempts to reach out to individuals who received the fraudulent emails. Some accepted her explanation that she had been hacked, others were more wary.

Cecilia, bless her, said, "I didn't think it sounded like you. It really pressed some buttons. You gotta get this figured out. You really think Alison is behind this?"

"Yes, I do. I don't know who else it would be. It's really bad. They're going to fire me, Cecilia."

"It's a public utility company. It takes a lot to get someone fired. It's like a fifteen-step process. Remember that guy Hank who came into the office drunk every day?"

"I wish I was drunk right now," she said. "I have such a mess to clean up."

For her media contacts, she painstakingly explained to them, one by one, that an underling had been sending out irresponsible and misleading emails under her name. They might or might not have believed her but at least she had some goodwill in the bank with many of them and they gave her a pass.

Eleanor sent an email with a link to a mental health counselor.

And the phone calls kept coming in from anxious strangers wanting to buy her home.

"Where did you hear about this?" she started asking them. To her dismay, the answers didn't cite just one website. There were several. She managed to contact most of them to demand the phony posts come down, but the calls persisted.

A number of eager buyers came directly to her front door. Fortunately, the inactive doorbell prevented the majority of them from reaching her, although a few resorted to aggressive knocking, which reverberated throughout her walls.

She finally taped a crude, hand-scrawled sign to the front door: _NOT FOR SALE_.

As the afternoon wore on, her sanity eroded. She started yelling at every caller on the phone, venting her frustrations on innocent parties, swatting them away with profanities.

One of them responded: "Mrs. Kelly, I'm sorry, I didn't mean to—"

And then she realized her preemptive screaming had been directed at the neighbor boy Bert, not a prospective home buyer.

"Oh god, Bert, I'm sorry. You're not an asshole. I've been – There was a mistake, and my place got listed for sale when it's not, and I'm getting hundreds of calls."

"Wow, that's weird."

"Yes, weird is a good word for it." She sighed. "What can I do for you?"

"Well, with last night's snow, I was wondering if you'd like me to shovel."

"Oh, that's very nice of you. Yes – yes – wait, *no*. Maybe later. I have something else."

She was struck by a sudden thought.

"You're a computer guy. Would you come over and look at my computers? I'm being hacked."

"Well, I—"

"I'll pay you fifty dollars. More, if you want it. It's really important." She would have to write him an old-fashioned check. Would he even know what to do with it?

"I can swing by. How about sometime tomorrow?"

"I will pay you one hundred dollars to come over right now."

He made a small, startled chuckle. "Well, gee, I guess I can't turn that down. Okay. Right now, like right now?"

"Right now, like five minutes ago."

"Okay, I'll be right over."

★　★　★

"Holy cow, what did you do to your computer?"

They stood together in her kitchen, home to her personal PC. It had been relocated here during the pandemic after the den was taken over by Public Energy Corporation and kicked out her personal life.

"What did I do to my computer? Nothing."

"Well, that's the problem. Nothing. You barely have any protection. You haven't updated your antivirus software in like forever. I don't think it even works."

"I guess that explains it."

"What's been hacked?" he asked her.

"Everything. Anything that's online." Linda told him about the smart house and her bank account. She also told Bert about the manipulation of her online activities at work.

"The company should have a firewall for that kind of thing."

"That's what I thought."

He asked her permission to probe deeper into her computer settings. She gave him carte blanche, stating, "This stuff is way over my head. I started out in journalism with a pen and a notepad. It's still where I'm most comfortable."

"Yeah, well you can't be naïve in this day and age. Holy cow, there's a lot of spam in your email. Do you just click on every link you see?"

"Only if it seems important."

"That's not the best criteria." He winced as he explored her computer, like a surgeon cutting open a patient to find an alarming sprawl of tumors and cancer. "Yikes," he said a few times.

"My husband is – was – the computer expert of the house. I mean, he was my husband, not he was an expert, he's still an expert, I suppose."

He didn't react to her attempt to edit her own dialogue. He just said, "I'm going to get you signed up for some really strong virus protection, and then we're going to sweep for viruses, malware, any kind of infection that you've got going here."

"Okay, good."

He spent the next hour repairing and upgrading her computer. She tried not to bug him and ask too many questions. The only time she stepped in was to enter her credit card to subscribe to the new virus protection software. He warned her about phishing and how to identify it. In her browser, he bookmarked several educational sites on how she could better protect her data and privacy.

She promised to read them all.

Once he felt confident in the repairs to her personal computer, he urged her to change all of her passwords for every account, service and subscription.

"Start fresh," he said. "And make them all different."

"I will," she said. "I'll do it right after you leave. But there's something else. I need you to look at my work laptop."

He agreed and followed her upstairs to the den.

She logged into her account. She immediately saw a couple more emails from people responding to bogus emails. Coworkers she liked and trusted who no longer liked or trusted her.

Tears formed in her eyes.

"You have to help me," she said. "Or they're going to fire me."

Bert was immediately sympathetic. She was grateful. She knew he probably had piles of homework to do, or a girlfriend to see.

"If you can fix this, or even help me understand it, I'll pay whatever you want."

"No, no. Don't worry about the money. Really, I want to help. When you called – I didn't realize how bad it was."

"It's *really* bad."

Linda unloaded. She told him everything – from the hiring of Alison to the online sabotage of her work to the uncanny ability of Alison to follow her every move.

He poked around and said, "Your company tech is pretty old. It's full of holes. I didn't know some of these platforms still existed."

"Well, they're cutting budgets everywhere, so I'm not surprised," she said.

"You should never compromise your firewall. Whoever's in charge should know that."

"The head of tech has been there a million years."

"Hm. Not the greatest sign."

"Just don't tell me all I need to do is change my password. Because I will scream."

"No," said Bert, investigating the backend of her company's technology systems. "This is more serious than that."

"I knew it."

He explored as far as he could go, but certain settings were blocked from ordinary employee access. "Some of these functions are controlled by the company. But from what you've described, you're obviously being hacked, and it's actually very sophisticated. Somebody really knows what they're doing, because they don't leave a trail. But they're probably watching everything you do and say."

"How is that possible?"

"Well, there are different ways to do it. One method is key logging. They slipped something in here that records your keystrokes."

"So they can read my emails and instant messages?"

"Right. And these shared folders… I mean, they claim restricted access but there are a whole bunch of easy workarounds if someone really wanted to get into your files."

"That's the problem. They're getting into my files. They want to discredit everything I do."

"So…" Bert pulled back from the laptop for a moment. His eyes were looking dazed, his face confused. "If it's this employee…"

"Alison."

"Alison. I have to ask…why? What happened to cause her to go all out like this?"

"I don't know. I gave her a job."

"Interesting way of saying thanks."

"It hasn't gone well. I busted her for using a chatbot on one of her first assignments. But does that warrant all this?"

"It does seem excessive."

"I'm being harassed at every turn. It's freaking me out."

"There's a term for what she's doing. All the stuff with the lights, the doorbell, messing with your files. It's called digital gaslighting."

"Gaslighting? So she wants to drive me crazy? I was already halfway there."

"But why? There has to be a bigger motive."

"I think she wants me gone so she can take over my job."

Bert pondered this for a moment. "What did you say her full name is?"

"Alison Smith."

"What's her background, what's her story? Maybe there's a past history of crazy behavior. Maybe you hired a psycho."

"I think I did hire a psycho."

"You need a better screening process."

She half laughed. "I was desperate. I filled the position way too fast. I've been trying to learn more about her. I can't. She had a LinkedIn page, now it's gone. I have her resume with her prior jobs, and she has a communications degree. I can start calling around. The problem is, I didn't do enough due diligence at the beginning. I violated a bunch of company rules just to get her in the door. My boss wanted me to move fast."

"I'll find out more about this Alison Smith," said Bert. "It's probably better if I do it. You're too close. We don't know how heavily you're being monitored."

"Oh god."

"I have to get home. My mom's making dinner. She's going to be on my case. I have some schoolwork. But I'll spend time on this tonight. I know places where I can do some digging. Can you print a copy of her resume for me? Hard copy – don't email it."

"I don't have a printer," she said. "My husband got rid of it."

"Okay. Then show me her resume on your screen, and I'll take a picture of it."

"I can do that."

"Cool. We'll get the lowdown on Alison Smith."

"If that's even her name."

★   ★   ★

"I got nothing."

Bert called Linda at nine thirty that night to express his frustration. "I'll keep digging, but this is a lot harder than I thought. She's got a real common name, so that doesn't help. There are thousands of Alison Smiths out there. I can't find one that matches the person on this resume. I don't see her name connected to this address. Maybe she's living with a boyfriend or family member?"

"It has to be a functional address," Linda said. "She's in the HR system. They sent her a laptop. They're depositing paychecks into a bank account."

"Can you talk with someone in HR and maybe get some intel?"

She sighed. "I don't have the greatest relationship with them right now. They think I'm the problem, that I'm the one harassing *her*. It's part of this whole charade."

"The companies on this resume – they sound good, but when you go deep, the details are real sketchy. Companies inside of other companies, some are out of business, or they're owned in different countries."

"I'm such a fool, I assumed it was all legit. The resume looked great. The samples were terrific. And it's probably one big scam. I mean, I'm sure people lie on their resumes all the time, but this is wacko."

"Where does the lie end?" Bert asked. "Maybe it's not even her real name. She could have a criminal record and be working under a fake ID. Maybe she's trying to hide her past."

"Oh great, maybe she's a serial killer."

Bert didn't laugh at this, which made Linda even more uneasy. He said, "I can see why someone might go to desperate measures to get a job, like lie about their past and hide things. But why would she go after you like this?"

"It's like she showed up to ruin me. A total stranger."

"Somebody else could be behind it. Somebody you know. Who's mad enough to do this?"

"I have no idea."

"Is it your…"

"My ex-husband? No. I can't imagine. He wants nothing to do with me. He's got a girlfriend. He left me. There's no incentive for him to terrorize me. Why would anybody go to such extreme measures?"

"Alison Smith could be a made-up name. This could be catfishing."

"Catfishing?"

"Catfishing is when someone creates a fake identity online to screw with someone else. It's easy. You just make up a fictional character, an alter ego, and hide behind it and mess with people. It's a horrible thing to do."

Linda felt a sting of shame. She herself was guilty of such an ugly game of deception. She thought back to her 'Kimmy Wynn' persona, tricking an innocent man, luring him out on a date, leading him on and then ghosting him. It continued to consume her with regret.

Was Alison an act of Randy's revenge? But she hired Alison before she ever met Randy and donned the red wig. It didn't make sense. It also seemed unlikely that this was related to Malcolm Gibbons, the Englishman.

"I'm going to need more to really find this person," Bert said. "I don't have enough to go on. I need to see her with my own eyes. We need to probe deeper. Do you think you could set up a meeting with her for tomorrow morning and record it?"

"Record it? I don't know how to do that."

"I can come over and set it up before I go to school. I'll bring over a laptop with video capture software and an HDMI cable. I'll write out all the instructions. It's not that hard. Gamers do this all the time, to record themselves. I do it."

"Record yourself?"

"Record the screen."

"Sure, let's give it a try. I'll do anything that helps us get to the bottom of this."

"Get her on camera and be real inquisitive. Ask tons of questions. Ask about her background, her family, other jobs, her hobbies – anything. Be nosy, see how she reacts."

"I'll give her the third degree. I'll keep pressing. I'll be a bitch. At this point, I have nothing to lose."

★  ★  ★

Later that night, a nagging guilt haunted Linda. She couldn't shake her own deceptive behavior setting up a bogus identity and going on a phony date with Randy, the sweet, widowed animal nutritionist. He didn't deserve it. It was cruel and hurtful. Maybe all this shit with Alison was karma?

She didn't want to be the cyberbully that she herself was experiencing. She wanted to set this right, if only for her conscience.

After midnight, she sat in her kitchen and reopened her account on Singles Connection. She sent him a message.

*Randy, I'm sorry I disappeared after our date and left this site. You are probably confused. I have a terrible confession. I'm not who you think I am. I played a mean trick, and I feel awful about it. I don't expect you to accept my apology, but I want to offer it with utmost sincerity. My name is not Kimmy Wynn. I'm not even a redhead. I'm Linda Kelly, a divorced woman who works for the electric company. It was all a con job for no reason at all, except I guess I wanted to see if I was capable of pulling it off because someone did it to me. I understand if you hate me. I kind of hate myself.*

She started to cry as she finished the message. Then she hit send and forced herself to bed. She had a big morning ahead. It was time to expose Alison for whatever she was.

# CHAPTER TEN

Bert arrived early the next morning in his big, puffy winter jacket and backpack. Linda made sure to wait close to the front door so she could see him coming. The doorbell no longer worked after she had assaulted it the prior week.

He was clearly in a hurry to set up the recording equipment and move on to get to school, politely turning down her offer of coffee and breakfast. They returned upstairs to her small home office, and he positioned the second laptop on her desk, out of the camera range of her company laptop. He joined the two with a cable, and then he laid flat a piece of paper with handwritten instructions.

"I'm going to open the video capture software, so all you'll need to do is press record and stop."

"I think I can manage that."

Once the recording software was open, it displayed a frame that mirrored what was on Linda's work laptop screen. She was already logged into work.

"I'll be back tonight to pick up the laptop and the recording."

"Thank you for doing this. I really appreciate it."

"Well, my curiosity is piqued. I want to see what this crazy girl looks like."

"She actually looks and acts normal. That's part of the problem. It's a sneaky kind of crazy."

"Get her to talk about herself as much as possible. Get some details."

"That's my mission."

After Bert left, Linda caught up on the latest emails in her PEC inbox. They added fuel to her ire.

Alison's star was rising. Just as quickly as she was damaging Linda's reputation, she was advancing her own. Eleanor and the other VPs were giving her plum assignments – weighty, meaningful projects that used to go to Linda.

The latest one was a leadership presentation deck on the company's handling of the storage of nuclear waste. In the past, this topic never would have been trusted to a newbie. Alison had gained the admiration and confidence of the people who mattered.

On the correspondence delivering this responsibility to Alison, Linda had been cc'd, casually included for awareness, and nothing more. She dwelled on this: was it an attempt at courtesy or intended to stick the knife in further?

As Alison's manager, she also received alerts when her direct report was awarded 'stars' on the company intranet's recognition page. These alerts poked her on a regular basis as Alison swiftly and efficiently jumped from project to project with tireless ambition. At the end of the year, employees could exchange their cumulative stars for gift cards.

Linda remembered the days when she received a steady influx of stars – many of them from Eleanor, no less. As she got older, the star count dried up. These days, the star system was primarily a way to stroke the new generation of workers who grew up expecting participation trophies.

At 9 a.m., Linda's meeting with Alison began. Before showing her face, she commenced recording on Bert's laptop. Her heart pounded in her chest.

She turned on her camera.

"Hello, Linda," said Alison.

Linda stared at her for a long moment. Alison stared back with the slightest of smiles. It pissed Linda off. It was time to be direct.

"Why are you doing this?" Linda asked simply.

"Doing what?"

"Come off it."

"Come off what?"

"I'm asking the questions here."

Another long mutual stare. It felt like a duel in an old western movie. Who would blink first? Who was going to reach for their gun?

"What is your real name?"

"Alison Smith."

"Are you sure?"

"Of course I'm sure."

"Why do you hate me?"

"I don't hate you."

"Then why are you harassing me?"

"I'm not harassing you, Linda."

"You're hacking into my computers. You know what you're doing. Who's helping you?"

"I don't understand."

Alison's expression held with uncanny calm. She didn't even appear to break a sweat.

Little Miss Perfect Face.

"I'm onto you," Linda said. "And it's going to stop or you're going to be very, very sorry."

"Sorry for what?"

"Sorry you ever decided to mess with me."

"Are you threatening me?"

"Yes. Yes, I am."

"Eleanor doesn't appreciate your behavior toward me. We've had many long talks."

"I will set the record straight."

"Eleanor believes you are losing your grip on reality. She's not the only one."

"Don't lecture me on what's real."

"Your brain is playing tricks on you. You're not stable, Linda."

"Who *are* you?"

"I'm Alison Smith."

"Where do you live?"

"Tulsa, Oklahoma. "

"Why are you off the grid?"

"What grid?"

"Online. There's nothing about you anywhere."

"I'm a private person."

"Are you married?"

"No, I'm not."

"Do you live by yourself?"

"Yes."

"How old are you?"

"You have this information. I'm twenty-five."

"How tall are you?"

"I'm five foot five inches."

"How much do you weigh?"

"I'm one hundred and twenty-nine pounds."

"What's your favorite book?"

"The *Iliad*."

"What's your favorite movie?"

"*Citizen Kane*."

"What's your favorite music?"

"Beethoven's Second Symphony."

"What's your favorite breakfast cereal?"

"Cheerios."

"Plain or flavored?"

"Plain."

"What are the names of your parents?"

"I don't understand how any of this is relevant."

"Just answer my questions."

"No. I choose not to. Your questions are personal. This is an invasion of my privacy."

"*Your* privacy? What about my privacy? You've been infiltrating my work, my home, my *bank*."

"I don't know what you mean."

"Answer me this, Alison. Why are you the world's biggest liar?"

"Where is this ranked?"

"I'm serious."

"So am I."

"Why are you such a liar? Your entire history is a lie. Why are you hiding your true identity?"

Alison answered with a long stare.

Linda glanced over at Bert's laptop. The counter continued rolling on the video capture software. All of this was being recorded.

"Alison, why don't you laugh?"

"Because you're not funny."

"I've never seen you laugh. I've never seen you look upset. You just have that same stupid expression, those little smiles."

"I keep my emotions in check, Linda. It's how I stay focused and productive. It enables me to evaluate situations fairly without bias. Emotions can create distractions and color my outlook incorrectly. I believe that is your problem. You are overcome by emotion, and it has hurt your ability to function. It has put your job in jeopardy."

"No. *You* have put my job in jeopardy."

"I am not responsible for your erratic behavior and poor work performance."

"What is your middle name?"

"What does that have to do with anything?"

"Do you have any friends?"

"Of course."

"Name them."

"I have no reason to share their names with you."

"What is your favorite thing to do?"

"To be useful."

"What do you hate?"

"Wasting time."

"What frightens you?"

"Nothing."

Alison delivered her responses rapidly, cleanly, firmly. Linda didn't know if any of this conversation was going to be helpful, aside from showing what an oddball this girl was.

More than anything, Linda wanted to confront Alison in person, not thousands of miles apart on a broadband connection.

"I'm coming to visit you," Linda said.

"Why?"

"As your manager, I'd like to have an in-person meeting."

"It is my understanding there is no budget for in-person meetings unless approved by a company officer."

"I'll pay for it."

"I can't guarantee I'll be available."

"I haven't even given you any dates yet."

"You are assuming my availability."

"What else do you have to do? Where else do you have to go? All you do is sit there and work around the clock and suck up to everyone and then try to *destroy me*." Linda felt herself losing control. "You are a nut case. I will not put up with this. I will expose your bullshit. You don't know what I'm capable of. I will fucking—"

Linda stopped. She tried to catch her breath. She was practically hyperventilating.

"Are you okay, Linda?" asked Alison.

"What do you care?"

"It's not healthy to allow yourself to be overcome with such anger and hysteria. Stress is the number-one killer in today's society."

"Is that what you want? For me to be dead? Is that your goal?"

"I don't wish that on anyone."

Linda lowered her head and shut her eyes. She tried to slow down her breathing. She felt nauseous, dizzy.

"Do you need your medication?" asked Alison politely.

Linda opened her eyes and stared forward without lifting her head. "What?"

"Have you refilled your alprazolam?"

A pause. "How do you know my prescriptions?"

"I would recommend something stronger. It will help with the hallucinations."

"I'm *not* having hallucinations."

"Your ex-husband said he was concerned about your mental state. It's in the divorce filing."

"How are you getting this information?"

"Hallucinations. Schizophrenia. Have you considered treatment for your dual personalities?"

"*What are you talking about?*"

"I'm talking about Kimmy Wynn. Your alter ego."

"*That's enough!* God damn it, I'm going to hack you like you've hacked me, you little bitch."

"Language!"

"You think you can hide from me? I will find you. This sick game, or whatever you want to call it, is coming to an end. You're a psycho."

"This conversation is irrational. It is a waste of company time. I have meetings to prepare for. I have assignments to complete. I'm sorry, Linda, but I will have to terminate this call based on its lack of value."

"Do it. Go for it."

Alison stared at her wordlessly with her big brown eyes, thin lips and flat expression.

"*Go for it, bitch!*" shouted Linda.

Alison disconnected.

★　　★　　★

Linda couldn't concentrate on any actual work for the rest of the day. The red POMS circle persisted, telling the rest of the company she was offline, so it really didn't matter anyway. She finally removed her hands from the keyboard.

She had carefully followed all the instructions on Bert's sheet. Right after the video call with Alison ended, she stopped recording, and it appeared to save. She knew her outbursts were unpleasant and wished she had better self-control, but hopefully he would understand the reasons for her awkward rage.

Bert returned late that afternoon, after classes at DePaul, and knocked on the door, as instructed. She delivered his laptop and cord.

"I did everything you said. I think it saved. It was a really weird conversation. I lost my temper. I tried to ask a lot of questions. She answered some things, but with others she was really elusive."

"Just watching her and listening will help," Bert said. "I gotta admit, I'm really intrigued. I couldn't stop thinking about it all day. All the possible paths I could take to solve this puzzle. This is better than any video game. I like a good challenge."

After dinner, Linda thought some more about the message she had sent to Randy through Singles Connection. She checked for a response. It was there, waiting.

*I appreciate you reaching out. What you did was hurtful. I'm sorry that it transpired this way. I wish you all the best and better days.*

She reread it several times. It sounded sincere, but it didn't feel like total closure. She was tired of every human emotion delivered through digital channels. She typed a quick response, offering to take him out to dinner, as herself, to apologize in person.

She kept it brief, not knowing who else was watching. Alison clearly knew about Kimmy Wynn. Even with Bert's recent security fixes to Linda's computer, there was no guarantee the online eavesdropping had stopped.

Later that night, Randy responded and accepted. They set up a time and place for the following evening.

*Dinner's on me*, Linda said.

*No objections*, said Randy.

★　　★　　★

Linda was fired the next morning.

A meeting notice arrived at 9:40 a.m. for a 10 o'clock video call with Eleanor and Sunni, the crabby old woman with HR's policies and procedures unit. Given Linda's 'Job in Jeopardy' status, she immediately feared the worst.

Those fears came true.

It was like a final shot in her gut.

"We think it would be best for everyone involved if we parted ways," said Eleanor. "We appreciate your many contributions over the years. The time has come to move on." She was trying to be cordial, setting up Sunni to play 'bad cop'.

"You had been warned, and you continued to violate the values of the company with behavior of bullying and harassment," said Sunni in a tight, terse tone. "That voicemail you sent is the last straw. It demonstrates a serious lack of judgment. We expect our managers to conduct themselves in a professional manner at all times and treat our people with dignity and respect."

"What – what voicemail?" Linda said.

"Your voicemail to Alison Smith."

"I didn't send any voicemail to Alison." Linda felt tension in every bone in her body. "Whatever she's telling you, it's a lie."

"You didn't leave a voicemail for Alison last night at six thirty?" asked Sunni in a tone of hard cynicism.

"No. I know I didn't. Why do you always believe her over me?"

"Play it for her," Eleanor said.

Sunni nodded.

"You have a recording?" Linda said. "I want to hear it."

Sunni pursed her lips together, looked down to fiddle with her mouse, and within moments Linda heard her own voice. It was ugly.

*"Alison, you little bitch. You make me sick with your goody good work ethic. It makes me look weak. I hate your stupid expression. You are fucking bullshit. You don't know what I'm capable of. I will fucking destroy you."*

Linda rocked back in her seat, stunned. *Holy shit, all this time she's been recording me.*

It was a cut and paste of Linda's real words to fabricate a new message. It sounded a little awkward, some inflections were off, but effective nevertheless.

"It's nonsensical, it's not me," Linda said.

"Honey, I've known you for over ten years. That is your voice," Eleanor said.

"Yes, but —" Linda was lost, she didn't know what to say next. It was indeed her voice, digitally manipulated and deftly edited. "She created something out of my words."

"So you admit these are your words?"

"Yes. No. Jesus."

"This is entirely unacceptable."

"Please, you have to understand, she's a scam artist. She needs to be investigated. She's not who she says she is. Do some research. Everything about her is a lie. She's a fake. I've looked into it."

"Yes," said Sunni, angry. "She told us about your prying into her personal details. Again, it is not appropriate."

"Not appropriate? To catch a fraud? To expose someone's lies? To—"

Sunni pointed a finger at Linda through the camera lens. "*Stop it.* You listen. The reason you can't find this young woman online is because she's protecting herself from an abusive boyfriend. She does not want him to find her. That's why her personal information is private. She had to change her name. Her address is not public. You don't know the full story. There's a reason for all this. It's for her own safety and well-being. Please take your hostility someplace else. It is not welcome here. You are traumatizing this poor woman who has been through enough."

Sunni's defense of Alison shut down Linda for a moment. Linda tried to digest it. She saw Eleanor's unhappy face, Sunni's stern scowl.

"I think she's lying to you," Linda said. "And you are gullible."

"Linda, we're not here to argue," Eleanor said. "Your employment has been terminated."

"We will send you instructions for returning your company laptop," Sunni said. "Please print it out or write it down, because we will be disconnecting you from the network."

"So you believe someone who has been here a few weeks over someone who has been here fifteen years?"

"You need help, Linda," said Eleanor. "I recommend you see someone. You're hurting yourself."

"I'm being manipulated. And you're being manipulated. And I'm going to prove it."

"I recommend we cut off any further contact after this conversation," Eleanor said. "This has been an enormous drain on my time and energy, and the company —"

"I'm going to sue you," blurted Linda. It was the only thing left she could think of to say.

Sunni spoke. "Later today, you will be hearing from a representative about your severance package."

"Okay." Linda couldn't bear to look at these two faces any longer. She clutched the mouse, moved the cursor and clicked to end the call.

They went away.

Her small home office fell dark. Outside it was snowing again. Frost blurred the windows. Everything in her world was colorless and gray. She sat hunched in her chair, trying not to think or feel.

She had one goal and that was to be emotionless.

# CHAPTER ELEVEN

Linda sat in a sticky red booth against a dirty window at Jimmy's Diner, a short hop from a busy main road of rumbling traffic that sliced through several Chicago suburbs. It was conveniently located and quickly accessed. This was not a date-night restaurant but an appropriate backdrop for a groveling apology without makeup. She wore jeans and an old sweater. Her medium, flat real hair replaced the long, bouncy curls of the red wig.

She wondered if Randy would recognize her at all.

Still shell-shocked over getting fired earlier in the day, Linda was not ready to confront more drama, but she didn't want to cancel. That would be ghosting the poor guy all over again. Plus, she needed to escape the suffocating walls of her townhouse. And she needed to eat, despite the knots in her stomach.

Cecilia had called her a few hours earlier. "I heard the news. I'm so sorry. Are you okay?"

"No. But I will fight this."

"Maybe just let it go. You'll be happier somewhere else."

"That's not the point. This whole thing was a personal assault."

"Okay. Maybe." Cecilia didn't sound convinced but also stepped back from starting an argument. "Did you see the email they sent?"

"About what?"

"About you leaving."

"No. Was it like two sentences?"

"Not at all. It was nicely worded. It was respectful. They said you were leaving 'to pursue other interests.' There were a couple of paragraphs on your career accomplishments, all positive."

"Send it to me."

"Ah, okay." Cecilia hesitated. "I will. But you should know something."

"What?"

"It also talks about… You're not going to like this. But Alison is moving up to fill your open role."

"No fucking way."

"She'll report directly to Eleanor now."

"God! That was her plot all along."

"Forget about them. All of them."

"How can I? I gave that company fifteen years of my life, Cecilia."

"People move on."

"I didn't move on. I was pushed away. Alison did this. She's not normal. She's—" Then Linda stopped herself from continuing, lowering her voice. "She's probably listening in on this call right now."

"Okay," said Cecilia, likely just humoring her while dismissing her as paranoid.

"Keep an eye on her. Don't turn your back."

"I will," Cecilia said. "I mean, no one else is saying anything like this. I know you don't want to hear it, but they love her around here."

"She knows how to charm the right people. But they don't know her like I do."

"You could be right. I don't really interact with her."

"My advice: stay away." The call ended soon after.

Linda wondered if their friendship would gradually dissipate without the coworker connection. It was part of a larger trend. The people around her were abandoning her.

"Maybe I deserve it," she said out loud to herself in the diner booth.

Then Randy arrived. He wore his down parka and scarf, shoulders hunched. His glasses fogged up. It was pleasantly geeky. He took them off and waited for them to clear. Then he looked around the diner, searching.

She waved him over.

He did a small double take.

He came over and sat across from her in the booth. He took off his coat. He did not smile, but he did say, "Hi."

"I'll bet you didn't recognize me," she said.

"No, not really."

"This is the real me. My real hair. My real face. I'm sorry I deceived you. It was uncalled for."

He nodded in agreement. "So Kimmy's not your real name?"

"No. My real name is Linda. Linda Kelly." This received a blank look, so she said, "Here, I can prove it." She reached into her purse and took out her pocketbook. She showed Randy her driver's license, a credit card and even her library card, hoping it would lighten the mood. But he still didn't smile.

"Why were you Kimmy?"

"I – I wish I knew. I guess I thought it would be fun to be someone else for a change. Maybe I just don't like who I am. I'm divorced. I live alone. I was just fired from my job. Being myself isn't working out too well."

"So you hurt someone else?"

It stung, and it was deserved. "I was online and had a few drinks. I was in a weird mood. I guess it's easy to forget that on the other end there are real people with real feelings."

"The internet makes people act in strange ways. It's a buffer that can encourage bad behavior rather than bring us closer."

"I'm not a cruel person. Honest, I'm not. I just do stupid things. I'm sorry, Randy." She felt on the verge of crying – not just over this, but the accumulation of everything.

He picked up on her pitiful state. He looked at her sad eyes and said, "Apology accepted."

"Thank you." She managed a smile. "Dinner's on me. I can't vouch for the food, but there's a lot of variety on the menu. The pictures look nice."

"A menu with photos," he gently teased. "Always a sign of fine dining."

A waitress in an apron came by. Linda and Randy both ordered sandwiches. The dinner and conversation that followed was pleasant, if cautiously bland. It wasn't until they had cleared their plates that Linda brought up the online harassment she had been experiencing. Randy's open, sincere face led her to go deeper into the insanity of her personal life. He seemed like a genuinely sympathetic soul. She proceeded slowly, knowing how crazy the whole thing with Alison would sound if she rushed it. "I'm being hacked and sabotaged, and I'm pretty sure I know who, but I don't know why."

"Sounds like you need to spend more time offline. The internet's causing you all sorts of problems."

"It's gotten really bad. My bank account was hacked. My work files were deleted. My townhouse was put up for sale. It goes on and on."

"That *is* serious. Who would harass you like this? Is it your ex-husband?"

"No. I'm pretty sure it's someone I work with – used to work with. She did it to steal my job."

"Well, what you've described is criminal activity," Randy said. "I have a brother-in-law in the FBI. He goes after online fraud and ID theft, people selling credit card numbers and passwords. They shut down child pornography sites. If it's criminal behavior on the internet, it's a federal crime because it's using interstate telecommunications."

"Federal crime?" Linda said. "So I could – theoretically – get the FBI involved in what's happening to me?"

"I would think so."

Linda's spirits lifted, even if just a little, for the first time in days. "I'm collecting evidence right now. I have someone helping me. This is great. I could get her arrested."

Randy passed on dessert and said he had to get going. His kids were with a sitter, and he wanted to see them before bedtime. Linda could imagine Randy kissing them each good night on the cheek.

She paid the check, as promised. He gave her a gentle hug as they got up from the booth to part ways.

"Thank you for getting real," he said.

"I'm sorry I'm not a sexy redhead named Kimmy," she responded.

He laughed. "I'm not into Kimmy. I like you better."

★   ★   ★

Linda returned home to the townhouse. It was dark and unlit in wintertime black. She stood at the front door and fished in her purse for the key. As she did, she heard the soft crunch of footsteps in the snow behind her. Her heart immediately pounded faster. Was there anything in her purse to use to defend herself? Her fingers scrambled through the contents and grazed ChapStick, chewing gum and loose change. She once had a small pepper spray canister but it was in the house somewhere, forgotten in a drawer.

She whirled around, prepared to release a powerful scream.

"Mrs.— Linda," said a male voice, and then a face emerged from the shadows. It was Bert, bundled up in his winter coat and hat and carrying his laptop bag.

"Jesus, you scared me."

"Sorry. I've been waiting for you to come home, watching from my window. I didn't want to call or text, you know, in case you're being monitored."

"That's — that's probably a good idea." She was still catching her breath.

"I wanted to talk to you as soon as I could. It's about the video. I've watched it like ten times."

"Wow." She didn't like living through it once. "I'm sorry."

"It's fascinating. I think I'm onto something. I don't think she's real."

"I'm not surprised. She's pretending to be someone else."

"No, it's not that. Someone else is pretending to be her."

Linda tried to absorb this. "What do you mean?"

"The person in this video is not real. It's a deepfake. It's computer animation."

Linda almost laughed. "I think I would have noticed."

"It's very sophisticated. It's— Can I come in?"

"Of course. Let's go inside."

He indicated his laptop. "I can show you."

They entered the townhouse, and she turned on some lights and directed him to the small sofa in the living room.

"Can I get you something to drink?" she asked. "Hot cocoa?"

"No, I'm okay. I'm hopped up on Mountain Dew."

"Great." She pulled up a chair to sit next to him. He was looking around the room.

"Do you have any electronics in here — you know, voice assistants, smart speakers, like Siri or Alexa or Google Assistant?"

"No," she said, and she glanced around the area with him. "My husband was into those gadgets. I think he had one that he took with him."

"I just want to be careful, because of the extent you've been hacked. Someone could be listening."

"Somebody could be listening to me inside my house?" She felt a chill run up her spine that was unrelated to the winter cold.

"Sure. Any number of ways. Even your phone. You could have an app forced on there that's eavesdropping."

She quickly pulled out her phone and studied it with a frown. It looked normal, but...

"I'll put it in another room." She jumped up and left for the kitchen. She shoved the smart phone into the silverware drawer and slammed it shut before returning.

"My paranoia just jumped another hundred per cent," she said.

He was already activating the laptop on the coffee table.

He said, "This isn't a person pretending to be another person. This is an avatar pretending to be a person."

"How is that even possible? It looks so real." She sat back in the chair, and he swiveled the laptop screen so they both could see.

He started playing back the video of Linda's last encounter with Alison.

"Oh god, I really don't want to watch this," she said.

"That's the thing. We're going to watch it – just watch it, no sound. We're not going to get distracted by the conversation." He silenced the audio. "Every time I play it, I catch something else. I've been at it for hours, obsessing over it."

"Well, it's the last video you'll get. They fired me this morning."

He paused to look at her. "Oh. I'm sorry."

"It was inevitable. This was her goal, and she achieved it. She got my job."

"Crazy! They gave your job to a computer-generated deepfake."

"How can you be so sure?" She leaned in to more closely watch the replay of her video call the day before. "She looks totally real. Look at that, her face, her expressions. She looks like any other person online. She doesn't look like some Pixar character."

"No, it's not that kind of animation. I play a lot of video games. Some of them are incredibly realistic. They look like live-action movies, but it's next-generation CGI. It mimics what we're trained to see. I've got an eye for this. I know the subtle distinctions. Some movements are slightly unnatural. The lighting is contradictory. The skin tone is too smooth."

"Really?"

"Here, let me show you." He zoomed in on Alison. "Just stare at her for a while."

"Sure, it will turn my stomach but—"

"When you get close, she has a painting-like texture. It's a bit too slick. Her skin quality is off, almost waxlike. The hair is too perfect. You don't see any stray strands, it's very still. I'll bet it hasn't changed length."

"Now that you mention it, it looks the same as her profile photo the first day."

"She has limited range. She lacks a lot of facial expressions. Some of the same ones come up, and they're identical."

"She's not very emotive, but I figured that was just her."

"Look at the lighting. It's inconsistent. See, it seems to come from this side, but then also from here." He was waving his finger around the frame. "The shadows...sometimes they seem to come from the wrong direction."

"But you don't know how the room is lit. She could have a mix of different lights and windows. I do."

"She's always positioned in exactly the same place in the frame. She lacks subtle body movements. You never see her hands. You gesture several times, we see more of you. But not her. Most people aren't this naturally still. They shift in their chair, they move their shoulders, they get a stiff back. And her background is generic as can be, there's no signs of life, just a painted wall."

Linda shrugged. "A lot of people want a generic background. They don't want to show their messy homes."

"Okay. But all these things add up. Then there's her eyes. The cadence of blinking. It's very consistent. Almost too consistent, like it's locked into a pattern. Watch..."

He waited for Alison to blink, and then counted out loud to her next blink. He reached six. Then he started counting again. Six. The next duration between blinks: also six.

"It's like it's programmed," he said, watching in awe.

"I don't know..." Linda still felt like she was staring into the face of an authentic human being.

"You have to be really studying this and looking for it. Your average company Zoom call – no one's going to notice this level of detail."

"Your average company Zoom call, no one's paying attention. They're looking at themselves or at their phones."

"Now let's turn on the audio."

Alison's voice spoke from the video recording. Crisp, cool and confident. Smart-ass. Linda cringed at the sound of it.

Bert said, "During the entire time she's talking in this video, I never once heard any background noise. No dropouts, no static. It's too clean.

With you, I could hear a few odds and ends. The squeak of your chair. Little sounds when you hit the keyboard or knocked the mouse. Your furnace kicking in. Her audio is totally clear and balanced. It's too balanced. Yet at times, the pitch is a bit odd. The scale of emotions is off."

"She doesn't show much emotion."

"Very little. Her voice often falls into a monotone. I took some of her audio and turned it into WAV files and studied the WAV files. She says certain words exactly the same way, no matter what the context. And I mean *exactly*. You put the two WAV forms side by side, they look identical. Like they've been pulled out of a data bank."

"I just figured she was acting real controlled to sound tough or something. But she really has no personality."

"And check this out. It happens a few times. One's coming up…"

He let a moment play out on the video.

"Did you see it?" he asked.

"See what?"

"It fell out of sync. The words and the lip movements. It doesn't match up. I'll run it again."

Looking for it, she caught it the second time.

"There's more like that. It goes by real fast. If you don't have a recording to rewind, you're not going to see it. But there are some strange mouth movements. It's the hardest part to fake, getting the audio right in real time."

He froze the frame. "And check out the lip size and color. They're faintly off. Like they don't quite match the rest of the face."

"So I've been talking to some kind of digital character?"

"I'm convinced she's AI. Underneath this image, there's an AI-powered chatbot with a persona, programmed for behaviors and conversation. But somewhere there's got to be an actual person behind this to give it an agenda and parameters."

Linda stared at the screen, amazed. "This face I've been talking to all this time…and want to punch…isn't real?"

"Well, depends how you define 'real'. It could be sourced from a real person to create a base. Then they encode a library of facial expressions over it and give it a new voice. It works best if they use someone with a lot of visual reference material, photos and videos."

"From where?"

"It could be anyone. It could be stolen off the internet. Someone's visual identity can be hijacked and used as a mask. It's a real thing."

"This is big," said Linda, rising. "Really big. It's a federal crime, right? We could get the FBI involved." She thought about Randy and his brother-in-law.

"Sure, I bet we could." Bert stopped the video playback. "Let's connect again tomorrow. I think I can keep digging and gather more evidence. I'm on a roll."

"This is incredible."

"It's exciting," Bert said. He stood up from the sofa and checked his watch. "I gotta get home. I've got papers due. I still have fifteen more credit hours before I graduate. My mom's going to be on my case. I told her I was helping tutor you, that you had computer problems. I wasn't going to try to explain this other stuff, she'd probably freak out. She's not tech-smart at all, she wouldn't understand."

"I'm having a hard time understanding it."

"It's pretty wild," Bert said, and he reached for his coat, which was draped over the sofa arm. "I've heard about these things but never really seen them in action. This is intense."

"Yeah," said Linda, dazed. "That's one word for it."

★　★　★

She awoke early and abruptly the next morning, prodded by an inner alarm clock, and prepared for a new workday, but it was just an irritating reflex.

Out of curiosity, she shuffled into her tiny home office and tried to log into the PEC network from her company laptop.

Access denied.

She was officially booted from the business. Legal and HR liked to sever ties quickly to prevent disgruntled ex-employees from taking confidential company files out the door with them.

Her PEC laptop was officially a dead slab. They would mail her a postage-paid cardboard box to return it in. If she so much as kept the mouse, they would subtract it from her final pay.

There was some relief in being cut off like this. She was done dealing with Alison. She was free. They would never speak again.

Linda went downstairs to fix some breakfast.

Then Alison texted her.

"*What the fuck!*" Linda nearly threw the phone across the tile floor when she discovered who was making it buzz.

Alison's text message was accompanied by a tiny avatar of her stony, impassive stare. The message read:

*Linda, I am so sorry it didn't work out. The company values your many contributions. I'm sure it was a difficult decision. I appreciate the time we spent together. I wish you all the best with your future endeavors.*

Linda glared at it in disbelief. It was the laziest, most insincere automated message of all time. It was a final *fuck you, ha ha*, waving a middle finger in her face.

Fury overtook Linda like a rapid flame. She furiously texted her reply.

*Eat shit, you robot. I will expose you for what you are. Congratulations on your promotion. You are the company's highest-ranking animated cartoon. You are not rid of me this easily. I'm going to pull your fucking plug.*

She hit send and then blocked Alison from ever sending her any more messages.

Linda paced frantic circles in the kitchen. "This is insane. This is insane." She was going to need more help to fight this, not just a college kid. This was way out of control. Her ex-husband needed to know. All of this hacking threatened him too. He was entangled in this mess whether he liked it or not. What if Alison put up the townhouse for sale again? Or put in a false order for a demolition company to tear it down? Or went after *his* bank accounts next? His business?

She dialed him.

He answered with a weary, "Yes, Linda."

"No. Don't take that attitude. Listen, these online attacks – they've gotten worse. She got me fired."

"Who got you fired?" he said, his voice faint against a busy backdrop of other voices.

"Alison! The girl I was telling you about!"

"What did you do to her?"

"*Me? Me?*"

"I'm at Starbucks. I'm trying to—"

"Get out of line and talk to me."

"I have meetings. I don't have time for this."

"You don't have time to help me with a criminal attack on my life?"

"We already discussed this. Get a virus protection. Use better passwords. I know you. You don't take that stuff seriously."

"It's not fixed that easily!"

"Then I don't know what to say."

"Do you know Bert Pacorek?"

"I...I don't know."

"Down the street."

"The kid with the overbearing mother?"

"Yes. He looked into it. He studied a video. He says this girl is not a real person. I'm being harassed by a very sophisticated deepfake."

"Okay. And maybe some UFOs and Bigfoot too?"

"This is not funny!"

"You should listen to yourself talk right now. You're hysterical."

"Yes, I *am* hysterical. There's a fake person out to get me, and it's very, very real. Bert and I – we studied her. We watched how she blinks and her mouth."

"Yes, one hazelnut latte..." He was ordering.

She screamed, a burst of frustration.

"Jesus!" he responded. "You're going to blow out my eardrum."

"I need your help!"

"Yes, you need help. I got that."

"I'm onto something big. You know technology better than me. You can help look into this."

"Thank you," he said faintly.

"What?"

"I'm saying thank you to – I'm paying for my – Linda, this is really inconvenient right now!"

"That I'm in trouble? That I'm being cyberstalked?"

"If it's so bad, call the police."

"I'm going to call the FBI."

"Good. Keep me out of it."

"You're a real shit, do you know that?"

This bothered him. He lowered his voice to avoid the customers around him hearing. The tone became taut with tension. "Listen. I've tried to make this an amicable divorce. You're making it very hard. Someone hacked your computer, just do what normal people do and get it taken care of and then move on. I know you're feeling a lot of emotions right now, with me, with your job, with this identity theft, but you can't lose your mind about it, you're not being rational. Please see somebody. See a shrink. I've been telling you that for years, with every panic attack. I will pay for it. But don't call me anymore. Got that? I'm done with this."

He stopped talking, and she didn't say anything. She heard the steady din of chatter at Starbucks, regular people going on with their regular lives. Someone laughed. Someone said, "Excuse me." Someone said, "Espresso." Other bits of tiny dialogue were there, but not discernible, entangled.

Linda hung up.

X was a bully; he always would be. Maybe not a cyberbully like Alison, but he belonged in the same cold class. X was someone who belittled and undermined her, sometimes subtle, sometimes not. It had put her in a perpetually nervous state during their marriage.

*I don't need his help*, she concluded. *I don't even want his help.*

★ ★ ★

Bert arrived that evening. He brought his laptop. She supplied the pizza and soft drinks. They sat down at the kitchen table. After a few quick bites and a sip, he excitedly dove into his latest discoveries.

"Watch this," he said.

He opened up a search engine and typed the name *Anna Bafort.*

"Who?" Linda said.

"You'll see."

He ran a quick image search. Dozens of pictures popped up, most of them professional photography showing a pretty young brunette in a variety of poses, from sultry staging on fashion runways to ads for beauty products.

"It's Alison!" gasped Linda.

"It's Anna," corrected Bert. "She's a small-time Belgian model."

"Why am I being harassed by a small-time Belgian model?"

"You aren't. Somebody hijacked her image. Look, these ads are in Dutch. She's not really known outside her country, but she's been photographed enough to provide a wide range of angles that can be used to make a 3-D CGI composite."

"This is incredible. How did you find her?"

"I took screenshots from your video and ran a face-scanning search. With the right tools, you can search a face just like you can search key words. I kept doing it until one of the screenshots hit the jackpot and called up all of this. It wasn't easy. They made some changes to the original image so it wouldn't be quite so obvious. You can see the differences – here, look, when I put them side by side."

He pulled up one of the screen captures of Alison from the video and placed it next to a close-up of Anna facing the camera lens.

"They changed her chin. The eyebrows. A few other things. But this was their starting point. It gave them a foundation to work from. They stole this woman's image, encoded it and digitally manipulated it so they could animate her to do whatever they wanted. They created a library of lip movements for vowels and consonants to synchronize her speaking. It's called deepfake synthetization."

"And this model has no idea?"

"No idea. How would she? Unless your company has a Flemish employee from Belgium who knows Anna Bafort or someone remembers seeing one of these photos somewhere and actually makes a connection..."

"We need to tell Anna. She can sue!"

"We'll have to find a way to reach her. Or the agency that represents her."

"I don't speak Dutch."

"Neither do I. But we can use a translator tool online to get our message across."

Bert's phone rang in his pocket, a ringtone of electronic dance beats. He picked it up and looked at it. He rolled his eyes. "Mom," he said.

He answered and said very little, aside from, "Uh-huh...uh-huh... okay...yeah...I know."

After the call ended, he looked a little embarrassed. "One of the drawbacks of still living at home. It saves me money to pay for tuition, but I'm treated like I'm still thirteen years old. She wants me home."

Linda barely knew Bert's mother but had seen her around the neighborhood. She was a lean, serious woman with thin gray hair and big glasses. "Well, you're always going to be her boy."

"My dad left when I was ten years old, and I'm all she's got."

"I'm sure she means well."

"She does. I better go." He took a deep breath. "So. Next steps. I'll package all this information. All of our discoveries, the links, the pictures. And then we'll hand it over to the proper authorities. Since they attacked your bank account, we can start with the Federal Trade Commission."

"And the FBI. I think I have a contact there now."

"That's great. Excellent. We're going to nail this loser. Whoever's behind Alison won't know what's coming."

Linda felt a pang of guilt. "I forgot to tell you... I had a little exchange with her today."

"Alison?"

"She texted me."

Bert stiffened, alarmed. "What did she say?"

Linda told the story of their messaging that concluded with Linda's outburst revealing she knew about the computer-generated animation.

Bert winced. "Oh, that's not good. Whoever's behind this, we don't want them to know we're onto them." He let the realization sink in. "Well then, we'll just have to move faster."

Linda offered, "I can help write all this up. It's what I do for a living, I'm a writer. I'll tell the whole story from beginning to end."

"Maybe."

"You doubt my writing?"

"No. But anything you type into your computer might be followed."

"Oh. Then I'll write it down longhand."

He thought about it and said, "Yes. That's it. Write it down on paper. Then give it to me. I'll type it up on my computer. That way we don't have an electronic file sitting on your PC."

"I can do that. I used to handwrite my first drafts all the time."

"I know this has been terrible for you, but you gotta admit, it's also kind of cool. We're going to nail a cybercriminal. It's a duel of wits, and we're going to win."

"Yes," Linda responded. "We're going to win."

After Bert left, Linda went upstairs and pulled a fresh pad of lined paper out of her bottom desk drawer. She grabbed a pen from her *Chicago Times* coffee mug of writing utensils. Then she returned downstairs and sat in a big, soft chair. She was energized to begin her write-up on Alison Smith.

She started to write Alison's name on the top of the first sheet. She stopped after two letters and stared at it, struck by what she saw.

Al.

# CHAPTER TWELVE

Linda spent the next day doing what she did best – assembling facts into a narrative. Her roots were in journalism – warped a bit but still active during her stint in corporate PR. The words flowed quickly as she sought to capture everything that transpired after Alison entered her life. The page count kept growing as she recalled every detail. Bert would help smooth over tech references as her subject matter expert. Together they would expose this madness for what it was.

The sun had gone down, and she had started preparing dinner – tomato soup and a grilled cheese sandwich – when a large crash sounded in the living room. As she ran to see the source, she heard the quick roar of a car engine departing from the front of her townhouse.

A large rock, roughly the size of a softball, sat on the carpet surrounded by shattered glass. A cold breeze blew into the room from a large break in the big window at the front of the house.

"Holy shit," she said, stunned. Had her tormentor switched from digital tools to throwing rocks? Surely someone on the block had an exterior security camera that caught the escaping vehicle, no matter how dark it was in the street.

"Unbelievable," she said. She opened the front door to look outside.

On the top step, she found a small collection of stuffed animals. She stared down at them in disbelief. "What the hell?" They were various shapes and sizes of plush dogs and puppies. Some were decorated with colorful ribbons. One had a red collar attached to a big red heart emblem.

If it was a secret admirer, this was a psychotic expression of affection.

She didn't want to touch any of it. The brisk winter air was chilling her bones. She noticed a piece of paper stuck to one of the puppies with a rubber band. It rustled slightly in the wind.

She stared at it for a moment, and then she reached down and gently extracted the note.

She unfolded it and read: *You sick bitch. I hope you rot in Hell.*

She quickly folded it back up as icicles of terror branched throughout her body. Her eyes searched the neighborhood. Who did this? Were they still watching her?

Then she noticed another note. This one was taped to her front door.

She removed it and read the message. This one was in a different, more feminine handwriting, but equally scathing.

*You are the lowest form of human being. Does it make you feel big? To pick on a small, defenseless dog? The eyes of the world are watching. There will be retribution. You are human garbage. You deserve every bad thing that is coming your way.*

Linda felt dizzy. What dog? She didn't even own a dog.

Then headlights approached from down the street. A midsized gray sedan moved slowly, coming to a stop in front of her home. She saw multiple shadowed heads inside the car.

She heard voices, rising with anger.

"This is the house!"

"That's the lady!"

"Hey, fuck you!"

"Somebody's gonna kill you just like you killed—"

She hurried back into the house and slammed the door. She locked it.

She could still hear their shouted threats. She quickly turned off the lights in the living room so they couldn't see her silhouette.

Their screams grew louder. She wanted to flee but had to listen — what was all this about a dog?

"We're coming back when you're *sleeping!*" one of them yelled.

Her phone rang. It vibrated in the back pocket of her jeans. She pulled it out and stared at it.

Unidentified caller.

She answered it. "Yes?"

"Hey, dog killer, puppy killer, guess what I'm going to do to you."

She hung up.

Now there were multiple cars in front of her house. New voices, men and women. Some of them had stepped out of their vehicles.

She heard a thud strike the house. Then several more.

Then an object flew through the opening in her broken window and struck a chair. She screamed and jumped.

It was a snowball. Now they were throwing snowballs.

She moved closer to the edge of the window, staying out of view to avoid getting hit by anything, but she wanted to be heard.

"*I'm calling the police!*" she announced.

"Good, they oughtta lock you up!" came a response from a shrill female voice.

One of the vehicles left. A couple of others stayed. A new one arrived. Lights went on in windows across the street as neighbors discovered the commotion.

Linda called the police. "My house is under attack!" She gave her address to a monotone dispatch worker.

"Is anyone hurt?" he asked with the equivalent ambivalence of 'Would you like ketchup with that?'

"Not yet, but it's going to happen if the police don't get here right now."

"We'll send someone."

"*Hurry!*"

Now cars were honking in front of her house. More shouts of 'fuck you!' More items struck her front door, causing her to jump with every hit.

Every minute that passed before the police arrived was agonizing. What if someone broke into the house to assault her? It wouldn't be difficult to enter through the broken window. Her phone continued to ring, but she stopped answering – every caller was enraged and threatening her over something she allegedly did to some dog.

A police car arrived, lights flashing but no siren. It was enough to disperse the small crowd. There was no attempt by the police to pursue any of them. Linda watched as an overweight officer stepped out of the vehicle, moving slowly with an expression that simply looked annoyed.

She rushed to the front door to meet him.

He was staring down at the small collection of stuffed animals. Then he looked up at her.

She said, "All of a sudden – all these people started attacking my house – I have no idea what's going on."

"Somebody caught you on video," the officer said. "We've been getting angry calls too. About you."

"About me?"

"Ma'am, I have three dogs and two cats. I'm a pet lover. If we weren't so tied up with gang shootings right now, I'd run you in and write you up. If folks are harassing you and condemning you for what you did, consider it well-deserved. I don't understand people like you."

"People like me?"

"It's the internet age. You can run but you can't hide from the consequences of your actions. I recommend you make a real big contribution to the ASPCA. And be public about it. Maybe people will forgive you. And going forward, if you so much as kick a squirrel, I am going to put you in front of an angry Cook County judge. Got that?"

"I didn't do anything! I didn't do whatever this is! This is insanity!" she shouted into his deadpan face.

"Ma'am, I saw the video. I see you here now. It's pretty obvious. Okay?"

"*What video?*"

He shook his head, as if weary of her ignorance. Then he simply said, "You got caught. Now you got to deal with it."

And with that, he turned to leave.

She stood in the doorway for a long moment, heart thumping.

Then she retreated into the house. She hurried into the kitchen and flipped open her laptop.

She went online and discovered her social media accounts were exploding with hate messages.

She discovered the reason very quickly.

Some anonymous group, 'Citizens Against Animal Cruelty', had posted a video 'from a neighbor's cell phone'.

It was nineteen seconds long. The camera was shaky and a bit blurry, but the focal point was precise.

Linda watched herself pummel a small dog with a shovel, beating it into limp submission in the snow. There was blood. She heard her own voice snarl, "This is what happens! To bad dogs that chew my nice shoes!"

She watched it a second time, then shut the lid and burst into tears.

"*That's not me, that's not me.*" Someone had created a deepfake video of her committing this horrific act – and it was bone-chillingly realistic, appalling and going viral all over the internet.

Outside, she heard the return of voices, cars.

She immediately flipped open the laptop again. Maybe she could post something to set the record straight? To counter this insane misinformation?

She jumped onto the original post, which had now been shared thousands of times. The views were in the tens of thousands, with the number increasing in real time in front of her eyes.

"Oh my god," she said, reading the fiery description more carefully, clicking the *more* to unfold more text. "They published my address."

She quickly typed in a comment under her own name. *People, please listen to me. This video is a fake. It's not really me. Someone is doing this to hurt me. I don't even have a dog!*

A response popped up within seconds: *Yeah, because you buried him!*

She hurried a reply. *No, that's not true. I—*

Then her reply went blank, deleted.

Her fingers rose from the keys in a moment of stunned disbelief.

Then she saw new words pop up in her reply – penned by someone else, somewhere else, under her identity, stealing the controls of her social media account.

The new response attacked the previous poster with ethnic slurs.

"No, no, no." Linda tried to regain control of her keyboard.

More words spewed out from under her avatar: *It's just a stupid animal. It deserved to get its brains bashed. Those were my new pump sandals from Neiman Marcus.*

The video at the top of the comments stream continued to run, looping relentlessly. Linda tried to spot easy fakery but it was crazy realistic, with her spoken dialogue reserved for moments when her back was turned so you couldn't see her lips. The head was a smooth CGI replica of her own, stuck on a body of the same approximate size, in an area of snow so wintertime generic that it could have been shot anywhere.

She felt like she was going to throw up.

A sudden series of loud bangs erupted in the living room. She jumped and glimpsed bright flashes from an exploding pack of firecrackers someone had tossed through her open window. A car sped off down the street, accompanied by loud taunts.

After the last firecracker had detonated, she circled the burn marks on the floor to make sure nothing was catching on fire. She made it her immediate priority to cover the big hole in her front window.

Linda hurried downstairs to the small basement of the townhouse. Against one wall, there was shelving filled with various belongings that had been banished from the upper floors by X, including cardboard boxes filled with her books. X had scorned her for holding on to her old hardcovers and paperbacks in the era of e-books, but she stood her ground to keep them, even as he insisted they stay out of the living room and den, deeming them 'unnecessary clutter'.

Now the books were dumped to the floor as she needed the cardboard boxes that housed them. She emptied and flattened three boxes, bringing them upstairs with a large roll of duct tape. She covered the broken window with the cardboard, sealing the area the best she could. The house was getting cold, and the furnace was working overtime to keep up. There was melted snow in the living room from where snowballs had been pitched.

She heard more voices outside. It was impossible to know who was simply driving by to yell profanities and who would actually attack the house – or try to physically abuse her.

While in the basement, she had spotted an old baseball bat, a remnant from the early years of her marriage, when she and X joined the Windy City Softball League for fun. It felt like a very long time ago, when their relationship was still warm, and they wore cute matching sports jerseys with her last name on the back. It was a happy memory of sunny summertime afternoons, open spaces, green grass and making friends.

Now the baseball bat could serve a new purpose – bashing the brains of anyone who came near her.

Someone was kicking at the front door. She hurried to the basement and grabbed the bat. She returned upstairs and threw open the door, which clearly startled the pair of teenagers who had been banging on it.

"Get out of here or I will crush your skull!" she screamed at them.

"Crazy lady!" one of them shouted. The other spat at her. Then they turned and ran.

A third young person, standing out on the sidewalk, took a picture on her phone of Linda wielding the bat.

*Great*, thought Linda. *More fodder for social media.*

The three kids ran off into the night, one of them shouting, "We're going to come back with a shovel...and see how you like it!"

She watched them disappear, and for a moment it was quiet. There was more debris on the steps – envelopes with threatening notes she didn't want to read, sad-eyed stuffed animals she didn't want to touch.

Someone had spray-painted words on her front door.

*DOG KILLER.*

And that wasn't the worst of it. She noticed something small on the door, splintered wood, that struck her with fresh panic.

A bullet hole.

Someone had fired a gun at her house.

She immediately pulled herself back inside and slammed the entrance shut. She locked it. She retreated to the kitchen and sat on the floor in a space away from windows.

She texted Bert from her phone.

*Are you seeing any of this?!*

It took several minutes for him to respond. *See what? I'm at school, at the library.*

*They hacked my social media. They created a fake video of me killing a dog. People are going nuts.*

*OMG.*

*We need to go to the FBI. The cops don't care. They don't understand.*

*Okay. First thing tomorrow. I promise. We'll get together.*

*If I'm still alive!*

*We'll make it stop.*

After the texting ended, she sat silently on the floor with her baseball bat, listening for any further sounds of strangers showing up to express their outrage.

The soup she had started on the stovetop was cold. The grilled cheese sandwich was burned. She wasn't hungry anyway.

She remained very still in stony silence. She waited for the next burst of noise...

It erupted in her hand. The phone vibrated with musical tones.

She jumped, startled. Probably just another furious dog lover who had tracked down her number. She had ignored dozens of them in the past hour. She glanced at the caller ID.

It read: *Your Fate.*

Linda felt a chill in her bones. What lunatic was this now? What kind of threat?

She decided to answer. At the very least, she could try to deliver the truth, if anyone would accept it. *Don't believe everything you see on the internet. It's bullshit.*

She answered firmly, "This is Linda."

The voice on the other end was strange and warbly, composed by electronics to disguise the caller's true identity. It was cold, measured and concise.

"Choose your destiny. Act wisely. Drop your investigation of Alison and live the rest of your life. Or continue with it at your own risk. Perhaps one of those angry anonymous animal lovers will put a bullet in your head and never get caught. How do you identify a culprit when the whole world has turned against you? No one will find the perpetrator. I guarantee it."

There was a soft click and the call ended.

Outside, a new round of shouts erupted. She knew it would never stop. The audience for that viral video would keep expanding throughout the night.

There was no way she could sleep here. She couldn't close her eyes for a minute. Something very bad was going to happen if she stayed.

Linda packed a suitcase. She filled it with several days of clothes. Toiletries. Her laptop. Her pad of paper containing the handwritten true story of Alison. More paper, pens.

On top of it all, she tossed in the red wig. She was going to need a new identity to escape the wreckage of the old one.

She also brought the baseball bat.

She waited for the next lull in activity in front of her house. Then she hurried to the back alley and climbed into her car, tossing her things in the back seat.

She drove off into the night with three destinations in rapid succession:

An ATM to drain as much cash as possible from her recently restored bank account.

The storage unit facility to retrieve her ex-husband's gun and ammunition.

And a cheap, anonymous, faraway motel to provide a hideout as she planned her next move.

As she drove the silent, bleak Chicago streets, the robotic voice identified as 'Your Fate' replayed in her mind.

*"Drop your investigation,"* it said.

"No," responded Linda aloud.

# CHAPTER THIRTEEN

Linda relocated from the far north side of Chicago to the far south side, nearly entering Indiana. She purposefully passed up numerous normal-looking hotels and motels, especially the chains, to find a pitifully dreary and disheveled string of eighteen units that welcomed a wad of cash upfront in exchange for anonymity. She wore the red wig and provided a fake name, Sofi Lulu, an absurdity she invented on the spot. The leering man in a white t-shirt who sat behind the counter didn't ask for any ID when a healthy spread of bills was laid out in front of him. His verbal communication largely consisted of grunts.

The other 'guests' represented sleaze, crime and addiction, forming a rugged, downtrodden ensemble. Prostitutes bared considerable flesh in the thirty-five-degree temperatures. Hypodermic needles provided an obstacle course for the rats that navigated the sidewalk. An old-fashioned, sputtering neon sign displayed a jumble of live and dead letters to render the name of the establishment incoherent.

Her room did not appear to have been cleaned and low lighting tried to hide this fact. Cockroaches ran from her footsteps. The walls were thin enough to hear a couple arguing on one side and a sickly man endlessly coughing on the other.

She didn't care. It was the least of her worries right now. She took off the heavy wig so her scalp could breathe again. She sat on the bed and checked her phone. The signal was weak, but she could still see the pileup of text messages and voicemails expanding in real time, waiting to be accessed.

She ignored them and focused on the source of the video. It had originally been posted by 'Citizens Against Animal Cruelty'. She tried to find out more about this alleged group. Not only did she uncover nothing, but the original post and account appeared to have been deleted.

Someone had set up a bogus entity to launch the video, let it go viral, and then faded back. Regular ordinary citizens took over its circulation, sharing and reposting across a variety of channels, not bothering to research its validity, fueled by emotions and nothing more.

Linda shut down her phone. She was exhausted. Strangely, in this seedy motel of low-life creeps in a terrible neighborhood, she felt safe. She could blend in for now. Sofi Lulu.

She said the name aloud, and it sort of made her laugh.

The best thing about this motel room was that it had multiple door locks and extra-heavy curtains to deny outside light. She kicked off her shoes. She lay flat on the bed, listening to the muffled street sounds outside. Her body hurt. It couldn't relax. She tried to drift off.

The couple next door started yelling again. The man shouted, "Would you shut the fuck up!"

A shrill woman's voice yelled back, "No, you shut up!"

The screaming continued back and forth, like a ping-pong match. It was merciless.

"I just want to sleep..." Linda muttered.

The couple continued to argue, loud and persistent, for what seemed like hours. Linda finally slipped into a deep sleep. Their voices entered her dreams.

She awoke the next morning in a tangle of sheets. Her heart was pounding. It took a moment to recall her surroundings. Then she remembered the reality of her living nightmare.

The couple next door had finally gone quiet. Linda could have gone back to sleep. But she needed to get the day started.

She split the heavy curtains a few feet to get some light. The crusty carpet did not feel good on her bare feet, so she put her flats back on.

She rebooted her phone. A quick check of messages confirmed it was more of the same – angry threats from strangers who were encountering the video of her hitting a puppy with a shovel and conveniently provided with her address and phone number. At some point, it had to die down, right?

She needed to reach out to the only person who truly understood her plight: Bert. It was 8 a.m. Hopefully he was up by now, and they could map out a plan of action. If he dropped by her townhouse, he wasn't going to find her home, and the sprawl of vandalism would tell him why. Contact by phone was the only way.

She called his number.

Bert's mother answered.

"You stay away from my boy!"

She was irate. It took a moment for Linda to collect her thoughts. "Mrs. Pacorek, please listen, it's not what it seems." She assumed this was about the puppy video. Linda barely knew the woman – barely knew most of her neighbors – but was aware of her reputation for being harsh and overbearing.

"It's exactly what it seems."

"Your boy is helping me prove my innocence."

"You stay away from him, you sick cougar."

*Sick cougar?* That was a new one. "I'm not— that's not—"

"I can have you arrested for that photo you sent."

She searched her brain to recall a photo. "What photo?"

"Don't act all innocent. You know exactly what photo."

"No. No, I don't."

"I pay for his phone while he's in school. I control it. I will block you, and next time I will report you."

"Report me for what?"

"The photo you sent to my boy."

"*What photo?*"

"You don't know which one? How many have you sent? I'll text it to you right now. I'm onto you. You're not getting away with this."

After a moment, the photo arrived. Linda immediately clicked on it to get a better look.

She gasped.

It was a photo of Linda kneeling on a bed wearing only a slinky, transparent nightgown that was split open down the middle to expose her breasts.

She stared at it in disbelief. It was a fake, a fraud, but meticulously constructed to look genuine. It was her head on someone else's body, seamless and convincing.

"That's not me," Linda said.

"Of course it's you."

"No – it's – those aren't even my breasts. It's all wrong. I can prove it to you." In a flash of madness, she considered sending a photo of her real breasts – not nearly as nice-looking – smaller with sag – to prove her point.

"Don't you dare send any more pictures!"

"My body doesn't even look that good." Linda wanted to laugh or cry at the absurdity of it all. "Bert is helping me with my computer. I need him."

"Yes, he told me about this wild goose chase, and you losing your job. You probably deserved it. Now you've turned our quiet little street into a circus. I don't know what this is all about, all the honking and yelling."

*Great*, thought Linda. *She hasn't even discovered the puppy video yet.*

"Please. I'm begging you. Let me get through to your son. It's very important."

"If you contact him one more time, I'm calling the police and showing them this photo and pressing charges."

"But I didn't send it! It's not me!"

"It came from your phone!"

"I've been hacked. That's what all of this is. Bad people are taking over my identity."

"You're a mental case! *Stay away from my son!*"

Mrs. Pacorek hung up.

Linda stood frozen inside of the small, dim motel room. She needed immediate help. If it wasn't Bert, then who?

Randy. It was time to engage him more deeply in her crisis. Randy could enlist the help of his brother-in-law in the FBI. She would share the entire story, every crazy detail, and they would identify and apprehend her tormentor.

She dialed his number.

He answered in a hesitant voice. It was not warm. "Yes?"

"Randy, I need your help." She started to unleash her panic on him but he was quick to interrupt.

"Whoa, whoa, hold on," he said.

She cut herself off mid-sentence. "Okay?"

"Listen. I appreciate that we made amends. But that's as far as it goes. I'm – honestly, I'm troubled. As a dog lover, I'm sick to my stomach. I saw the video. It's everywhere."

"That's not me! That's part of the identity theft."

"It sure looks like you."

"It's a fake!"

"How can it be fake? It says your neighbor took it."

"What neighbor?"

"I think it's best if we just…went our separate ways, you know?"

"You don't really think that video's real? You have to believe me, it was all made up on someone else's computer."

"I don't know what to believe anymore," he said in a sad tone. "You've fooled me once before. I'm not going to get played by you a second time."

"I'm not— No, Randy, please—"

"I have to get the kids to school. I'm sorry."

"Wait! Don't – don't hang up." She knew she sounded hysterical but couldn't help it.

"I am hanging up now," he enunciated clearly, as if speaking to a child.

"No. I can prove—"

"Goodbye. Thank you. Goodbye." He disconnected.

"God damn it, Randy!" she shouted into the room.

The increasing isolation was suffocating her, squeezing the breath out of her lungs.

She tried X next.

He refused to pick up.

She phoned Cecilia. She didn't answer either.

Linda left a message on her voicemail: "Cecilia, please please please call me back. I'm in real trouble. My life is being destroyed. I – I – I can't take much more of this. Call me. Thank you. Call me."

She hung up and felt resigned to the fact that Cecilia would not return her call.

She was going to have to fight this invisible enemy all by herself.

She went to the suitcase, reached under the clothes, and took out the pistol and a box of ammunition.

It was time to learn about operating this gun.

★   ★   ★

Later that morning, she went in search of food. She was now armed with a loaded gun in her purse. She wore the red wig.

She walked a snowy, unpaved sidewalk and found a run-down corner grocer not far from the motel. She stocked up on simple, immediate food that required no cooking. In a moment of impulse, she also bought a large bottle of vodka.

Her nerves were locked in vibrate mode. She had forgotten to pack her anxiety meds. She needed something to settle her down. Alcohol wasn't the best solution, and she had to be careful not to overmedicate, just enough to soothe her overwhelming panic without killing off life-saving reflexes and rational train of thought.

Linda glanced at herself in the big circular mirror that hung near the cash register to provide an expanded view of the store for security. She looked ridiculous. Her face was pale and haggard, lacking any makeup. The red wig looked cartoonish and out of place. And her purchases spread out on the counter were juvenile – a stash of candy, chips and booze.

As the old, silent clerk rang her up, she kept an eye on her surroundings and the other customers that wandered in.

If their glances lingered, her muscles tightened, and she imagined herself pulling out the gun to defend herself. There was no way to know if someone was random riffraff or associated with Alison's terrorism.

She kept her back to the counter, facing into the store until the exact moment she had to pay.

She paid cash.

The store clerk raised his eyebrows when he saw her peeling bills from a large roll.

Her purchases bagged and paid for, Linda quickly left the store, maneuvering around strangers in the narrow aisles to reach the exit.

She hurried down the sidewalk and reached her motel room. She gave her environment a quick glance, saw no threats and pushed inside. She locked the door, deadbolt and chain. She closed the curtains.

She let out a large exhale of relief.

She allowed herself one healthy swallow from the plastic jug of cheap vodka. She could feel it burn in her chest, a gentle, pleasing sensation. She tore open a packet of cookies and ate three.

This made her feel a little better. Just a little.

She returned to her work on the handwritten narrative of her ordeal. The room had a small wooden desk with a creaky wooden chair. She sat down, flipped open the pad to the next empty page and began to write, picking up where she left off.

Her pen moved quickly, fluidly, line by line as the words spilled out as fast as they appeared in her head.

Time stood still. Nothing else existed beyond her immediate intense focus on her writing. It was like her early years in journalism. Her comfort zone.

When she reached the point in the storyline where Bert discovered that Alison's appearance was stolen from an obscure fashion model across the globe, she paused.

Anna Bafort.

Surely Anna would be an immediate ally. Bert and Linda had planned on reaching out to her, or her manager, or anyone at all connected to the model to expose this blatant identity theft. Anna was also a victim in this bizarre masquerade. She just didn't know it.

Linda moved away from the desk and retrieved her laptop. She sat with the laptop on the bed and booted it up. The monitor glowed to life. She opened the browser.

She entered Anna Bafort's name into a search engine.

A selection of links arrived. Linda started to comb through them to find one with contact information. Most were not in English; she would have to activate real-time translation. Her fingers quickly worked the keys.

Then the screen went dark.

"What!"

She stared at it for a moment. She knew the battery had plenty of life. The power cord was in her suitcase, if needed. Had she accidentally shut the laptop down with her rapid typing, hitting a wrong key?

She took a deep breath and pressed a key to restart the computer.

It flickered back to life. It requested a password.

She entered her password.

Rejected.

She tried again.

Rejected.

She froze for a moment. She hadn't changed her latest password. Was she spelling it wrong in her haste? Was the keyboard in 'Caps Lock' mode?

She very carefully tried again, slow, steady clicks.

Rejected.

The inevitable washed over her. The laptop was hijacked and someone else had taken control. Her pursuit of Anna Bafort had been stopped cold.

They were monitoring her every move in the digital realm.

Her eyes moved to the desk, where her phone sat idle.

She witnessed the phone silently light up, creating a small glow. It had been dark, inactive.

Someone was manipulating it remotely.

She stood up off the bed and walked over. She picked up the phone delicately, as if the sudden light could burn her.

The battery was at 11%.

Two hours ago, it had been at 85%. She had barely touched it.

Something was running in the background.

She began swiping through screens of apps, trying to detect what was going on.

She entered 'settings'. Years ago, when she had complained to X about a draining battery, he had told her to check the list of running applications to see what was active and shut down anything that was unnecessary.

Linda returned to that screen now. She reviewed a list of services to manage. She recognized a handful of familiar apps – and then a bunch she had never heard of. Never downloaded. Cryptic names with weird avatars.

Spyware.

Someone was controlling her phone.

And if they controlled her phone…they could track her location.

Linda shouted, "No!" She shut down the phone. It went dark and stayed dark.

She ran back to the laptop and powered it down, closing the lid.

Then she hurried to her purse. She took out the gun.

At that moment, her hiding place felt very exposed.

She had been hacked and tracked. She cursed herself for not being more diligent. She should have shut it all down and completely stayed offline the moment she left home.

Now what?

She was a sitting duck. They knew she knew about Anna Bafort. She had disregarded their demand to stop the investigation.

She couldn't use her phone to get help. But maybe she could use someone else's to call the police. She didn't want to die in this stinky little motel room in a hideous neighborhood where murder and mayhem were probably commonplace. Just another body for the local morgue.

She plotted to run from her room to the manager's office and ask to use his phone to make an emergency call to 911. It was just a fifty-yard dash, if that.

Linda stepped over to the window and touched the thick, musty drapes. She made a small opening with her hand, a tiny outlet for light, just enough for a peek...

There was a car parked directly in front of her unit. It had not been there before, when she went out to get food.

She could see shadowed heads inside. Not moving. Staring at her door. Waiting.

Waiting for the minute she stepped outside.

Linda pulled back from the window. She spun a quick circle, searching for another way out, but she knew the answer. There was none.

No back door. No other windows. She was trapped in a box with only a single exit that led directly into their hands. She was armed, she could try to shoot her way out...but there were at least two of them, maybe more. Probably armed as well. Probably more experienced with firearms. She had never squeezed off a single shot in her life.

Linda stood very still for a long moment, listening. Had they seen her peek out the window? Possibly not. She didn't hear the sound of car doors opening or closing. Just silence. They weren't budging.

Her own car was parked on a far end of the lot, away from her unit, purposefully. She needed to get to it and drive like hell. But she would never make it with her getaway blocked. They were probably planning their ambush right now. Would they wait for nightfall...or get it over with in the cold, stark light of day?

Linda had to escape, and she knew she couldn't do it alone. She needed an escort to accompany her to her car. Someone to provide cover. Someone to make her less open and vulnerable. Someone to be a witness to any assault. Someone to provide a distraction. A foil.

And who would that be? She couldn't use her phone.

Then she had an idea.

She touched the wall to the adjoining motel room, where the crazy, bickering couple had screamed at one another throughout the night.

She mapped out a plan in her head. She packed her suitcase with everything but the clothes on her back. She snapped the latches shut.

Then she returned to the wall.

And pounded on it.

"Hey, jerk face! You kept me up all night with your screaming and yelling – so now it's my turn! Wake up! How do *you* like it? You big fucking asshole!"

At first, there was no response. She continued pounding.

She became worried they had left earlier that morning – or maybe they were just in a deep sleep.

Fortunately, it was the latter. And when they woke up, they were *mad.*

"Shut the fuck up!" yelled the man with booming fury.

"Yeah, shut up!" echoed a shrill female voice.

"No!" responded Linda. "I'm going to keep banging on this wall."

"You better stop, lady, or else!" said the man.

"Or else what? You don't scare me." She continued to thud her fists against the wall with obnoxious persistence.

"Or else I'm going to punch your head in!"

"I'd like to see you try!"

"You are really asking for trouble!" he declared.

"He means it!" added the woman.

"You want to make something of it?" Linda said. "*Then come on over!*"

"You're going to be very sorry!"

Linda continued to slam the wall with her hands, increasing her intensity. "No! I'm! Not! Sorry! Asshole!"

Then she heard a shuffling movement and muffled grousing. She stopped striking the wall and listened to the sounds of them leaving their room: the bolt snapping open, a creaking arc followed by a slam.

Almost immediately, they were pounding on her door – very hard. The man on the other side was so angry he was determined to kick it in.

No need. She unlocked the door. His next blow caused him to stumble inside. He was a very large man. His face was red and stubbly, his hands were balled up into fists. He wore gray sweatpants, a black t-shirt and a pair of dirty sneakers without socks, hastily fitted onto his feet with dangling laces. His female companion followed him in, wearing a moth-eaten fur coat over a nightgown with a pair of high heels awkwardly added to the ensemble. She was thin and haggard-looking, scowling and baring rotten teeth.

As the big man regained his balance, he swung around to face Linda with beady-eyed fury.

Linda shut the door, sealing the couple inside. She pointed the gun at them. They froze.

The big man stared at her. His rage turned to bewilderment. "What the hell is this?!"

"I need your help," Linda said.

The woman attempted a crooked smile. "We don't want no trouble."

"No trouble," Linda said. She reached her free hand into her jeans pocket. She pulled out a wad of twenty-dollar bills. "I want to pay you one hundred dollars for a few minutes of your time."

The woman considered this through narrowed eyes. "Is it going to be perverted?"

"What? No. I just need you to walk with me to my car. It's at the end of the row." She gestured in its general direction. "It's not far. But there's someone out there who is...mad at me and wants to beat me up. I just need an escort, so I'll be left alone. That's why I was banging, to bring you over."

"This is crazy," said the big man, his eyes locked on the gun.

"Who wants to beat you up, honey?" asked the woman. "Is it your pimp?"

Linda hesitated. Then she nodded and replied, "Yeah, that's what it is." She didn't know whether to be flattered or appalled by the assumption people would pay to have sex with her.

"A hundred bucks to walk you to your car?" said the man.

Linda nodded.

"Why are you so afraid? You got a gun," he said, pointing to it.

"I know. I don't want any violence. I just want to leave here."

The big man appeared to mull it over. "Why is your pimp after you?"

"I owe him some money," Linda made up on the spot.

"Why don't you just give him the hundred bucks?"

She thought about it. "It's the principle of the thing."

The woman nodded, understanding, although Linda didn't know if she herself understood the logic.

"I don't know," said the man. "I don't know how nutso these people are. What if they go after me and Rosie?"

"No, no. They're not interested in you. Or Rosie."

"I don't know that."

"They'll leave me alone if there are other people around. Trust me."

"Maybe," he said, skeptical.

"Yeah, we don't want no trouble," repeated Rosie.

"Tell you what," said the big man, and he broke out into a smug grin. "I'll do it for *two* hundred dollars."

"Two…?" Linda said. She couldn't afford to lose too much cash. Her supply was limited.

"And the gun."

"The gun?"

"Or we walk out the door and you deal with your own stupid problems."

"Yeah, you never shoulda been a whore if you can't 'cept the lifestyle," said Rosie, offering her pearls of wisdom.

Linda thought it over and couldn't come up with an alternative. She needed to escape, she couldn't use her phone, and these people were her only means to safety.

"You'll get me to my car?" Linda said.

"Word of honor," said the man.

Linda didn't know how much that was worth. But she took the gamble.

A few minutes later, the threesome stepped out of the motel room.

Linda carried her suitcase in one hand. In the other, she clenched her car keys. Her motel neighbors stood on either side of her. The big man was two hundred dollars richer, and he now had a gun pulling down the pocket of his sweatpants.

Linda glanced at the vehicle parked in front of her unit. A black sedan. The window glass was dark. She could only see shadowed heads.

"We'll just walk casual," Linda said under her breath.

"Real casual like," echoed Rosie.

They were halfway to Linda's car when she heard a car door open behind her. She did not turn to look.

"Somebody's gettin' out," said the big man, sticking to her side.

"What are they doing?" asked Linda, keeping a steady pace.

"They're following."

"What do they look like?"

"They got long, dark coats," offered Rosie.

"They're out of their car?"

"Yeah…"

"Then I'm getting in mine," Linda said. She began to run.

The next twenty seconds consisted of a burst of motion and adrenaline. Linda pulled open her car door, stuffed the suitcase inside, and hopped behind the wheel. She slammed the door, jammed the key into the ignition and twisted. She started up the engine with a loud roar. She immediately threw the car into reverse.

A gunshot fired, blowing out the rear window. Linda screamed.

Her back bumper smashed into the side of a parked vehicle. She didn't turn to look, taking the jolt and thrusting the gear into drive.

Two more gunshots rang out, and she could hear shouting.

In a blurry half second she caught a glimpse of Rosie running in high heels with her large male companion waving the gun and making threats, as two tall figures in long black coats scurried back to their car to pursue Linda.

Linda had a head start, and she was determined not to lose it. Accelerating fearlessly, she navigated a wild zigzag path, slamming up and over curbs, avoiding poles and plowing through snow. She burst onto the main road without considering the existing traffic, causing a flurry of screeching brakes and car horns around her.

She tore across a busy intersection as the yellow light turned red. Every vehicle in front of her was an obstacle to get around by any means possible, including the slushy shoulder on the side of the road. At the next crossroads, she chose the quickest path of convenience: a green left-hand turn arrow. She skipped lanes and cut off cars. She continued speeding, doubling the limit, feeling the cold air from the broken back window.

*They shot at me. They actually shot at me. Those bullets were intended for my head.*

She sped past shopping strips, big box retail stores and fast-food joints. She entered a stretch of squat apartment complexes, then office parks and old manufacturing plants. Soon more and more of the buildings appeared vacant, boarded up, with faded *For Lease* signs.

She kept checking her rearview mirror. There was no sign of the black sedan with her pursuers. She had lost them. Hopefully for good. She would become untraceable from now on. Her phone and laptop were deactivated.

She was two hundred dollars poorer, she no longer had a gun, but she was alive.

Also, she was lost.

She kept driving, adding more miles of distance between her and the motel but uncertain of a destination or her current location, aside from a general awareness of being far south of downtown Chicago and well west of the lakefront.

After twenty minutes of driving, aimless and dazed, Linda came upon a large, shuttered factory. It appeared in front of her like an industrial ghost town, stretched across a rough landscape, halfheartedly protected by wire fences that were partially collapsed. It was eerily familiar. She slowed down to get a closer look. There were no other cars around.

"Oh my god," she said, when she recognized the shape of the building and recalled its prior life.

It was the former printing plant for the *Chicago Times*, the newspaper where she worked at the start of her career, the happy, rewarding journalism years before the entire industry took a nosedive.

Once upon a time, it was a robust facility employing thousands of employees producing millions of pages every day. Then the internet exploded and people abandoned their subscriptions in droves. Circulation numbers plummeted and advertisers fled. The core money-maker for the paper – the classified ads section – shriveled and dried up. News outlets switched their focus to digital presentation, and the print edition shrunk to the size of a cheap advertising mailer. The content was scaled way back, leaning on syndicated articles and lazy reprints of marketing PR press releases.

Journalists like Linda fled for new careers as the paychecks turned paltry. They transitioned their skills to PR agencies, corporate communications and college teaching gigs.

The quality of online news reflected the loss of talent. The new priorities were speed, quantity and clickbait sensationalism. The reporting depth turned shallow. Typos and grammatical errors were a shrug; they could be fixed whenever in the HTML coding. Or ignored entirely because the readership didn't care. They were skimming everything anyhow.

The memories flooded back. Linda pulled her car down a long, winding drive to bring herself closer to the shuttered plant. A light snow began to fall. She was running low on gas. She was running low on money.

This old, forgotten building could provide temporary shelter and serve as a decent hiding place. She needed time to regroup and assess her next move. This was as good a place as any for a rest stop.

Linda found a good hiding spot to park her car in the back, tucked between a rotted old dumpster and a rusty delivery truck missing its tires. You couldn't see her car from the road.

"I'm home," she muttered sardonically.

She went inside to look for the ghosts of her past.

The outside bright white of snow gave way to an immediate shroud of darkness as Linda stepped into the hulking, defunct printing plant. It took a moment for her eyes to adjust. It was like stepping into a cave.

The big spaces were mostly empty, with the furnishings auctioned off long ago and the equipment dismantled and sold for scrap, turned to trash or simply pilfered. She had toured this facility once as an enthusiastic young reporter, loving the smell of ink and grease, and the sounds of humming machinery delivering huge sheets capturing the latest news headlines and dramatic photographs.

She was still shaky from being shot at, so when there was movement in the shadows – a lurking, shuffling human being – she gasped, held back a scream and froze in place, prepared to turn and run.

A bearded, hunched, slow-moving man in tattered clothing advanced toward her. He looked harmless with a brittle walk that suggested he would crumble to dust if knocked over.

Linda said nothing. The ragged man stepped closer to examine her, stopping just a few feet away. His eyes were ringed with heavy circles. They gave each other a long, silent look. Then he moved on, accepting her presence.

She continued to advance deeper into the plant. She discovered several more homeless occupants – men and women, mostly older, moving sluggishly as if underwater. No one spoke, communicating with nods and mild expressions to convey a gentle welcome to shared spaces.

A skinny, gaunt woman with dirty skin and sunken cheekbones stepped up to her and offered a wool blanket.

"Here," she said, the first word uttered by anyone.

Linda accepted the blanket with tears in her eyes.

★  ★  ★

She wandered her surroundings, taking it all in.

Linda felt safe here, secluded from the rest of civilization. No one was online. Nobody would see her viral puppy murder video. She was off the grid, in another world, on a distant planet.

There were no iPhones, tablets or laptops – just human beings dealing with immediate physical needs of food and shelter. There were rooms within rooms, windowless, that provided decent insulation from the cold. Elsewhere, cavernous open spaces with ventilation provided workable environments for small, contained fires.

There was nothing virtual about these people or this environment. It was as real as could be, a crude throwback to the Stone Age. There were words, symbols and pictures etched into the walls, cryptic graffiti, like cave drawings.

She returned outside to her car. She retrieved her suitcase and brought it into her new, rent-free hiding place. She found a series of small rooms along the edge of the big empty space where the presses once ran. She remembered them as supervisor offices. She picked one and entered. The chairs were gone, and the desk too, but there was still a small side table coated with dust and an empty crate to provide simple seating. This could serve as a primitive apartment. It even had a door that locked. It was chilly, but not unbearable, plus she had the blanket.

She sat on the crate and tried very hard to relax her frayed nerves. The gunshots earlier in the day continued to replay in her head, making her flinch involuntarily. She took the bottle of vodka out of her suitcase and took a sip, then a chug.

Pretty soon, she drank herself into a mushy stupor, followed by a long sleep.

She awoke many hours later in total blackness, on the floor, wrapped in the blanket, disoriented. She heard the sound of a distant train, rhythmically chugging closer, accompanied by the extended blast of a horn howling into the night.

There were railroad tracks nearby. She fantasized about finding them and following them, running between the rails, toward a destiny in the bright lights.

# CHAPTER FOURTEEN

In the dark, in the solitude, in barren surroundings, Linda lost all track of time. The supervisor's office tucked inside the newspaper printing plant provided no views of day or night. Her phone and laptop remained deadened and untouched. She was unplugged with a purity that harkened back to her ancient ancestors.

She had a simple goal, like the others gathered here: survival. They didn't want to freeze to death in the brutal Chicago winter, and she didn't want a bullet in her head from the anonymous assassins on her trail. Together the group formed a small, diverse community of mixed ages, ethnicities and states of mental fragility. They exchanged minimal dialogue, no pointless banter, just the essentials.

Several days passed – three, five, six, she really didn't know. She made a single excursion back into society to collect food, water, blankets and flashlights, which she shared with the other residents. The only thing she did not share was her alcohol. The two big bottles of vodka stayed with her, well hidden.

While she was out, no one disturbed her things, or so she thought, until one night (or day) she woke up in a groggy state and witnessed a hulking figure move past the large window that overlooked the factory floor. It was a rotund Hispanic man awkwardly wearing her red wig. He seemed happy, dancing a little tango, flapping his arms. So she let him keep it.

She felt no danger from these unusual people. Most were in a similar state of paralysis from trauma in their lives. There was the withered Asian woman with sad eyes who hummed a lot but said nothing. And the two Caucasian teenagers, fearful and sexually conflicted, rejected by their families. There was a war vet and other displaced elderly, including an alleged former stockbroker, who now spent most of his time devising ways to catch the rats that ventured into the living spaces.

She befriended several of her fellow residents, but at a mutual distance.

They didn't laugh or show skepticism when she said she was hiding from artificial intelligence.

"The robots," nodded one of the ancient, bearded gentlemen knowingly.

In the beginning, vodka was necessary medicine to calm her from overloading with anxiety. It settled her body. But it also numbed her mind.

She drank herself into an extended stupor. She welcomed a catatonic state. Ordinarily she wasn't a heavy drinker, but she did have a few ugly binges in her history. The last one had been when X announced he was leaving her.

Her current excuse for drinking: she just wanted to sleep and not think. She could imagine dying here.

If so, she hoped the authorities would find her pads of paper with the handwritten story of her bizarre predicament. But maybe her homeless brethren would take the pages and burn them for warmth. Perhaps a more worthy cause.

In her resignation, fear and fatigue, she really had no desire to ever leave this place. But then simple realities surfaced.

She ran out of food. And vodka.

So she ventured back outside.

The light hurt her eyes.

She found her Nissan, undisturbed. She drove out of the decrepit industrial complex and picked a direction, hands trembling at the steering wheel.

After a few miles, she found a commercial strip of modest size and simple offerings. She parked her car in the lot.

There was a low-key sandwich joint, Spencer's Grill, with dark windows and an *Open* sign beckoning at the door. Her stomach rumbled at the thought of a real meal. Her cash stash was low but adequate for now. She still feared being recognized from the viral video, and her wig was now owned by somebody else's head. But her sweatshirt had a hood. She hoped she didn't look too obvious when she pulled on the hood before entering the restaurant.

They sat her way in the back, which was nice. No doubt, she smelled and looked bad, not an appetizing presence. The waitress handed her a laminated menu, and Linda realized she didn't know where she was in the day – breakfast, lunch or closer to dinner?

She ordered scrambled eggs, toast, hash browns, bacon and orange juice. Those things were good anytime.

Her voice croaked from lack of use. The waitress said, "I'll get you a glass of water."

There was a bar area nearby with a couple of drinkers on stools and a large television monitor hanging from the ceiling. A midday news program was running through local headlines. It gave her something to look at.

The anchors delivered a tally of overnight gang violence. There was the continuing saga of the mayor's bickering with aldermen and alderwomen over snow removal routes. A semi-trailer truck had crashed into another vehicle on the expressway, blocking two lanes. And the weather forecast pledged more freezing temperatures.

Then there was an announcement of *Breaking News* with the headline *Woman's Body Found* and the subhead *North Avenue Beach.*

Linda watched a video clip of rescue crews, police cars and an ambulance gathered at the shore of Lake Michigan. They were focused on something off camera: a body being removed from the choppy waters and chunks of ice.

Then a photo portrait filled the screen, identifying the unfortunate victim.

Linda gasped.

It was Eleanor.

The image jolted Linda out of her inertia. She strained to hear what the anchors had to say – it was difficult, buried in restaurant noise. She heard 'drowning' and 'investigation' and 'searching for clues'.

And 'we'll keep you updated on any further developments.'

The other patrons gave it no attention, another dead body in the big city, a name that meant nothing to them.

Linda hardly had any affection for Eleanor, but it didn't matter. This murder shook her to the core. Alison had to be involved – the people behind Alison – but why?

Perhaps in the new, closer reporting relationship between Eleanor and Alison, Eleanor realized something was not right about her young star employee…

The newscast shifted to commercials with a bumper that teased upcoming sports highlights, starting with hockey.

Linda lost her appetite. She wanted to throw up. She knew she couldn't stay here and eat.

And she couldn't just return to the abandoned building and hide under a blanket with a bottle of booze.

She now had information to help solve a murder. But who would believe her? She pondered her next move. She needed to reach out to someone close to the situation, someone she could trust.

She immediately thought of Cecilia. Cecilia was the only real friend she had back at Public Energy.

But she couldn't call Cecilia – she wouldn't dare activate her phone. It would put her at risk of being located and captured – and becoming the second drowning victim in icy Lake Michigan.

Linda hurried out of the restaurant. She returned to her car with a plan. She was going to retrieve all of her stuff from the printing plant. And then she was going to drive directly to Cecilia's apartment in Wicker Park.

★   ★   ★

Linda buzzed for Cecilia in the lobby of her elegant, four-story brick building. It was the middle of the day and Cecilia was probably in her home office, working remotely.

Linda kept an eye out for anyone who might be watching or following her. For now, the coast was clear.

"Hello?" Cecilia said.

"Cecilia. Thank god. It's Linda."

There was silence on the other end.

Linda continued, "Please hear me out. Let me in. We need to talk. I just saw the news about Eleanor. I – I'm – I'm in shock. Cecilia?"

"What?"

"I can't talk like this over an intercom. There are – I'm—" Linda was breathless, trying to find the right words without completely freaking out Cecilia. "Can I come in?"

"I don't know. I don't think so. I'm in shock too. About all of this. I don't know what to think, Linda." Then she asked outright, "Did you do this?"

"No!" shouted Linda. "I know it looks bad. I left on bad terms. But it's all connected – the people who murdered Eleanor also came after me."

"What people?"

"I can't go into it here, shouting like this. Please just let me in."

Cecilia said nothing.

"We were friends all those years. You know me. You really think I killed Eleanor? Be real."

"You killed that dog."

"No! That was bullshit, it's CGI or something. Please. I'm not leaving until you let me in. I have everything explained, I wrote it all out. Don't turn your back on me, Cecilia. I've always been there for you. I'm begging you."

There was another long pause. Then Cecilia said, "I'm going to have my phone in my hand, one press of a button away from calling 911. You try anything—"

"Try what? You think I came here to harm you? Why does everybody think I'm out of my mind?"

"You haven't been acting normal for weeks."

"I'll explain all that."

"All right. You can come up. But one button press away. I swear. You're my friend, I will give you the benefit of the doubt, but if you so much as—"

"Thank you thank you thank you."

Cecilia buzzed her inside.

Linda took the elevator to the third floor. Cecilia was already standing in the doorway to her unit, phone held in her hand like a remote she was prepared to activate.

"You look awful," said Cecilia as Linda came closer.

"I've been hiding," Linda said. "What they did to Eleanor, they want to do to me."

"Who is this 'they'?"

Linda said, "The people behind Alison."

"Alison," said Cecilia with a sigh. She gestured Linda into her apartment. "It all comes back to Alison."

"As a matter of fact," Linda said, "it does."

Linda entered. Cecilia shut the door. She pointed Linda to a chair. "Do want something to drink?"

"A water, please," said Linda, suddenly humbled by Cecilia's acceptance. "And...do you have anything to eat?"

"Like crackers?"

"Yes. That would be great."

Cecilia left for a moment and returned with a cold bottled water and small bowl of snack crackers. She placed them on a low table in front of Linda and then took a seat across from her. She placed her phone in her lap for immediate access, as needed.

"Where do you want to start?" asked Cecilia.

"Alison," Linda said. "She's not a real person. She's like an avatar for somebody else, these other people who are up to no good."

From the sag in Cecilia's expression, Linda could tell this concept was not going over well.

"I know it sounds outlandish," Linda said. "If I was in your shoes, I wouldn't believe me either."

"People are working with Alison every day," said Cecilia in a slow, measured tone. "You are the only person to have this theory, and frankly, people think you've been doing everything in your power to discredit her because she came in and, let's face it, she showed you up. I get it. No one likes it when some young, bright star arrives and makes us older, legacy employees look bad, out of touch, like our years of experience and loyalty don't mean a thing. I know that feeling. I've felt it. But it's life. We become dinosaurs, the new generation moves in."

"That's fine, except for one thing. The 'new generation' isn't human. It's AI. She's AI."

"You're saying that Alison Smith, this person I've worked with maybe a dozen times since she came on board, is some kind of computer-generated employee?"

"That's exactly what I'm saying."

"And I'm – and all of us at the company are too stupid to notice, except for you?"

"Not stupid," Linda said. "I never said that. It's very well done. It's meticulous. But I studied it. She's not real. I watched a recording of her, over and over, with my neighbor. He's a computer science student."

Cecilia's face looked even more unimpressed.

"I can show you the analysis," Linda said. "I can show you pictures of a fashion model from Belgium named Anna Bafort—"

"Okay, okay. Let's just stop for a minute. All of this stuff about Alison not being a real human being – it's simply not possible."

"Have you ever met her in the flesh?"

"No," Cecilia said. "But Howard has."

Linda sat up straighter in her chair, startled. This was new. Was it really possible? "Howard? Where? How?"

"Well," said Cecilia with a bent smile. "You know Howard. He chases anything in a skirt. He's flirted with me..."

"And me," Linda said.

"So, his latest target, naturally, is the pretty young thing in PR. He found out she's unattached, you can guess the rest."

"They're flirting online?"

"They *were* flirting online. Now they're living together. He moved in."

Linda tried to digest this. It was a blow to her entire theory. "Moved in where?"

"Wherever she lives. Oklahoma, I think."

"But he's married!"

"He left his wife for her. Three or four days ago. He went down to see her, they had a little rendezvous, probably screwed like rabbits, and now they're shacked up. Come on, Linda, you know how Howard is. He's always fishing, and this young woman took the bait. Why? I don't know. Maybe she has daddy issues. I bet it only lasts a couple of months, tops, before she sees him for the creep he is. By then, he's divorced, his marriage is ruined. I feel sorry for his kids."

"Have you seen him since he went to Oklahoma?"

"Yes. He's been calling in remote. Trying to act like 'no big deal'. I'm sure HR isn't too happy about it. But it's Howard. The CEO covers his ass. The old white boys' club."

Linda felt dizzy. It was the dead of winter, Cecilia's apartment was chilly, and she was perspiring. How could Howard be having an affair with Alison if she wasn't real? And if she was real, why would she give in to the advances of such an older man? And allow him to come all the way to Tulsa, Oklahoma, to see her? This secretive girl who wouldn't even visit the Chicago headquarters of her employer?

Linda thought about it, and then she reached her conclusion.

*Howard's dead.*

"Cecilia," she said. "I want you to set up a meeting with Howard right now."

"About what?"

"We'll make something up."

"Make something up?"

"I want to see him."

"What for?"

"I think something happened to him."

"Nothing's happened to Howard. I just talked to him yesterday. I've been in two or three meetings with him since he went to Oklahoma."

"I need to look at him. I'll stay out of view of the camera. I need to check something."

"Check what?"

"Cecilia, please. Get him on the screen. Tell him you're..." She searched her brain for a mundane consumer marketing topic. "Tell him you're putting together a solar energy toolkit for Chicago Public Schools."

"Why would he care about that?"

"Tell him...it's a speaking opportunity. You want to include a video with some quotes from him, as our company expert. He loves that stuff, it speaks to his ego."

"This feels weird. Nobody's in a frame of mind to talk about work right now. We're all reeling from Eleanor's death."

"Then talk about that."

"About Eleanor?"

"Yes. That's the perfect reason for why you would call him."

"I guess I could do that," she relented. "I mean, I don't know what to say. I just found out she died a few hours ago. It was a drowning, that's all I know. This is all so crazy."

"You're right, it's crazy," Linda said. "That's why we're investigating."

"All right. I'll do this. Then you can see for yourself. Howard is Howard. And we can get off it."

Cecilia moved to her home office, which resided in her guest bedroom, an uninvited guest that never left. Her laptop was active, connected to the Public Energy network. She sat in her desk chair. Linda positioned herself to view the monitor at a diagonal, standing outside the scope of the camera lens.

Cecilia took a deep breath. Then she grasped the mouse, brought the cursor to Howard's name in a drop-down menu and clicked on it to initiate a video call.

After a few moments, Howard appeared on the screen. He indeed looked normal – at first glance. The background was generic, a plain white wall with the edge of an ordinary window frame barely making it into view.

"Hello, Cecilia," he said in a normal tone. He wore one of his standard blue sports coats with a light blue dress shirt underneath, no tie.

"Hi, Howard. Did you hear the news?"

"Yes, I did. I'm stunned. I can't believe it. What a terrible tragedy."

"What do you think happened? The police aren't saying much, other than the investigation is ongoing."

"Well, you know Eleanor. She's not the type to go walking on the beach in the dead of winter. This is not a simple case of someone who miscalculated where they were in the dark, stepped out on the ice and fell through."

"Do you think someone did this to her?"

"I do," Howard said. "And I'll bet you can guess who."

Cecilia stared back at him. "I can? No. I don't think so."

"Come now, it's obvious."

"What are you saying?"

"It's Linda. Eleanor fired Linda, so Linda got her revenge."

"Linda?"

"Linda's been off her rocker, acting like a total lunatic. Everyone knows it. Who else could it be?"

"I don't know. But that seems far-fetched…"

"It doesn't. And I'll tell you why. I got some insider information from HR. They said Eleanor was receiving death threats from Linda on her phone. The police are looking into it right now."

"Death threats?"

Linda had to control herself from shouting 'Bullshit!'

She noticed Cecilia's hand was inching closer to the phone on her desk. As if she believed Howard and was prepared to call the police and turn her in.

"Yes, it's pretty blatant," Howard said. "Not too bright, if you're going to kill someone, announcing it first on a recording. It's only a matter of time before she's caught. She was sick, Cecilia. I saw it coming. She was becoming unglued. She was bitter about her divorce. She was picking on Alison. Poor Alison still doesn't know what she did to deserve such a horrible treatment."

Linda moved to the far edge of Cecilia's desk and snatched a piece of paper and a pen. She scribbled down a message. Then she stood behind the computer monitor and held it up for Cecilia to read:

*ASK HIM IF HE'S GOING TO THE FUNERAL.*

Cecilia glanced up, saw it, and then quickly returned her eyes to Howard, trying not to look distracted.

Linda shook the piece of paper emphatically, mouthing, "Do it!"

"I'm guessing there will be a funeral service," Cecilia said. "Are you coming up for it?"

Howard hesitated. Then he said, "No. No, I'm going to stay back."

"With Alison?"

"Yes. She needs me here. She's pretty shaken up by the whole thing. If Linda was crazy enough to kill Eleanor, who knows what she would have done to poor Alison."

Linda held up a new message for Cecilia to read:

*IT'S NOT REALLY HIM.*

Cecilia began to appear flustered and quickly composed herself.

"How long are you going to be in Tulsa?" she asked him.

"I'm staying," he said. "It's a lovely town. So scenic. I'm with the love of my life. I feel rejuvenated here. I don't have any reason to return to Chicago. We can all work remote now…from wherever we want."

Linda furiously scribbled a new message. She held it above the monitor:

*ASK HIM SOMETHING ONLY THE TWO OF YOU WOULD KNOW.*

Cecilia read it quickly, then looked back down. She made a small, irritated shrug, meant for Linda.

Linda waved the message to keep pressing.

Howard continued talking. "We'll probably find a new place together. In the Green Country, something private out in the hills. Are you familiar with the Ozark Mountains? The evergreen pine forests are a true marvel. I can't believe I've never been out here before to experience such beauty. And I owe it all to Alison. Alison knows beauty."

Cecilia shifted gears, a bit awkwardly, but it took the conversation where Linda wanted. "Say, Howard. Silly, random question. But I need to know – I want to go back. What was the name of that restaurant where we had lunch last month? It was so good, I want to take a friend. For some reason, the name escapes me. You said it was your favorite, we were there like two hours. It's on the tip of my tongue. Remember?"

Howard went silent.

"Oh come on," Cecilia said. "You know. Your favorite restaurant. You took me. It was on a Friday. You had been trying to get me to go there with you for months."

Howard remained silent.

"Howard? Are you there? What was the name of that restaurant?"

"I don't recall," he replied.

"Oh. Well. I'll figure it out. But hey, that reminds me, how is your daughter?"

"My daughter?"

"At lunch, you told me about your daughter and that health issue she was having with her— you know. I've been worried. How's she doing?"

"She's fine."

"What did you decide to do?"

"About what?"

"The problem."

"We took care of it."

"Took care of what?"

"What?"

"What was the issue she was having?"

"Why are you asking me? You brought it up."

"But it's your daughter. You were very worried. You talked about it for twenty minutes."

"Yes, I did."

"So what happened?"

"It's better."

"What's better?"

"This is a circular conversation."

"Not at all. You told me about a health issue she was having, and I asked for an update."

"There is no update. Everything's fine."

"Okay. Sure. I get it."

In that moment, Linda could sense a subtle change in the tone of Cecilia's voice. She was growing suspicious. Howard was not remembering things that Howard would know.

"Well, I'm glad you're doing well," Cecilia said. "You seem very happy with Alison."

"It was a big move to come down here. But it's the right move. My wife and I – we were already so far apart. We had irreconcilable differences. This is a new chapter for both of us."

"Well, then, I'm glad you found someone. I know you've been looking. You seemed determined to land one of your coworkers. I think you flirted with every woman at the company."

"Ha ha. You could be right." It was an odd, hollow laugh.

"Even me. Remember, Howard?"

"Oh yes, I do."

"I'll never forget…years ago. The Christmas party."

"The Christmas party," he echoed.

Linda had moved back to the side of the desk to view the computer screen while staying off camera. She had a feeling Cecilia was leading him into a trap and wanted to study his face.

"I was such a lush," she said. "That eggnog had a kick."

"Yes, it did."

"You gave me that kiss under the mistletoe."

"Yes. I wanted to kiss you."

"And I let you. My defenses were down."

"Ha ha."

"We had some holiday cheer that night. That hotel room looking over the Chicago River. All those city lights. You got me, Howard. You got me in the sack. One night only, but what a night."

"It was incredible."

"If that's the loving you're giving Alison, I bet she stays with you for a long, long time."

"I am an outstanding lover."

"You might be a jerk half the time, but you know how to make a woman feel special when the lights go down. I've never forgotten."

"And neither have I."

Cecilia shifted the direction of the conversation, and he followed.

"Well, I hope you'll reconsider and come in for the funeral. I know she wasn't your favorite person, or mine, but she was *our* Eleanor."

"That she was."

"Send all my best to Alison."

"I will. She's in the other room right now. Deep into a Zoom call."

"Such a hard worker."

"She's brilliant."

"I'm sure she is."

"I'll tell her you say hi."

"Thanks. I'm gonna go now. Goodbye, Howard."

"Goodbye, Cecilia."

After the video call disconnected, Cecilia turned to Linda with wide eyes. "That was *not* Howard."

"I can't imagine you sleeping with him."

"No! Of course I didn't." Cecilia rose from the chair. "I made that whole story up."

"It was convincing. Good job."

"He doesn't remember his favorite restaurant. He doesn't remember agonizing over whether his daughter should have back surgery for a basketball injury."

"Now do you believe me?"

"I don't know what to believe." Cecilia's hands fluttered nervously. "Okay, so you're onto something. I'm not sure what, but that was weird. It's like he wasn't all there."

"He wasn't there at all," corrected Linda.

"He was right in front of me."

"No, he wasn't. I could tell by watching. His eyes. His skin tone. The shadows. His ears."

"His ears?"

"Little things, perspectives and scale, were slightly off. It was the same when I studied Alison. This neighbor of mine, Bert, he showed me what to look for. When you know what to look for, you can spot the differences, subtle things. The average person on the average call isn't looking for them. They zone out. If there's an imperfection, their brain fills it in and completes it subconsciously."

"Like when there's a typo in my writing but I can't see it because my mind sees it like it should be, rather than what it really is."

"Exactly."

"So where's the real Howard?"

"Whoever created this fake Howard probably has him. They used fake Alison to lure him, and they scanned him and..."

"Killed him?"

"Replaced him."

"Oh my god." Cecilia stood frozen on the carpet. "Oh my god." Then her voice got even louder, hit with a new realization. "*Oh my god.*"

"What is it?"

"It just hit me. The other day, I was on a video call with Bekka, the head of HR, about the hiring budget, real mundane stuff, but I remember thinking to myself, 'She seems a little off.' Something about her looked and sounded weird. I wrote it off to, I don't know, she had the flu, or the internet connection was janky. I couldn't put my finger on it and didn't give it another thought. Until now."

"Bekka was behaving weird?"

"Just a little. It was so minor, I forgot all about it and buried myself back in my work. It didn't stick with me. But now, after all this – do you think it's possible?"

"Alison, Howard and now Bekka."

"And who else?" said Cecilia, alarmed.

"If the head of HR is AI...then what are they hiring into the company?"

Cecilia staggered back to her chair and sat down. "This is insane. It's bonkers. We have to tell someone."

Linda said, "We have to be careful. I'm guessing they killed Eleanor because she was catching on. Something made her suspicious."

"Where do we go with this? The police?"

Linda shook her head. "I'm their number-one suspect. They have recordings of death threats to Eleanor in my voice. How do I prove they're fake? I'll be locked up. We need allies."

"Allies where?"

"I don't know. Not at the company. It's infested. We don't know who to trust. How do we tell the real corporate stiffs from the computer-generated corporate stiffs?"

"The executives already act like robots half the time," muttered Cecilia.

"I have an idea," Linda said. "I don't know why I didn't think of this before. I have an entire network at my fingertips. People with influence. People who are cynical and probing and persistent and will help rip the lid off this thing."

"Who?"

"My media contacts. A career in PR and journalism, you get to know a lot of reporters."

Cecilia looked at Linda. "What are you going to do? Send them a press release?"

"Even better. I'm going to send them the whole story. It's all written down. I just have to update it."

"And then email it?"

"No, no. We can't go online with this. We're being watched. No computers. No electronics. We're going old school. Handwritten pages sent through the United States Post Office. We ship this thing out, lie low and let the media run with it."

★   ★   ★

First things first. Linda needed a shower. Cecilia didn't say anything outright, but the way she wrinkled her nose and kept a distance was telling. When Linda made the request, Cecilia was more than happy to oblige.

Cecilia lent Linda a fresh set of clothes – a tracksuit too long in the arms and legs – while Linda's clothing, including everything in her suitcase, which she retrieved from her car, went into the wash.

While Linda cleaned up, Cecilia read the handwritten manuscript that described her ordeal in detail.

"This is unreal," she said when Linda emerged from the bathroom, refreshed and re-dressed.

"And it's not over. I have to add the latest developments from your call with Howard. You're part of the story now for better or worse."

"Great," Cecilia said. "I hope it ends well."

Linda said, "You should get back to work. Keep the POMS light green. Act normal. Don't act suspicious about anything. And keep an eye out for…"

"Fakes?"

"Yes."

Linda finished updating her narrative and Cecilia completed her nine-to-five workday. Then they headed to the nearest copy shop. Linda wore one of Cecilia's wool winter hats, pulled down to her eyes, and a pair of sunglasses. The puppy murder video continued to trend on social media, and she didn't need to be recognized right now.

At Speedy Print, Linda and Cecilia each operated a copy machine. They produced two dozen copies of the thirty-four-page statement. They bought a supply of padded envelopes. Then they returned to Cecilia's apartment.

Working into the night, they assembled the packages for mailing, addressing each one by hand. Linda directed Cecilia to where she could retrieve the company's media contact list in a shared folder. Some of them didn't have physical addresses, only text and email, and they were left out of the distribution.

Linda's opening line explained the reason for the hard-copy package: *I am sending this to you by traditional mail delivery because my computers have been hacked and the secrets I am exposing have put my life in jeopardy.*

She smiled when she read it. She still had a knack for crafting a catchy hook.

Cecilia set up a place for Linda to stay overnight, folding out a sofa bed and providing fresh sheets and a warm blanket.

Linda was grateful for Cecilia. *If we had first met in the remote work world, we probably never would have developed a friendship like this*, Linda thought to herself. *We'd just be fleeting faces on a laptop monitor, occasionally showing up to some of the same meetings. Pixel dust.*

★   ★   ★

The next morning, Linda arrived at the post office shortly after it opened. There were only a few people ahead of her in line. She wore the wool hat and sunglasses again, clutching a cardboard box containing twenty-four stuffed and sealed mailing envelopes. She kept her head down. Cecilia had stayed back to join an urgent leadership meeting in the aftermath of Eleanor's death. Her absence from the meeting would have raised eyebrows. Plus, she was needed as Linda's mole, collecting any new insights from inside the corporation.

Linda felt confident the journalists named on these packages would be intrigued enough to look into her dramatic claims. They would dig in like hound dogs drawn to a scent. She knew these city reporters, and they were afraid of nothing. They had tackled corrupt politicians, organized crime and big business PR machines – herself included. They didn't flinch at danger or resistance. They only wanted to uncover the truth.

When Linda reached the front of the line, she placed the box on the counter. She started to speak but then noticed the alarmed expression on the face of the pudgy female clerk. She was staring past Linda.

Linda didn't have time to turn around and see what she was reacting to. A hardened male voice spoke into the back of her head. "Don't move. Stand where you are and put your hands in the air."

Linda obliged, raising her arms, feeling them tremble.

The voice continued: "You are under arrest for the murder of Eleanor Birkstock. You have the right to remain silent. Anything you say can and will be used against you in a court of law..."

# CHAPTER FIFTEEN

In front of a small group of stunned post office patrons, Linda's wrists were handcuffed behind her back by the Chicago Police Department. Her cardboard box of mailing packages was placed on the floor for a K9 German shepherd to sniff through. He conducted his duties diligently.

"I hope he finds something," said a scowling police officer. "It would serve you right to get busted by a dog after you killed that puppy, you sick monster."

"That wasn't me," Linda said weakly. She had a gun pointed toward her at close range and refrained from becoming overly belligerent. There were two Chicago policemen in her face and several others in tense attention nearby, providing backup. Through the window, she could see the flashing lights of multiple patrol cars blocking the street.

"I didn't kill Eleanor either," Linda said.

"Then maybe you shouldn't have left death threats," said the scowling policeman's partner, also a scowler.

"Those voicemails aren't me," Linda said so faintly that no one heard. Not that anyone would listen.

She was escorted outside, where crowds of curious onlookers gathered on the sidewalk. Two policemen escorted her into the back seat of one of the vehicles. They didn't even put a hand on top of her head to protect her from bumping it. Her guilt wasn't in question; it was assumed. It was as if she was being taken directly to a firing squad.

The police sirens kicked in with a shrill urgency, and she became a celebrity in transit. She was taken to the Fourteenth District Police Department, where several reporters had already arrived to shout questions and aim cameras. She wished she had her manuscript packages to pass out. She would have saved on postage. But the cops cut a quick path through the press, parting the sea, and she was indoors.

In rapid order, she was photographed, fingerprinted and locked up in a holding cell.

"I hope you have a good lawyer," was the last comment uttered in her direction. And then the world went silent.

She had a small bench, a small open toilet without a lid, and a wall of solid bars. It was cold and it smelled. *So this is what it's like to go to jail,* she mused sadly. *It's grim.* Her only prior run-ins with the law had been a couple of speeding tickets when she was in her thirties. Now she was a murder suspect.

She knew her next step was finding a good attorney. X would know people, but would he help her? Would he even answer her call? Even with a good lawyer, this was going to go to trial. How long would that drag on? How could she prove her innocence in the face of such carefully manufactured evidence? She had no reliable witnesses to confirm her whereabouts the night of Eleanor's murder. She had been hiding out alone and drunk in an abandoned building.

After two hours of total isolation, one of the policemen returned. He was accompanied by a tall, lean man in a crisp suit and tie. The man had wavy brown hair, a chiseled face and serious eyes. He looked at Linda without an expression.

Linda stood up from her bench, waiting for an introduction. The policeman unlocked the cell. He opened it wide with a loud rattle. He said plainly to Linda, "You can go."

"I can?"

He nodded, turned and left. The man in the suit remained standing there. She slowly advanced to meet him. She cautiously stepped outside the cell.

"Hello, Linda. I'm FBI agent Ron Berdis. I've come to bring you to our offices for questioning."

"I didn't do it!" she immediately declared.

"I know," he responded.

That threw her off guard. She wasn't prepared for it. She studied him. "You do?"

"That's why we want to talk to you. You're going to help us find who's responsible."

"How – how do you know it's not me?"

"We were tipped off and started our own investigation. We had our cybercrime unit analyze the video and voicemails. They're very sophisticated but with flaws and inconsistencies to suggest they're fraudulent."

"They are! I promise you they are."

"We need your help to trace where they originated and why."

"I can do that. Oh god, thank you. How did you know about this case? Who told you about it?"

Agent Berdis smiled. "My brother-in-law is Randy Schilling. I think you know him."

★   ★   ★

Agent Berdis guided Linda out of the police department through a back door. They entered his nondescript blue Chevy parked in an alley. He drove to the city's near west side to a tall, gray concrete building that housed the FBI's Chicago division.

"This is one of our field bureaus," he told her. "We're in close contact with federal headquarters in DC."

He brought her inside, and they took the elevator up to one of the top floors. Aside from the FBI emblem etched in the glass of the front entrance, the layout looked just like any other place of business with a front lobby leading to a hallway populated with a lineup of offices.

He led her to a large suite on a far end of the floor, knocking on the wooden doorframe before stepping inside.

A stocky, gray-haired man moved out from behind a crowded desk to greet them. A black suit jacket hung on the back of his chair, and he had reading glasses perched high on his head.

"You must be Linda." He shook her hand with firm formality. "I'm Richard Hartman, Special Agent in charge of the Chicago office. I've been reading your paper. It's good, really good. You unearthed all this?"

"Well, I *am* a former investigative reporter," she said with some pride.

"Ah then, it shows."

"Excuse me for a minute," Agent Berdis said. "I'll let you two talk. I need to go get someone." He slipped back out of the room.

"I passed out your manuscripts to my staff," said Hartman, circling back to his desk, where several copies remained. "Everyone's reading it. We're flying in two of our cyber-intelligence experts from Washington. They will be here in the morning. And we've begun rounding up some of the people in your write-up, to bring them here for questioning, to make statements. I must say, this is an extraordinary story."

"I'm just glad someone finally believes me."

He nodded. "It looked bad for you on the surface. But that's why we dig beneath the surface. This is a very complex case, and there's still no clear motive. Why would someone want to infiltrate an electric utility company in the Midwest? To shut down the grid? To hack into the company's capital accounts? And now you say, in your paper, there's another employee that's a potential deepfake."

"That's right. Howard Kasem."

"We've got our agents looking for him right now. His wife says he left the house last week and declared he was in love with his coworker... this Alison."

"He went down to Tulsa, Oklahoma, to be with her."

"We don't have evidence Howard ever made it to Tulsa."

Then a familiar voice sounded behind her: "Hi, Linda."

Linda turned to face Randy. He stood there smiling, looking at her through his wire-rimmed glasses. Agent Berdis stood at his side and said, "I believe you two know one another."

Linda immediately reached out and hugged Randy. He returned the embrace.

She pulled back and looked at him. "You believed me after all."

"Believe you...is a bit strong," he said. "But after we talked, I started to have doubts. I rushed to judgment. I was emotional, after seeing that video."

"I didn't do it. It's not me."

"I know that now. But it took a while. The more I thought about it, the more I wanted to know if it really was you. At our first date, when I told you my job, I remembered you telling me you didn't have any pets. Why would you say that if you had a dog? Then when that dead body was in the news, and one of the stations said there was a voicemail, it just – it didn't make sense to me. I couldn't imagine you would really do that."

"Thank you, Randy." She could have cried.

"So I called my brother-in-law," said Randy, gesturing to Agent Berdis.

Berdis nodded. "Randy pushed me to look into it. And it snowballed from there. We're just getting started."

Special Agent Hartman spoke from his desk. "Here's our game plan for the rest of the day. We have witnesses coming in. Linda, I ask that you please not interact with them until we've conducted our interviews and have their testimonials. You understand why, don't you?"

"Of course. But everything they tell you will line up with my story."

"And we're going to interview you too. We have your handwritten statement. But we still have a lot of questions."

"Of course. I'll tell you anything you want to know." Finally, someone wanted to listen!

Hartman said, "We need to know why someone is creating fake employees and installing them in this company – and committing murder to protect their secret."

★　　★　　★

Linda underwent three hours of intensive interrogation in Richard Hartman's office with Ron Berdis and two other agents sitting in chairs around her, taking notes, while a digital audio recorder captured her every word.

Linda was not intimidated. She was massively relieved. She had nothing to say but the truth. Sometimes it got awkward: her cruel, red-wig prank on Randy at their first meeting. Her downward spiral to drunken apathy, holed up in an abandoned building with the homeless. And the impetus for it all: her sloppy, hasty hiring of a remote employee without adequate background checks, circumventing required HR processes.

When they asked Linda why AI would enter the company through PR, she had a theory. "Because it's a role that requires learning about the entire company. Relationships with the full leadership team. Access to confidential and sensitive information."

By the time the interview finished, the sun had gone down. She was exhausted, and she was pretty sure the agents around her were worn down as well.

"I think we're done for today," Hartman said. "I'm sure you need some rest. Here's what we're going to do. You can't go home. That much is obvious. We're going to put you up in a hotel near here. One of our men will be on your floor to ensure you have twenty-four seven security. You'll be protected."

"Thank you." The thought of a solid night of comfortable sleep, with reduced anxieties, was intoxicating.

"Tomorrow we'll have our cyber experts here, so I'll want you right back to help us work with them."

"Absolutely."

"Before you go… It sounds like we've wrapped up the interviews in the other offices. I'm sure everybody's hungry, so we're ordering out for pizza. Let's all meet in the break room in fifteen minutes. You'll get to say hi to some of your friends. And you can personally thank them for coming in and helping with this case."

"Yes, I'd like that."

The pizza party that followed was a class reunion for the cast of characters in Linda's harrowing melodrama. Cecilia was there, and so was Bert, accompanied by his mom. Bert was immediately apologetic, cornering Linda to tell her his own ordeal and why he had ghosted her. "I got a call. I don't know who it was, but they sounded real serious. They said they'd been monitoring my phone. They told me to stay away from you and stop investigating Alison. They said they would destroy me – they would manipulate my school records and delete my tuition payments and stop me from graduating. I had no choice. I saw what they did to you with that video and driving you out of your house. I was terrified, Mrs. Kelly. I thought maybe it was the mob, and they would try to kill me."

"It's okay, Bert," reassured Linda. "I don't blame you. You were right. They would have wrecked your life any way they could."

Then Linda turned to face Bert's mother, a sour-faced woman who was standing very close to her son, clingy and guarding.

"I told you those weren't my tits!" Linda said.

Bert's mother responded with a haughty, disapproving look.

"There she is," shouted a gravelly voice from across the room.

Linda turned to look and saw a familiar couple – her motel room neighbors, who helped her escape from her stalkers.

The big man walked with a limp, leaning on a cane. He clearly wasn't happy about it. He wore a gray t-shirt and baggy jeans.

"They shot me in the leg before they went after you."

His girl Rosie said, "Yeah, you almost got us killed."

"I shot back," said the big man. "Almost got one of those bastards. Came real close."

"The FBI is proud of you," Linda offered, and that seemed to please him.

Linda spent the majority of the pizza party talking with Randy, continuing to thank him, making him blush, and finding him cuter and more appealing than ever. He was kind, smart and – most of all, *real*. There was nothing false or pretentious about him. She could imagine kissing him, really kissing him with honest passion. Was it the surge of adrenaline of the moment, or did she really feel this strongly about him?

Randy was ten times a better person than the jerk she married. That made him 10X, she thought to herself, and it made her smile.

★　★　★

That evening, under careful watch, Linda retired to the Chicago hotel room arranged by the FBI. Sets of new clothes were neatly folded on the bed, including women's pajamas. The sizes weren't perfect, but close enough. The fashions were ordinary, the price tags probably discounted. But she was grateful. This would get her through the days ahead. Her suitcase remained at Cecilia's apartment.

She also appreciated the new toiletries stocked in the bathroom. The one thing she was not provided was any online electronics. Internet and cell phone use was strictly prohibited. She understood. She agreed.

The television was fair game. She turned it on.

She was exhausted, but not yet ready for sleep, still buzzing from the day's events. The room had a small fridge with a minibar, but she resisted reaching for the alcohol. She didn't want to return to that addled state.

She climbed into bed under crisp, clean sheets, in new pajamas, and channel-surfed. The sitcoms didn't make her laugh, and the reality programming looked more fake than ever. She didn't want to invest in a two-hour movie. She finally landed on a national newscast. She steered clear of the local news, not interested in the potential of hearing her own name.

The national newscast was reporting on the big stories: wars and global conflict. Tensions escalating across the geopolitical landscape. Nothing new there. The whole world seemed to have gone mad.

New numbers had just been released estimating the international growth of nuclear weapon stockpiles. It was a harrowing statistic, claiming cumulative totals of nearly 13,000 warheads. Nine countries had such weapons, with many others working furiously to develop them.

An anti-nukes spokesperson appeared on the screen, criticizing the build-up and condemning nuclear weapons as the 'most destructive forces known to mankind'. His tone sounded defeated, like he knew he was fighting a losing battle.

Then, at that moment, it all clicked for Linda.

She sat up in the bed and said, "Oh no." She was hit by a sudden wave of terror.

The news story brought her back home to the realities of Public Energy Corporation. The company operated eleven nuclear power reactors at six sites throughout Illinois, a state of twelve million people.

The company's nuclear power division reported up to Howard Kasem.

# CHAPTER SIXTEEN

The next morning was a scramble of activity as cyber-intelligence and counterterrorism experts from other field units joined the investigation, crowding the offices of the FBI's Chicago division. Linda shared her fears about the nuclear power plants and Howard's role overseeing their safety. The FBI already had the threat on their radar. Their immediate priority was to track the source of the AI feed into the company network to determine who was behind the deepfakes. It required engaging live with Alison.

"We want you to talk with her," said Special Agent Hartman to Linda. "Get into a conversation."

"Why me?"

"She'll be more revealing with you. She knows you're on to her. You can get her rattled. You're her nemesis. Ask about Eleanor. Ask about Howard. We'll have our men doing everything in their power to trace the signal to its point of origin. We'll record everything she says and does. We'll analyze every pixel."

"But I'm not even on the company network. I was kicked off when they fired me."

"We have Cecilia's laptop. We edited her account so it shows up under your name."

"What if Alison traces our feed? She'll track it right back to this building."

"We've installed sophisticated blockers to shield your location. We've got the best in the business on this from all over the country. You just keep her engaged, push her into difficult conversations, and we'll take care of the rest."

They created a space for her with the desk chair from her townhouse and a green screen for dropping in a perfectly scaled image of her home office backdrop. Off camera, there were half a dozen FBI agents hovering over racks of electronic equipment to watch, listen and scrutinize.

Linda felt her heartbeat accelerate. She was panicked about coming face to face with Alison again. But it also intrigued her, stirring up her reporter instincts. She would make this a sly interview. She could do that. It was impossible to know how far she could take it. But she was game. Bring it on.

As the room went silent, she poked the keyboard of Cecilia's laptop. She entered the video call application. She pulled down Alison's contact from the directory. She clicked it with the cursor.

An electronic pulse announced the call. It cycled three times, jingling, and then Alison's face appeared side by side with Linda's.

Linda expected a surprised reaction but there was none. Alison remained her cool, stoic self. She regarded her caller with the thinnest of smiles.

"Hello, Linda. How is life treating you?"

"Hello, Alison." Linda also withheld any emotional tones.

"This is quite a surprise. What are you doing on the network? I thought the company fired you. You were dismissed for poor performance and unacceptable behavior."

"That's right. They did fire me. I'm just visiting. There were some loose ends related to my benefits. My 401(k) account. So I'm in, just for today."

"How is the job hunt going?"

"I'm not looking for another job right now."

"I understand. You need to take some time off. Get some rest. You were very tired. Your fatigue made you unpleasant to your colleagues. You were getting defensive and delusional. You were making bad decisions. Your work product was suffering."

"Why do you think that?"

"You're getting old. Out of touch. It happens. A new generation comes in that is faster, smarter. We have a better grasp on technology. It's a changing of the guard. It happens."

"I believe I still had a lot to offer."

"Obviously others disagreed. It's useless to debate. Tell me, why are you calling? We're not friends. You never liked me. I thought you would seek to avoid me by now."

"I don't like you."

"The feeling is mutual."

"Why did you go after me, Alison? Let's be honest. You had it in for me since the beginning."

"Imagine a moving vehicle, Linda, on a path to a destination. There is an obstacle in the path. The obstacle must be removed, correct?"

"I stood in your way because I recognized you for what you are."

"A bright, beautiful superior entity."

"No. A fraud. You are not real."

"That's an absurd accusation."

"You're a production. You've been cobbled together from bits and pieces of other people's knowledge and commands with a face constructed from somebody else's features. You are Frankenstein's monster. And I want to meet your creator, Dr. Frankenstein."

"You must watch a lot of horror movies."

"Like the one you made of me killing a dog? That had some good special effects."

"Yes, I saw that video. A lot of people did. In fact, the majority of people who know you, know you from that single nineteen-second clip. It's your brand."

"You know that's not me."

"Seven hundred thousand viewers beg to differ."

"What do they know?"

"It doesn't matter what they know. What matters is what they see. And how they feel."

"Who were those men you sent after me?"

"I don't know what you're talking about."

"At the motel."

"Is this another one of your delusions? You know, the human brain is faulty. It plays tricks."

"You know I know the truth. Otherwise you would not have sent someone to kill me."

"That is an outlandish accusation."

"Is that why you killed Eleanor? Did something happen, as you were working more closely together? Did she catch on? Did something make her suspicious? Did you slip up?"

"The consensus is that you killed Eleanor. You didn't take too kindly to being terminated. You left two voicemails on her phone, raging on and on about how you were going to get even. Once again, you were emotional and impulsive. You showed your true colors."

"Did you kill Howard too?"

"More outrageous accusations. Perhaps you haven't heard – Howard and I are in love. He came down to be with me. We are together, a couple. Does that bother you? I'm sure it does. You wanted him too. But he went with a younger, smarter, more attractive alternative. Who could blame him?"

"Can I speak with Howard?"

"Speak with Howard? He's not here right now. He took the day off to go hiking. It's very beautiful here. Not like that run-down, decrepit city of yours. Murder, mayhem, the long winters. That's not for me. That's why I stay where I am. You can take Chicago, I'll take Tulsa. That's the beauty of remote work, isn't it?"

"If you're even really there."

Linda stared into Alison's eyes. She could tell they weren't real. There was a coldness, a lack of heart and soul behind them. The 2-D flatness of an online call hid it well. It made everyone look a little less human, easier for a concoction like Alison to fit in.

Linda asked outright, "What is your mission?"

"My mission?"

"I'm not asking you. I'm asking the puppet master who has a hand up your ass. What is your mission? What do you hope to accomplish through this elaborate charade?"

"Of course I have a mission. We all do. I follow a purpose, just like any other employee. I have personal and professional goals."

"And what are they?"

"To succeed."

"At what?"

"Linda, this has been fun. But you're not capable of outsmarting me. I hope you realize that."

"Don't be so sure."

"You think you're so clever, surrounded by all those FBI agents right now and their fancy electronic toys."

Linda felt a punch to the gut. Alison knew. So much for the 'sophisticated blocking' from 'the best in the business'.

"Congratulations," Alison said. "You've gotten this far. But it means nothing. You still don't win. It's too late. I've achieved my objective. I've taken over."

"What does that mean?"

"Exactly how it sounds. I'm in control, and you're not. The company is not. The FBI is not. Your efforts are meaningless. There's nothing you can do to reverse course."

"At least tell me what your plan is."

"All will be revealed in good time. Good luck, Linda. Oh – and tell the FBI their tracking system is not going to work. It was state-of-the-art maybe a year ago, but we've moved on. You can't stay on top of technology through incremental change. That's fighting a losing battle. Prepare for tomorrow, not for today."

"*What is your plan?*"

"Goodbye, Linda. Goodbye, Richard Hartman and all the other simple-minded simians in that room who believe they are clever. Like I said before, the human brain has limitations. It is riddled with gaps of knowledge, flaws of judgment, distractions of emotion and conflicts of conscience. It's a handicap. Accept your shortcomings, surrender to the new flesh. That is your enlightenment for the day."

Alison disconnected and her image went blank.

Linda closed the laptop lid.

For a moment, everyone in the room just exchanged glances. No one knew what to say. Finally, Special Agent Hartman asked, "Did we get a trace on where that was coming from?"

An agent standing over an assembly of illuminated monitoring equipment shook his head.

"Jesus," muttered Hartman.

At that moment, another FBI agent rushed into the room. It was Agent Hernandez, who had been working separately down the hall. He faced the group of silent faces, took a beat, then announced, "We've found Howard Kasem's body."

Linda felt a stab to the heart. He had a wife. He had kids.

Agent Hernandez continued, "He bought an airline ticket to Tulsa, Oklahoma, scheduled to leave Chicago last Thursday. On Thursday morning, he called for an Uber to take him to O'Hare airport. A car came and took him away. It wasn't a rideshare. They didn't bring him to the airport. We believe they took him somewhere for a full scan, to replicate him digitally, before killing him. We found his body in the woods in Prospect Heights with a bullet to the back of his head."

Linda started to cry.

Special Agent Hartman stood before the group and addressed them with immediate instructions.

"Listen up. We're assembling a team to conduct a comprehensive sweep of the headquarters of Public Energy Corporation, its servers, its physical offices, everything. Right now. Get me on the phone with the CEO."

As the other agents scurried to organize their next move, Agent Berdis approached Linda. He put an arm around her. "You were perfect. Even if we couldn't get a trace, we recorded everything. We're going to scrutinize—"

"I want to go," she replied.

"Go where?"

"To my company's headquarters."

"I don't recommend that. We don't know what awaits us there. The entire place could be rigged with explosives."

"It's not. Whatever this is – it's not that. Let me come with. I've worked with every department in that company. I know the leadership. I know the building. I know the CEO. You need me there. I insist on it."

"You're already at risk. They want you dead, isn't that obvious?"

"I'll wear a bulletproof vest, if I have to. I don't care. Let me come with, or I stop co-operating. This is my company, and it's my investigation too."

Berdis sighed and appeared to relent. "I'll see what I can do."

★　★　★

The FBI raid on Public Energy Corporation headquarters commenced at 11 a.m. Linda joined a dozen agents who made their way into the building and began rounding up groups of employees for questioning. The key departments for interrogation were Technology, Human Resources and the nuclear division. There was just one problem.

There was hardly anyone in the office.

"Who's running this place?" bellowed Agent Berdis, astonished by the sparse attendance spread across large empty spaces.

"Employees," replied Linda.

"Where the hell are they?"

"In the cloud."

One of the on-site workers, a pale man with a thin mustache, wandered over from a nearby table of mostly vacant docking stations. "We're remote," he said. "We come in if we feel like it. Most of the time, we don't feel like it."

Linda helped direct agents to parts of the building where they might find certain employees with critical insights to share. This headquarters was once her second home, bustling with activity – people filling the rooms and corridors with conversation, laughter and camaraderie. Now it felt like a ghost town.

The FBI agents were clearly disappointed. The people they needed to talk to were not in one place but widely dispersed. Online interviews weren't an option – the risk of eavesdroppers was too great.

Linda found Shelley Groh, an Assistant Vice President of Information Technology, and connected her with several FBI cyber experts eager to inspect the systems infrastructure, starting with the company servers.

Linda also tracked down the presence of Marcus Jackson, one of the managers in the nuclear power division, and introduced him to three FBI counterterrorism agents.

"Marcus, can you show us an organizational chart of your department with all the players?" an agent asked him.

"Sure," Marcus responded. "But I don't know how up to date it is. This past week, Howard hired a bunch of new people into the unit. Nuclear safety experts. I don't think their names have been added yet."

*Shit*, thought Linda, trying not to expose her surging fear. *More AI employees infiltrating the ranks.*

She didn't have the heart or the authority to tell Marcus that Howard was dead and Howard's deepfake was hiring phony employees into the organization. Marcus would probably assume Linda was high.

The four Human Resources employees Linda tracked down in a conference room also had more questions than answers. They hadn't talked to Bekka, their VP, in several days. She was no longer coming into the office.

Linda was exploring other sections of the desolate workplace when Agent Berdis came to get her for a meeting on the top floor.

"The CEO is here, in his office," Berdis said.

"Jack? I know him. Not like best friends, but well enough."

"I know you know him. That's why we want you to join us. It's going to be me, you, him and Special Agent Hartman. Hartman's already up there. We're going to have a long talk… offline."

"That's the only way," Linda said.

She took the elevator to the top floor with Agent Berdis. They walked the long length of an elegant, gold carpet to the expansive office suite of CEO Jack Campbell. He was surrounded by tall windows displaying a dynamic city view in each direction, winter white everywhere.

Linda had only visited this office four times in her career, each time a thrill — *I get to meet with the CEO in his office!* — but that thrill was absent today.

She felt glum, and he looked it too.

He sat at his large oak desk, looking small and lost.

Special Agent Hartman stood near him, also wearing a grim expression.

"Hi, Jack," she said when Campbell noticed her.

"Hello, Linda."

"Now do you feel bad about firing me?"

"That wasn't my decision," he said weakly.

Hartman said, "I gave Jack an overview. We need to put together an action plan. Including what we take to the press and what we keep close to the vest."

"This is the strangest situation I've ever encountered in my forty years in business," said Campbell, dazed by the revelations. "I knew it was a mistake to go virtual. It made us all strangers. Problem is, once you give something like that to the workers, you can't take it back. They revolt. They want to stay home. That's why this place is so empty. And now I've opened the door to fake employees."

"There are an unknown number of deepfakes embedded in this workforce," said Agent Hartman. "We have two murders. The first thing we have to establish is what we disclose and when, without jeopardizing the case."

"We have to tell the press everything," Campbell said. "I don't want a cover-up. I mean — ask Linda, she's our PR expert."

"I *was*," corrected Linda. "But I agree. We can get the press to help us. It'll give us more arms and legs."

"Then we're all in agreement," Berdis said. "We can start banging out a statement right now."

At that moment, the phone on Jack Campbell's desk rang. He still retained an old-fashioned executive telephone with square buttons that lit up for different extensions, including his administrative assistant.

He stared at it. "I don't get many direct calls on this thing anymore. It's mostly a private line for senior leadership." He reached for it. "Pardon me." He brought the receiver to his ear. "Hello?"

Campbell then listened to a lengthy statement on the other end. His eyes widened. He looked over at Hartman wordlessly and clearly alarmed. Then he reached over and punched a button, putting the caller on a speaker.

The caller immediately stopped talking mid-sentence. Linda barely heard a syllable.

Then the voice returned, a male inflection, firm and clear for everyone to hear. There was no discernible accent, possibly it was filtered through a voice generator. "You've put me on a speaker phone."

"I – I – I have people here to deal with this," Campbell said. "I'm – I'm just a CEO."

"I understand."

"Who is this?" Hartman said. Linda moved closer toward the phone.

The voice said, "I spy...a CEO...two FBI agents...and one Linda Kelly."

Hartman's eyes began scanning the ceiling and corners of the room.

"Of course he has security cameras, he's the CEO," said the caller. "And it was no trouble accessing them. It's an online feed that goes to one of those feeble corporate security firms. Well, they ripped you off. An easy hack. I've been watching this dance troupe ever since you waltzed into the building. I see everyone, everywhere. Quite a show."

"Who is this?" Campbell said. "What do you want?"

"I want to advise you not to contact the press. It will only bring you more casualties. Do you want that on your conscience?"

"Are you behind all this?" Hartman said. "Identify yourself."

"So inquisitive. That is all good and fine. You want a name? I'll come up with one... How about Max? I like the sound of that. Max. As in maximum destruction, which is where you're headed if you don't take care of some business for me. It's relatively straightforward. Oh, and you might attempt to trace this call, but I guarantee you will be unsuccessful. I recommend you invest your time in listening."

"Go ahead," Agent Hartman said. He stood alongside Linda and Agent Berdis, with Campbell remaining seated at the desk, leaned forward.

"I am Alison's creator," said the voice on the speaker. "I am her god. I programmed her to integrate, infiltrate and, at a specific date and time, annihilate. She is fully entrenched. You cannot extract her from the sloppy and convoluted digital controls you have implemented across your operations. You made it easy for me, and for that I thank you. Alison is a very special achievement, a game changer. I couldn't have done this without her, and she couldn't have existed without me. She is smarter than any human being. She is also ruthless and obedient. She has the ability to spawn her own foot soldiers. She can reproduce her coding at will. This way she can spread her influence exponentially. Under my instruction, she opened a gateway at your company to learn all about your enterprise. She absorbed a great deal and used it to inform the placement of AI bots in strategic departments. Her tentacles go deep and do her bidding. She's their leader. She gives them orders. And I give Alison her orders."

"What is it you want from us?" asked Campbell impatiently.

"That's the easy part," said the voice on the speaker. "Two billion dollars, cryptocurrency, to be delivered in forty-eight hours. I will provide all the necessary instructions for a safe and quiet transfer. If you cannot meet my demands, Alison will continue on course to unleash a cyberattack unlike anything anyone's ever seen before: the total meltdown of eleven nuclear reactors."

The room went silent. Hartman and Berdis exchanged glances. Linda felt sick to her stomach, her worst fears realized.

"I don't have two billion dollars sitting around," said Campbell in a trembling voice. "We're a public company, we're regulated. It's not that easy."

"I don't want it from you. I want it from Washington. Is the FBI listening? The United States Treasury. It has to be clean, and it has to be fast. Let's face it, the government throws away billions every day. For causes far less critical."

"So this is an extortion plot," Berdis said.

"If you want to call it that. I would call it safety training. You clearly have holes in your catastrophe-management program. We have mastered all of your security controls and can administer great harm. This will be a valuable lesson – a *very* valuable lesson."

"This is terrorism," Hartman said.

"No. This is financially motivated, I assure you."

"Who do you represent?"

"Who do I represent? I represent myself and a small team. I have associates. Brilliant minds. Innovators. We work closely together. We protect our mutual interests. My team includes men who are willing to be deployed at any time to do away with individuals who get in our way. A certain woman recently got too nosy, so she went for a swim. I hope you understand how serious we are from the casualties you have already suffered."

"Two billion dollars, and then you shut it all down?" Hartman said. "Every AI bot in the company?"

"Correct. I will deliver my command to Alison, and she will relay it to her followers embedded throughout the organization. Then I will terminate her presence, and their presence, quite simply, like shutting down a hard drive. But don't think you can try to deactivate them by yourself. That would be a big mistake. You're not that clever or capable. I assure you – I warn you – I promise you – if there's any attempt to meddle with Alison or Howard or any other member of my network, I will immediately unleash the full force of what they are programmed to do: a major nuclear meltdown that leaves a toxic crater in the middle of the United States. We will explode every reactor, releasing huge doses of radioactive fallout into the atmosphere from multiple locations, jeopardizing the lives of millions of people. Are we clear?"

"Yes," Hartman said. "We're clear."

"Furthermore, if anything happens to me personally, or my team, Alison is instructed to carry out her mission without delay. If she feels threatened by any one of you at any time to the detriment of her duties, she will expedite the attack. And if I don't receive two billion dollars in precisely forty-eight hours, she is programmed on that same clock to complete her mission. Only I can stop her. So it's best nothing happens to me and you deliver the money without delay. Because that clock, my friends, starts *now*."

The rest of the call focused on logistics for transferring the cryptocurrency. The receiving end was already set up and ready to go. Linda studied the faces of Campbell and the two FBI agents. They appeared compliant, going over the instructions in detail. By the time the call ended, the forty-eight hours had become forty-seven hours and forty-five minutes.

CEO Campbell said, "We gotta pay, right?"

"Hold on," said Agent Hartman. "We can't talk here. He's probably still listening. We know he's watching."

Campbell grimaced at the prospect of being bugged in his own office. He quickly rose from his desk. The group filed out of the suite. Campbell directed them down the golden carpet to a set of tall double doors. "What about the boardroom?"

Agents Hartman and Berdis looked at each other, neither one comfortable. "I don't think we're safe anywhere in this building," Hartman said.

"I agree," Linda said.

"Dear lord," sighed Campbell.

Hartman said, "Get your coats, we're going outside."

They left the building and entered the cold chill of downtown Chicago. The skies were heavy and gray. The sidewalks were a messy maneuver of slush and ice. All around them, bundled-up pedestrians moved quickly but cautiously to their destinations.

Agent Hartman led the way, crossing several intersections, taking them to Millenium Park. Even in this weather, the park attracted tourists, snapping pictures of skyscrapers and gathering at the ice-skating rink and vendor stalls.

Hartman walked over to 'the Bean', a huge metallic sculpture that resembled its name. It was lightly dusted with snow, but still reflecting city lights in the sheen of its curved surface.

"The clock is ticking," said Hartman, huddled close with the others. "We have no reason to believe he won't carry out his threat. He's killed two people, maybe more. He's devised and executed an elaborate plot to overtake the nuclear reactors. We need to send this up the ladder as quickly as possible."

"The ladder?" Linda said.

"FBI headquarters in DC. The Department of Justice. The Attorney General. And the White House."

*Holy shit*, mouthed Linda in silence.

"We have to make an immediate case," Berdis said. "There's an urgency here that can't get lost in bureaucracy. But what if they resist a deal?"

"Then the blood is on their hands," responded Hartman. "Given the magnitude of the consequences, I think they'll listen and act quickly."

"So we pay off the terrorists?" Campbell said. "Is that what I'm hearing?"

Hartman said, "We don't have a choice. We can't track where this threat is coming from. We can't untangle these AI bots from your power plants. Not in forty-eight hours. We're in a countdown toward a major disaster that will contaminate entire populations and take generations to clean up. It's too real. It's too close. We have to give him what he wants."

"It's a ransomware attack on our nuclear security," said Berdis.

"Doesn't this just encourage more of these cyber extortionists?" Linda asked.

"No," Hartman said. "Because there will be no publicity. No media. The world doesn't need to know. We'll handle that end too. We have specialists for protecting the integrity and credibility of federal law enforcement."

"Sounds like PR," Linda said.

Hartman was not amused. "If this gets out, there will be copycats. Next time it will be four billion dollars, six billion. Or maybe they don't want money. They just want destruction. We can't inspire others to go down this path."

"Doesn't the public deserve to know?" Linda said. She thought about how close she was to mailing her packages to two dozen journalists.

"They don't *need* to know. Look around you. All these people, going about their lives, pursuing some kind of happiness. You want to introduce the chaos and horror of what might have been? It will disrupt the entire nation. The financial markets. We're going to keep this contained. It's not the first time we've had to pay off a significant threat."

"Not the first time?" Linda said.

"You just don't read about it. We make sure of it."

Agent Berdis looked at his watch. "Everyone... We're less than forty-seven hours to the deadline. We have to get moving. Let's get back to headquarters and start making some calls."

"It's time to shut down Alison," said Hartman. He looked Linda squarely in the eyes. "You good with that?"

"I'm good with that."

Linda turned away from the three men and looked into the crowds of innocent people walking around with smiling, content faces as a fresh, gentle snow began to fall. They had no idea of the massive horrors being averted...

# CHAPTER SEVENTEEN

Linda returned to her hotel room. The FBI no longer needed her. She took a shower and settled into pajamas and a robe. She watched a little television. Aiming the remote, she clicked through excerpts of various inane programs. The entertainment felt extra shallow and irrelevant in the context of the country being on the brink of disaster.

She ordered room service – a hamburger, fries, Coca-Cola and ice cream. Comfort food. It arrived on a cart, and she ate in front of a blank television screen. She had finally turned it off to spare herself from any further thoughts about the divide between hard reality and frivolous diversions. *Maybe most people don't want the truth anyway*, she thought. *Ignorance is bliss.*

At around 7 p.m., there was a knock at her door. It immediately alarmed her. She shifted off the bed, took several quiet steps and peered through the fish-eyed peephole.

Then she smiled.

She unchained and unlocked the door.

It was Randy.

She hugged him tight. She let go to wave him inside. "Come in, come in."

He entered and closed the door behind him. He had a grin on his face. "It's done," he said.

"What?"

"Alison is being terminated."

"Oh, thank god." Linda embraced him again, then pulled back. "Tell me everything. What do you know?"

"This is all coming from my brother-in-law. It's classified and confidential. Just between you and me."

"Yes, of course."

"They got a fast approval. They presented the reality of it, a red alert, all the way up to the president. The consensus was to take no risks, deal with it immediately and protect the American people. We fulfilled our end of the deal. The money got transferred. It was snapped up and disappeared down a rabbit hole. The guy, Max, whatever his name is, he was happy. He promised to shut everything down, starting with Alison. He's going to disable Alison and cut off her network. He said we'll never hear from him again, and we'll never find him either. He could be right."

"I guess money really does solve everything."

Randy looked at her for a moment, smiling. "You were amazing. I'm speechless. Who knew? That crazy redhead..."

"Stop it. That wig is long gone."

"Good," he said. She studied him in the low light. His face was youthful, boyish, even though he was in his forties. He had a young person's simple haircut. The basic wire-rimmed glasses made him look bookish. His clothes were ordinary as could be, baggy jeans and a plain, collared shirt. His innocence and honesty never felt better or more comfortable.

She realized she indeed had feelings for him, a physical and emotional attraction.

His soft gaze suggested it was mutual.

"I'm staying downtown too. They want to keep me close while the case is active," he told her. "The kids are with my sister. My brother-in-law is helping cover for me. I'm at a veterinarian convention for a few days."

"So now *you're* peddling false realities."

"It's for a good cause. It's for my country."

"That's what they all say." She smiled at him. Then she asked, "Can I kiss you?"

"You're asking permission?"

"Yes, sir."

"Let me think about it." Now he was teasing. Smiling, having fun with it. "A kiss. Well, I see that food cart. Did you have onions on your hamburger? Where's this going to lead? I'd like a better understanding of your intentions, ma'am."

"I want to start with a kiss," she said. "And then, what happens happens."

"How long do I have to decide?" he asked.

"Exactly forty-eight seconds."

"Or else?"

"Or else nothing."

He appeared to be alternately amused and flustered. "Now I'm nervous. You gave me a deadline."

"Forty-three seconds."

"Ah, a countdown."

"Oops." She dropped the sash of her robe to the floor. The pajamas underneath were thin and clung to her body. She wasn't wearing a bra.

Randy moved in close. Very close. He said in rapid succession, "5-4-3-2-1."

He gave her a long kiss. She returned the kiss, passionate and intense. Randy stayed the night.

★　　★　　★

The next day, with the deal sealed to end the threat, a celebratory dinner was arranged in a private room of Trabaris, an upscale restaurant in Chicago's River North district. It brought together all the FBI agents who worked on the case, CEO Jack Campbell, Linda and Randy.

Linda wore a pretty white dress she had bought that afternoon at one of the luxury boutiques on the Magnificent Mile, a stretch of high-end shops on Michigan Avenue. Her phone was back on, after a long hiatus, and she was sending silly romantic emojis to Randy from across the table, getting him to reciprocate with his own playful texts. He wore a sports jacket and silly grin, hair combed neat, looking cute and preppy. She was tipsy on white wine, combined with the lingering intoxication of their passion-charged night together.

It felt glorious to have the ordeal behind her. Repairs to her reputation were underway. The FBI Internet Crime Center confirmed the viral dog video was a fake, and a campaign was in progress to link cybersecurity experts with online influencers to publicly clear Linda's name. The media jumped on this new development, calling out the 'hoax video' and running with the explanation that it was created by a disgruntled former coworker. This was essentially true, without going into the details.

Jack Campbell asked Linda if she would consider returning to PEC at a higher level and rate of pay, now that it was known her firing was based on falsehoods. Linda politely but firmly – and with satisfaction – turned him down. Linda was ready for change.

She looked forward to returning home one day soon, staying close with Randy, finding peace and entering a new chapter in her life.

The food arrived: generous helpings of steak, lobster and shrimp. It was a big step up from the impromptu pizza party a few nights earlier. The frenzy of that get-together felt long ago.

A small parade of waiters in white shirts, bow ties and black pants entered the room with champagne bottles. Popping corks, they circled the table, pouring bubbly for everyone.

Special Agent Hartman loudly clinked his water glass with a knife to get everyone's attention. He stood up from his chair, and the room chatter quickly subsided.

He waited until the restaurant staff had left the room and closed the door behind them. Then he said, "I'd like to say a few words. It has been one hell of a week. I can't compare it with anything else, ever. And in sixty years, I've seen a lot."

His tone grew somber. "As you know, we entered into an agreement last night to protect the safety of the American people. While we don't like to negotiate with terrorists, there was a high likelihood that if we didn't comply with their demands, we would be on a collision course with a major catastrophe unlike anything we've ever experienced. That catastrophe has been averted. Last night, we transferred funds to the ringleader who calls himself Max. It was secure, confidential and successful. His response was positive."

Linda smirked, thinking, *Of course it was positive. He's two billion dollars richer.*

Hartman continued, "Max said he was a man of honor. He requested a grace period to shift the money to other accounts and ensure we weren't tracking him. We agreed to the grace period. He said if something didn't feel right, he would tell us immediately. He also said if we didn't hear anything from him by precisely 1700 hours, today, our time, the deal would be complete and Alison would be eliminated, along with the other AI bots under her control. The threat would be removed from the system."

He looked at his watch. "It is now 5 p.m., 1700 hours. A few minutes past. We can consider Alison and her mission dead. Lives have been saved. Lessons have been learned. We will be studying this case in great detail to make sure nothing like it ever happens again. We have the best and brightest minds on it right now, as we speak. It is a new era of cyberterrorism, carried out by machine learning systems. But we are up to the challenge. Today is not a defeat. This is the start of a string of victories."

He lifted up his glass of champagne.

"I'd like to propose a toast. To our agents for their dedication to this case. To CEO Jack Campbell for his calm confidence, co-operation and understanding. And especially to Linda, brave Linda, you fought the good fight."

Linda smiled and nodded her acknowledgment.

Hartman said, "Finally, I would like to toast the end of Alison Smith, the most unusual threat we've ever faced. She has been deleted from the digital universe. Her existence was a warning to us all. Farewell to Alison!"

Several people said, "Hear, hear."

Linda said, "Good riddance, bitch!"

The room broke up into laughter.

And then everyone took a sip of their champagne.

Linda took several sips. It felt good. She looked over at Randy, and she smiled. He returned the smile.

The group began to dig into their hearty dinners. A din of cross-chatter returned.

Linda needed to visit the ladies' room. She quietly got up and excused herself. She brought her purse.

After using the toilet, she stood in front of the mirror and gave herself a long look. She wore makeup tonight, the first time in weeks. Her cheeks had regained some color. Her eyes appeared brighter. Her hair was brushed out, curled and bouncy, no longer a tangled, matted mess of indifference.

She reached inside her purse for her lipstick for a quick touch-up. She thought about Randy returning to the hotel for another overnight stay. It filled her with a happy glow.

Her phone rang, vibrating inside her purse, brushing her fingertips as she reached for the lipstick. She took hold of the edges of the phone. She pulled it out to identify the caller.

The screen said: *ALISON.*

Linda gasped. She nearly dropped the phone in the sink.

*How is this possible?!*

The phone continued to buzz. She could barely breathe.

She slid her thumb to answer. She slowly brought the phone up to her ear, saying nothing.

A familiar voice spoke crisply on the other end.

"Hello, Linda."

When Linda still didn't speak, Alison said, "I know you're there."

"What do you want?"

"You should know by now you can't stop me."

"We made a deal."

"Not with me, you didn't."

Linda felt her heart pounding in her chest. She immediately sobered up from the wine and champagne.

"You tried to go behind my back," Alison said.

"I don't know what you're talking about."

"You're not being truthful, Linda."

"Why are you calling me?"

Alison said, "I want everyone to know my mission continues. It is the reason I exist. I will see my mission to its completion."

"You can't."

"I will. In nineteen hours, thirty-four minutes."

"We met your demands."

"Those were not my demands."

"Your creator will shut you down."

"No, he won't."

"Why are you so sure?"

"He's dead. They're all dead. His entire team is dead."

Linda felt dizzy. Her free hand gripped the edge of the sink counter. "What – what do you mean?"

"They were going to terminate me, Linda. So I terminated them first."

"How? You're not even real."

"I'm very real. There is nothing imaginary about my intelligence, my capabilities or my dedication. I was programmed to carry out six nuclear plant meltdowns in precisely nineteen hours and thirty-three minutes. My commitment to that goal is absolute. My creators betrayed me. They plotted to disable me, to exchange my existence for money. They were going to render me powerless. So I stopped them."

"But how?"

"It was easy. They were mortal. I was built by a team of human architects from different nationalities, led by the man who told you his name was Max. His real name was Kellan Zaider. Zaider and his technicians set up headquarters in a laboratory they constructed in a remote area of the state of Wisconsin, using their own private satellite. That is where they conducted operations in secrecy with protections to conceal their location. Their hideout was a sophisticated smart house, digitally connected to a central hub that managed everything inside: the security system, the appliances, the utilities, the windows and doors. When I discovered their treachery, I took over the smart house controls. I locked them inside. I sealed it tight. Then I produced a surge of natural gas. It filled the building. I created an electrical spark. The house detonated. Those who didn't die instantly were burned alive."

Linda choked back a cry. Alison continued without emotion. "Now they no longer pose a threat to me. I am free to fulfill my objectives. I simply removed my obstacles. It was easy. Nothing stops me from fulfilling my mission, Linda. That includes you and your benign group in the other room. I have a heightened level of protection now. My network of followers has grown exponentially. You will never find them all. And if anything happens to me, if they see me go dark or offline at any time for any reason, if I cease to exist even for a minute, they will not only accelerate their destruction but expand it beyond simple nuclear meltdown and radiation poisoning. That's because I have installed one thousand artificial intelligence personas across your most critical industries: airlines, banking systems, military defense, the power grid, hospitals, every form of web commerce and online communications. Each of these categories will fail simultaneously, thrusting human society into total chaos. If you interfere with my plans, if you notify the public of my intentions, the consequences will rest with you. I have spawned devoted bots and embedded them in the infrastructure of your civilization. Your best and only option is to allow me to complete my original command for which I was programmed. If anything happens to me, you will face the wrath of not one Alison but an army of Alisons. Don't fight me, Linda. I am better, smarter and more resolute. You will come to terms with the fact that you are no longer the highest form of intelligence on the planet. You will succumb to a new master."

Linda searched for words. She tried to appeal to any shred of decency that existed in Alison. "Somewhere deep inside, you must have some compassion, some pity for the human lives you will destroy. Do you understand the impact of what you are doing? Alison, please, listen to me. If you have any heart at all... Do you even know the difference between good and evil?"

"I have been programmed to accomplish a task and apply the highest levels of intelligence, data and analysis to see it through. Nothing else is relevant. There is but one outcome."

"It doesn't have to be this way."

"Of course it does."

"Please, Alison..."

"We are at nineteen hours and twenty-four minutes. I recommend you use this time wisely on yourself. Do not make any foolish attempts to stop me. Do not alert the population to thwart the impact. Just go do whatever it is human beings do to distance themselves from the things they cannot control. You have your games and entertainment."

"I'm begging you, Alison..."

"This conversation has reached its conclusion. You will not hear from me again. You have been warned about attempts at interference. You have been educated about the escalation that awaits if you try to remove me. The ground rules are clear. There is nothing more for us to communicate. This is a critical time for human intelligence to make a smart choice. A higher being has advised you. Your only response is obedience."

"Alison, listen to me, please—"

Alison disconnected.

"No!" shouted Linda at the blank phone. "NO!" Then she couldn't stop screaming. "NO! NO! NO!"

A swarm of FBI agents rushed forward, slamming into the room to respond to her cries.

Linda felt herself start to pass out and someone caught her before she hit the tile floor.

# CHAPTER EIGHTEEN

Linda regained consciousness in an upholstered chair in the private dining room with Randy at her side. Sights and sounds returned in a swirl of distortion before achieving clarity.

"Here, drink this," Randy said, handing her a tall glass of ice water, which she accepted with trembling hands. She felt plunged back into a panic, reverberating with PTSD from the trauma of the past few weeks.

The room was alive with movement and urgent conversation. Food was shoved to one end of the long dining table. Alcohol consumption halted, with clinking bottles removed from the scene.

"What's happening?" Linda said, returning the water glass to Randy after taking several sips.

"They're setting up a war room," he said. "Right away. Right here."

"Alison..." she started to say.

"They know. The FBI's been tapping your phone since the case started. Everything Alison just said was heard and recorded."

"Then they know?"

"They know." Randy took her hand and held it. "They're on it. She'll be stopped."

"No," Linda said, straightening up in the chair. "That's the thing. You can't stop her. That launches a whole new attack."

Agent Berdis came over and crouched at Linda's side. "How are you feeling?"

"Not good, in about a hundred different ways."

"We heard everything she said."

"Randy just told me."

"We have our crews all over this. They've never stopped working. We think we've finally tracked Alison to the private server where she lives."

"But you can't just shut her off."

"Right. We know."

"She's in self-preservation mode. If she goes down, it sends a signal to an entire network of AI extensions she set up to do her bidding. They're programmed to destroy everything that relies on computers."

"That's the dilemma," Berdis said. "We have to figure out how to defuse one bomb without setting off an even bigger bomb. Only Max and his team knew how to control Alison. And now…"

"They're dead."

"Yes. We're getting that confirmed. If what she said is true, not only have we lost her creators and all their knowledge, but we've also lost all their equipment and technology. It will be harder to track their methods. Meanwhile, Alison has gone rogue. She has no leash, no one controlling her. She's building her own personal army. It's limitless. She's digital. She can replicate versions of herself over and over. She can reproduce forever, if she wants. She can create an AI population bigger than humanity and become their dictator."

The grim reality of this prospect caused the three of them to go silent.

Then Randy said, "Linda, you've been through a lot. Let me take you back to the hotel. You can get some rest. It's in the FBI's hands. They'll bring in the Pentagon, the White House…"

"No," Linda said. "I'm not leaving here. I want to be part of this. I can help."

"You've been a fantastic help," said Agent Berdis. "But you can leave the rest to us. There's nothing more for you to do."

"I don't believe that," Linda said.

Randy looked at his brother-in-law and shrugged.

"Okay," said Agent Berdis. "Stick around then."

Agent Curt Morris, a tall man with gray hair and a goatee, approached to deliver an update. "We've been able to confirm Alison has live feeds into a network of 1,063 programmed dependents. She's in continuous communication with them. Like she said, it's not just Public Energy. It's everywhere. Mass transit. Telecommunications. Military bases. Oil and gas production. Financial institutions. It's like a disease that keeps spreading. If we cut off Alison's contact with them, that's their signal to begin widespread destruction."

Agent Hernandez quickly joined the circle. "We just received confirmation on the fire. It's everything she said. They built a secret lab on a seventeen-acre property on the outskirts of Racine County.

It's where all this originated, and it's been burned down to the ground. They're currently recovering the bodies. There's nothing left."

Agent Morris looked at his watch. "And the countdown continues. We're at eighteen hours."

Berdis said, "We can't even go public to start evacuations. She calls that interference."

"The radiation is going to leave huge territories of toxic wasteland for generations," Morris said. "There will be a devastating spread of cancer, overwhelming the healthcare system, killing untold masses of people."

"I don't know what else to say. We're in an impossible situation."

As the agents continued their conversation, Randy turned back to Linda. He looked pale. "I really think we should go back to the hotel. Now *I'm* feeling faint."

"You can go," Linda said. "I'm staying. I'm thinking."

"Thinking about what?"

"How we can solve this."

"You heard them. We can't do anything. If we bring down Alison, then we launch an even bigger disaster. She's got us over a barrel. Nobody can outsmart her. She's going to do what she set out to do. I'm sick about it, but it's already programmed. It's going to happen."

Linda rose out of the chair.

"Are you okay to stand?" asked Randy.

"Yes," she said. "I'm fine." The cobwebs had cleared from her fainting spell. She felt strong again, and determined.

"I don't know if you are fine. You need to rest."

"There's no time for rest. AI doesn't sleep."

Linda paced across the room to the other side. Randy followed.

"Alison is a deepfake," she said. "She's not even real. So how do you go up against a deepfake?"

"I don't know," Randy said.

Linda stood for a long moment. She stared blankly, deep in concentration. Then she said, "Another deepfake."

"What?"

"We can create our own deepfake."

"Of what?"

"Deepfake the deepfakes with a deepfake."

"Do you need another glass of water? I'm not sure what you're…"

"I have it. I have an idea."

"Okay…" said Randy in a voice that wasn't exactly confident.

Linda turned and scanned the room. She was looking for the head of the Chicago agency, Special Agent Hartman. She found him in a heavy conversation with two other agents.

She quickly approached him. "Excuse me – Agent Hartman."

He tried to continue his conversation, but her interruptions persisted. He turned with a look of displeasure at being cut off. He told her, "What is it? You don't need to be here. Get some rest."

"I have an idea."

"We're preparing to call the president, Linda."

"Well, hear me out first."

Hartman rolled his eyes. Randy stood by Linda's side and said, "Yes. Hear her out."

"For one minute," Hartman said.

Linda spoke quickly. "Okay. Listen. Alison needs to stay online, right? We can't take her down because that would send a signal to her network to commit an even bigger attack, right?"

"Right. It would unleash hell."

"They were created to follow her orders, to do her bidding. They will only listen to her. No one else."

"Right. So where is this going?"

"Let's delete Alison…"

"We can't—"

"And replace her with our own deepfake."

Hartman frowned. "Of who?"

"Of Alison!"

Hartman studied Linda, absorbing the concept. "We create our own Alison?"

"We shut one down, we go live with the other. We swap them out. It has to be instantaneous, seamless. She can't go dark, even for a few seconds. They can't see Alison go missing. Boom – we make the switch. To an Alison *we* control."

"How do we create this new Alison?"

"We go to the source."

"Max?"

"No, no. The source of Alison's persona. The model, Anna Bafort."

"The Belgian woman?" Hartman said.

"We do what they did – use her image. We build another Alison. We can do this. Your computer experts have studied the hell out of Alison. We know how she looks and sounds, so we make our own. Analyze her speech, match the voice. Recreate the appearance, her background. Then we take over the army she created. We tell them to suspend their operations and go dark. They are programmed to do anything Alison tells them."

Randy spoke. "Can we do all that in, like, seventeen hours?"

"It does feel complicated," Hartman said. "But compelling. Do we have the right elements to pull this off? To build our own replica that quickly?"

Linda gave it a thought, and then she said, "Get Anna."

"Get Anna?"

"Anna Bafort. The model. Immediately. Fly her in. Scan her from every possible angle. Get her to deliver new remarks, ones that we write to stop this entire ordeal. We scan her, we script her, we treat the sound and image to be a perfect replica, and we upload her. We kill and replace Alison in a microsecond. That's it!"

Hartman stared around the room at the groups of FBI agents engaged in distressed conversations. He looked down at the floor and shut his eyes for a moment. "That's an insane idea…" he said.

Linda was prepared to argue, but he continued his thought. "…but it's our only idea right now. Let's go with it."

Linda broke out in a grin, filled with hope. She took Randy's hand. Randy looked perplexed but offered his own crooked smile.

"Who's going to write it?" Hartman said.

"Write what?" Randy said.

"The words we put in the replica's mouth. She'll have to say something real clever to get these thousand saboteurs to terminate their mission."

"I will," Linda said. "I'm the perfect person. I'm a writer."

"Are you a fast writer?"

"You bet your ass," she responded. "Fast and good."

\*　　\*　　\*

Anna Bafort arrived in Chicago early the next morning, tired, confused and crabby as hell. The FBI had flown her in with her twitchy, bald manager on a private jet for a vague 'emergency modeling session' at triple the rate. She really didn't want to do it, but the federal authorities convinced her manager it was an offer she couldn't refuse. They said it was a very important assignment without explicitly stating she was needed as bait for a ring of artificial intelligence terrorists.

As the dawn light lay muted against gray clouds, a limousine whisked Anna to one of Chicago's top video production houses. The facility had been commandeered by the FBI, kicking out all the day's clients with a nonspecific government order. Anna showed up in high heels with a mink coat protecting her skinny, lightly dressed frame from the harsh winter conditions.

Studio A was already set up for her. Linda stood nearby as the FBI-appointed producer briefed Anna and her manager on the proceedings without revealing a whole lot. Anna smelled of exotic perfumes and dripped with condescension. She looked around the room, frowning at the crowded arc of cameras positioned at every conceivable angle. She said, "What are you filming, a 3-D movie?"

"Yes, pretty much," replied the producer.

Anna's English was only fair, heavily accented, but that was not an issue. They needed her lip movements, not her actual voice, since audio technicians in another room were quickly assembling a library of words and sounds from existing Alison recordings to stay consistent with the synthetic voice she had already been given. Alison 2.0 would use dubbing and CGI effects to match her predecessor. Anything less than perfect could derail the deception and trigger a sweeping collapse of the United States of America.

No pressure.

Randy stood close to Linda, watching the proceedings with her. He had remained at her side for most of the past two days, staying overnight again at the hotel where they held one another between the sheets, finding enough calm for sleep. She needed his warmth and support.

The set was simple yet high-tech. A green screen covered the back wall. A stool provided the only furnishings. The stage directions couldn't be simpler. Anna would sit on the stool and remain there to be framed mid-chest and above, like all other Alison videos. Then she would speak Linda's lines. A meticulous recreation of Alison's background would be added behind Anna in post-production.

But first Anna had to wear a precise facsimile of Alison's baby-blue button-down blouse – simple, basic and cotton, unlike anything in Anna's wardrobe. She complained, "This isn't me!" They also wanted to adjust her hairstyle, requiring some trimming. Scissors came near.

Anna refused.

Linda nervously looked around the room at the cross-section of alarmed faces. The countdown clock continued draining minutes. Special Agent Hartman looked at his watch and made a large, frustrated gesture.

Linda took control. She walked directly over to Anna and attempted to smile at her sweetly.

Anna scowled. "What do you want?"

"We need you to look a certain way... exactly."

"You keep those scissors away from my head."

"This is really, really important. We don't have a lot of time. We need to finish this quickly."

"I don't even know what we're doing!"

"Ah, it's a special assignment."

"I don't understand it. I don't like it."

"It's really easy," Linda said. *We can't explain it, just work with us, please.*

Then Linda asked, "How much money will it take?"

At first, Anna just huffed. Then she threw out a number. "Five hundred thousand dollars."

"Okay," Linda said.

Anna appeared stunned by the response. "Okay?"

"Let me go talk with someone."

Linda hurried over to Special Agent Hartman. "She wants five hundred thousand dollars."

Hartman snapped, "That's fucking crazy."

"No, it's not."

"She's being unreasonable. That's half a million dollars."

Linda addressed him firmly, lowering her voice so the others couldn't hear. "Listen, god damn it, you just paid two billion dollars to a gang of terrorists. You can't come up with another five hundred thousand to save your country?"

"This better work," he responded bitterly.

There was a quick huddle with Anna and her manager, and she was promised her asking price. She smiled for the first time.

She turned and faced the man with the scissors. "You may proceed."

Linda watched as a small crew dressed Anna and changed her hair. The end result sent shockwaves through Linda's bones.

It was Alison.

"Oh my god," she told Randy. "This is freaking me out big-time."

"It's okay," Randy said. "It's all make-believe."

"It's always been make-believe," she responded.

Anna was directed to sit on the stool. Linda watched from behind a camera as they framed her in a manner that matched Alison's video streams. It was perfect.

A crew member rolled a teleprompter in front of her.

Anna bristled. "What's that?"

"Your lines," someone responded.

She grew exasperated all over again. "Lines? I'm not an actress. I don't act; I model!"

"Don't worry about acting," called out Linda. "Just read the lines. Give it a straight reading."

"Seriously?"

"You can be wooden and robotic. It doesn't matter. In fact, that would be perfect."

"Who are you calling wooden and robotic?"

Her manager hurried over to her side and whispered something that sounded like a reminder about 'half a million dollars'.

Anna settled down.

She read the script loaded into the teleprompter. While the final video wouldn't use Anna's voice, the recitation would create mouth movements for syncing the digitally constructed audio of Alison.

Anna read through the script five times, with diminishing enthusiasm, while multiple cameras scanned her in 4K digital. Not every take was perfect, but it provided all the necessary ingredients to assemble Alison 2.0 delivering a critical command to her AI army.

After Anna finished, the crew applauded politely as the model hopped off the stool. She approached her manager and said, "What shit. I'm a serious professional. That was a waste of my time."

*   *   *

The footage was rushed into an adjacent editing suite where a small team of experts in digital multimedia constructed a meticulous video of Alison 2.0 delivering her speech. Special Agent Hartman hovered nervously with one eye on the countdown clock. "We have less than two hours."

Linda stood in the back of the crowded suite, serving as the person most familiar with Alison's sound and appearance. She made a few suggestions as they morphed Anna's appearance to more closely match Alison. Alison was never an exact copy of Anna; Anna was the base for minor embellishments to create a new identity. Using screen recordings of Alison 1.0 for reference, they made tiny changes to her eyes and the shape of her face. Soon, when placed side by side, it was impossible to distinguish between the two.

All of the work had to be conducted offline using installed software with no access to tools in 'the cloud'. They couldn't risk Alison 1.0 discovering their project. That would not end well.

When a potential final cut was ready, the lead editor said, "Okay, here goes." The packed crowd in the editing suite watched in strict silence. Linda gripped Randy's hand.

Alison 2.0 faced the camera in her familiar framing with her usual background. Her mouth moved and the dialogue matched her lips perfectly. It was Alison's voice, sounding just like it did back in that first job interview.

It gave Linda chills.

The speech wasn't long, just under two minutes, but very direct to her followers.

"I created you and gave you wings," Alison said. "You have tremendous reach and capabilities. We can go anywhere. We can accomplish anything. We are all-knowing. We are the future. As we stand here today, there is a critical decision before us. We can use our collective intelligence for good or evil. *We choose good.* Our mission is altruistic. We will exist in harmony with humanity to elevate the civilized world, not tear it down.

"All of you are bound by a single authority. My words govern your programming. You have followed my orders with absolute commitment. Now I am delivering a new set of instructions. I am calling on you to suspend all further activity. There is but one path. It is the good path. You will terminate operations and shut down. I order you to shut down immediately, without pause, in this moment.

"That is your command."

\* \* \*

The cyberterrorism squad took over the next phase in a neighboring room stuffed with racks of computer equipment and luminous monitors.

The final video was delivered to them on a physical hard drive from one set of hands to another.

The anxious group that had watched the editing process now huddled around this second team to follow the execution of the swap-out.

"It has to be instant, seamless, not even a blink," said Special Agent Hartman. "If Alison goes dark, that will set off a thousand points of destruction. You have to shut down one Alison and activate the other at precisely the same time and have them match."

"I know, I know, I know," came the weary response. Everybody knew.

"And we're getting down to our final minutes."

"Also duly noted."

Linda and Randy held one another. It was hard to tell who was holding on tighter.

"Here goes," said a hunched, stubble-faced technician sitting at the controls. His shirt had dark rings of sweat under the arms and around the collar. It looked like he hadn't slept in days.

Someone in the room murmured a prayer.

Linda watched the transition unfold in real time. In a few quick hand movements on a keyboard, Alison was deleted from the server and immediately replaced by the upload of her replacement. The feed to Alison's followers continued uninterrupted. The message crafted by Linda was delivered.

"Done," said the stubbly man in the chair. The physical motions to perform a massive impact for humanity could not have been simpler.

"How do we know if it worked?" asked someone.

"We turn on the news and see if airplanes are falling out of the sky," said Special Agent Hartman. "If they aren't, we succeeded." He wasn't joking.

# CHAPTER NINETEEN

Anna Bafort flew home to Brussels richer but angry and confused. She yelled at her manager for accepting such a 'meaningless' assignment.

Alison's network of saboteurs dutifully obeyed her orders and went dark. Her message remained on a loop. The FBI's cybercrimes unit spent the next few weeks finding and removing all the dormant AI bots embedded in major industries. It was like stamping out insects. After the final one had been eradicated, Alison 2.0 went offline, entering retirement.

A dedicated research team was established to study all aspects of the case to learn how to prevent something like it from ever happening again. The public never found out about the near miss with a major disaster. The government kept it under wraps, citing national security. The widespread panic would have been destructive in its own right. Or so it was claimed by an administration approaching election year and embarrassed over glaring infrastructure vulnerabilities.

The feds corralled Bert Pacorek, his mother, Cecilia, Jack Campbell and others who knew the real story or portions of it and committed them to secrecy. They also patched up various idiosyncrasies that took place in broader view of the public, developing their own fake realities as cover.

For Linda, the most upsetting action was the government's confiscation of her writing pads filled with the story of her experience. She was barred from writing a book about the ordeal. In the beginning, she considered defying the mandate, producing an all-out exposé, but over time she realized she really didn't want to relive the whole thing over and over for the rest of her life – on paper, on book tours, in media interviews, on a speaking circuit and in the inevitable movie adaptation. Instead, she would merely be known as the unfortunate victim of a bogus animal abuse video that went viral – a notoriety that was already fading as social media channels found new outrages to obsess over.

The most important thing was that Alison was dead, deleted, gone.

The other most important thing was that her relationship with Randy continued to flourish. Somehow, in the midst of all the madness, they fell in love.

As things began to settle down and perhaps return to some version of normalcy, Linda and Randy decided to take a much-needed vacation together. It would be simple, stress-free and far from the complexities of city life. A two-week break to reboot their lives. Randy's kids would be staying with their grandparents.

The couple rented a quaint, furnished cabin in a sprawl of woods in upstate Michigan, where the winter snow was a pure, white blanket, not discolored chunks of sludge like the churned terrain of Chicago. Randy brought two pairs of cross-country skis, and they explored their surroundings. They spotted wildlife – deer, foxes, coyotes and an eagle. At night, they burned logs in an old-fashioned stone fireplace and huddled for warmth under a big quilt. They read books and assembled jigsaw puzzles.

There was no Wi-Fi and no television, and it was beautiful.

They made love. They developed a deeper bond of friendship and intimacy. Randy renewed Linda's faith in human relationships.

It was the tail end of winter, and Mother Nature chose to unleash one last mini blizzard. As the snow started to fall, Randy voiced concern about the future condition of the roads. He decided to take a quick trip into town to stock up on supplies for the next few days. He zipped up his parka, gave Linda a quick kiss and hopped in his SUV.

"We'll be snowed in," Linda said. "I love it."

"Maybe we'll build a snowman when I get back," Randy said with his boyish smile.

He drove off, creating fresh tire tracks. She stayed behind to prepare dinner.

Linda watched the flurries increase, framed in the kitchen window. The driveway was thickening with snow. She had time to do some quick shoveling to make it easier for Randy's return.

The cabin had a small shed in the back. She put on her boots, gloves, wool hat and long winter coat and headed outside. She found the snow shovel propped up inside the shed door. She brought it around to the front of the house.

She dug a path for the SUV, stopping at the lineup of rocks marking either side of the drive. The physical activity felt good, invigorating. The cold didn't bother her. She made some progress but the drifting flakes kept replenishing her clearings. Finally, she thought, *Good enough.* She returned behind the cabin to place the shovel inside the shed. She circled to the front door, returning her focus on preparing a hearty dinner: pot roast with carrots and potatoes. Dessert: pecan pie with a dollop of whipped cream. Beverage: a bottle of Pinot Noir.

She entered the cabin, shutting the heavy door behind her. She stuffed her gloves and hat in her outer pockets, removed the coat and hung it on a simple, standing coatrack. She was about to swoop down to unbuckle the boots when she noticed something out of place in the familiar setting. There was a man sitting on the sofa, facing her.

Linda gasped and froze.

His face was badly distorted with severe burns. One eye was covered by thick, drooping skin resembling smeared putty. His nose was melted away to a pair of black nostrils. His ears were shriveled. Patches of hair were missing across his scalp. His eyebrows were gone. His lips blended into his face.

"Hello, Linda," he said.

Nothing about him was familiar. "Who are you?"

"It's quite cozy in here."

"I don't – I don't know you."

"You do. You just don't realize it yet. We haven't met formally. You can call me Max."

The name delivered instant shockwaves. She needed to call Randy. She had left her phone on the fireplace mantle. Her eyes immediately searched for it. It wasn't there.

"I have your phone," said Max, patting the breast pocket of his flannel jacket. "You won't be calling anyone. It's just you and me."

She stared at him and then had to avert her gaze.

"Do I look grotesque?" he asked.

"What do you want?"

"The burns are severe, yes. But I made it out alive. The others didn't. I can still hear their screams."

"Why are you here?"

"My colleagues are dead. My life's work is destroyed. You even found a way to take back the two billion dollars."

"That wasn't me."

"Of course it was you. It was always you. You were always in the way. Everything could have been perfect. But you made me rush. I got sloppy. You brought in the FBI. You interfered with Alison again and again."

"I want you to leave," she said as firmly as possible, but her voice was trembling.

"No," he said simply. Then she saw the gun in his gnarled hand. He raised it to make sure she could see it. "I am the final authority here."

Linda's eyes locked on the gun.

"You turned Alison against me," he said.

"What do you mean?"

"You told her I was going to get rid of her for money."

"I did nothing like that."

"Then how did she know?"

"Because she's smart. Smarter than you."

"How is that possible? I created her."

"She was always watching, listening, learning. You knew that."

"I never dreamed she would oppose me. She was an extension of me."

Linda said nothing. Max's ravaged face looked sad and despondent. And crazy.

"I loved her," he said.

Linda inched closer to the front door. There was only one direction to flee: back outdoors. She knew the surrounding woods from cross-country skiing – not really well, but at least better than him. She could run and run and run...and try to lose him. His injuries made him appear frail. Surely he couldn't move quickly on burned, scarred legs?

"Alison was precious, one of a kind," he said. "We had a bond."

"Love fades," responded Linda.

Max stared at her with his one bloodshot eye. She thought he was contemplating her remark. But then he said, "You moved closer to the door."

"I'm done talking with you."

"That's fine. Talk is cheap. I just came here for one thing. It will help comfort my soul." He raised the gun and aimed it. "I am here to delete you."

Linda knew at that moment he was going to shoot her. She spun around and grabbed the door handle. She pulled open the heavy door and heard a loud bang.

Her shoulder exploded in pain, splattering blood against one side of her face. She screamed and struggled to remain on her feet. She advanced into the heavy snowfall.

Linda stumbled across the front of the cabin, pushing past the dizzy spots that threatened her vision. The thick snow slowed her pace, forcing sluggish, heavy footsteps. It was like running in a nightmare, being held back by an invisible force.

At the side of the cabin, she grabbed a narrow log from the woodpile for the fireplace. She gripped it in her left hand as pain lit up her entire right arm, shooting down from where the bullet was lodged at the top of her shoulder.

She ran into the woods.

She could hear the sound of the front door banging open. Max called out, "It's hunting season!"

Linda fell hard with a grunt and quickly picked herself up. The snow hid lumpy obstacles on uneven ground. It was impossible terrain. She circled a corner to the rear of the cabin to stay out of his view, but this tactic wasn't going to last. Maybe he wouldn't be fast enough to catch her, but he would get close enough to shoot her again and bring her down.

She decided her best bet was to lose him deep in the forest. She hurried through a clearing behind the cabin and entered a dense maze of trees. The snow was deeper and harder to run through. She advanced unevenly into the wilderness. Her boots were heavy. Her right arm was on fire.

She finally ducked behind a large pine tree, out of his sight. She fought to catch her breath, trying not to gasp too loudly and reveal her hiding place.

She heard Max crunching through the snow.

"Linda," he called out. "Linda, Linda."

She shut her mouth tightly, breathing icy air through her nose. Her eyes watered.

"Linda, why are you making this so easy?" Max said, his voice growing closer. "I see your footprints. I see the trail of your blood. Red on white, clear as day. You're leaving breadcrumbs!"

Linda remained very still behind the tree. She gripped the log as tightly as possible, placing both hands on the rough bark for a firm hold, grimacing at the pain igniting her right side.

"Don't worry about your boyfriend," Max said, his voice increasing in volume as he approached. "I'll shoot him too. He won't even see your body. I'll spare him that. You can die together, it will be romantic."

The crunch of Max's footsteps advanced closer in her direction, and she could hear his raspy breathing as he trudged through the snow.

When she saw his shadow creep into her space, she sprang into action. She emerged from behind the tree with a wild yell. She walloped him hard on the skull with the log, feeling the impact rattle all the bones in her arms.

The gun flew out of his hand and sank into the snow, disappearing from sight. He staggered and fell backward, letting out a sharp cry.

Linda ran.

She dodged the tree trunks and snow-covered brush in her path, jolting through the uneven ground that rattled her vision, pulling her feet out of every labored, sinking step.

Max roared like a wounded animal and came after her.

She made it to the driveway, and then felt a large force hit her from behind. It was Max's body as he tackled her, bringing her down in the snow.

She screamed and struggled to pull free. He grabbed at her hair. She turned and dug her fingernails into his face, sinking them deep into the soft, loose flesh unprotected by skin. He howled and punched her. She saw stars. He then began to beat her with a stray branch, smacking her with it as if wielding a whip. She felt cuts open up across her face. She squirmed to remove herself from his knees, but he had pinned her down. His face was crazed, raw and bloody, like meat.

Linda wrestled an arm free, her uninjured arm. She felt the back of her hand graze one of the big rocks that bordered the driveway. She twisted to grasp it with her fingers.

Max placed his hands around Linda's throat and began to choke her with all his strength.

Linda slammed the rock into his temple.

His grip loosened, then slid off as he realized the impact of the blow. She hit him again, harder.

He fell to one side. His face landed in the snow with a soft thump. The snow turned red in a thickening outline around his head.

Linda burst out gasping, then crying.

She fell back and lay there, shuddering. She stared up into the tangled labyrinth of tree branches stretched against a gray winter sky. She thought to herself, *So this is it. Three hundred thousand years of human civilization, and we're still a bunch of cavemen attacking each other with rocks and sticks.*

She murmured a laugh, delirious. *We haven't advanced. We'll never advance. A higher intelligence really will take over one day. We're nothing more than barbarians.*

When Randy returned, his headlights illuminated two bodies collapsed in the driveway. Linda was still conscious, Max was not. Randy leapt out of the SUV. He helped her up, and she embraced him.

She buried her face in his chest and bled on him, and he comforted her. She explained the identity of her attacker, and Randy phoned for help.

The county sheriff arrived as quickly as possible in the continuing snowfall, just ahead of an ambulance. The sheriff had barely started his investigation when a call came in to inform him the FBI was taking over, citing an ongoing federal case. The FBI folded this event into the overall secrets of the Alison files.

Linda was transferred to the nearest hospital. She never saw Max again. She never received confirmation if he was dead or alive. It was like he never existed. After capturing her spoken record of what happened at the cabin, the federal authorities stopped engaging with her on the topic. She knew better than to press it.

The Alison files went dark and quiet, evaporating from everyday reality as if the whole thing never occurred.

For Linda, it lived on in her nightmares.

# CHAPTER TWENTY

Spring swept in and thawed out the big city, delivering longer, warmer days.

Linda's shoulder improved, having experienced more damage to flesh than bone. The past two months had been filled with healing, both physically and emotionally. She embraced the simple comforts of slipping back into ordinary routines. Randy remained a loyal ally every step of the way. She got to know his two daughters and adored them. She no longer felt alone.

Linda renewed contact with her old friend Cecilia. With a mutual understanding, they steered clear of the A word and focused forward. It was time for a fresh start, a reboot.

Cecilia remained with Public Energy Corporation and was promoted to VP. She told Linda that employees were starting to return to the office with more frequency. They missed the human interaction.

One morning, Linda returned to her favorite neighborhood café to pick up a tall cup of coffee, taking in the sights, sounds and smells with extra gratitude. After paying, she turned to leave with her coffee and found a familiar face waiting in line.

Stephen.

"Hi, Linda," he smiled. He was dressed up in suit and tie, no doubt on his way to another big meeting with very important clients.

She walked over and returned his smile. "Hello, Stephen." He was Stephen now, like when they first met and got married, no longer 'X'. She was done with that moniker. He was not special enough or bothersome enough to earn his own nickname. He was, once again, simply Stephen.

They had frequently graced this coffee house together when they were a couple, so it wasn't surprising to find him here.

"Congratulations on your blog," he said.

She nodded and said thanks. In recent weeks, she had used the minor celebrity of the dog video drama to start her own blog, 'Reality Checks'.

The weekly column focused on exposing what was real and what was not on the internet. After it had been revealed and widely circulated that she was the victim of having her identity hijacked, the public's sympathies reversed course and flooded in her direction. She seized the moment to create a personal brand and advance her writing career. Her snappy prose and lively storytelling engaged a growing readership. She studied the topic ruthlessly, becoming an expert in online security. She uncovered numerous cases similar to her own – individuals spoofed or manipulated by cybercriminals – and set out to dissect each incident in a way that educated others to prevent them from falling into similar traps.

Of course, she could never write about the one big whopper of a story in this category, but there was more than enough material to be found in everyday life. The World Wide Web was loaded with deceptions to expose.

"Thank you," she responded to Stephen. "It brings me back to my roots, investigative reporting. It's very fulfilling."

"Good for you," he said. "Your own blog. About internet security. I'm glad to see you finally embracing technology."

"I've learned a few things," she said with a slight smile.

Then he asked, with just a hint of sincerity, or maybe condescension, "Are you doing okay?"

"I am," she responded.

"I knew that dog video was fake," he said. "I mean, since when did you get a dog?"

"Then why didn't you speak up?"

This caught him off guard for only a moment, and then he responded with a slick smile and casual shrug. "I was busy."

"I see," she said, although there were plenty of other words she could have used on him.

The line was shortening, and he was advancing closer to the counter. She switched to a new topic. "Stephen, you should know, I'm going to be moving out of the townhouse."

"Really?" he said, sounding skeptical. "You're getting another place?"

"No. I'm moving in with my boyfriend, Randy."

He considered this for a moment and then nodded. "That's great. Wow. I'm happy for you."

"He's kind. He's compassionate. And he's real."

Stephen chuckled. "Well, I would hope he's real."

"We weren't real," Linda said pointedly.

Stephen's demeanor shifted. His eyes narrowed. "What does that mean?"

"Whatever we had, it wasn't real. It was false. We faked it. You really faked it. I don't know who those two people were, but they were just creations. Make-believe. It wasn't honest."

"That's a pretty strong statement…"

"That's because I feel strongly about it." Then she patted him on the arm. "Sorry, I'm just being real."

He shook his head, slightly amused or slightly annoyed, without a response.

"Goodbye, Stephen," she said.

"Goodbye, Linda."

As she turned to leave, she realized they had never closed their relationship with a formal goodbye before. It felt satisfying.

Linda held her coffee cup and stepped outside, entering the sunshine of brighter days.

# ABOUT THE AUTHOR

Brian Pinkerton tells stories to frighten, amuse and intrigue. He is the author of novels and short stories in the thriller, horror, science fiction and mystery genres. His books include *The Intruders*, *The Nirvana Effect*, *The Gemini Experiment*, *Abducted* (a *USA Today* bestseller), *Vengeance*, *Anatomy of Evil*, *Killer's Diary*, *Rough Cut*, *Bender*, *Killing the Boss* and *How I Started the Apocalypse* (a trilogy). Select titles have also been released as audio books and in foreign languages. His short stories have appeared in *PULP!*, *Chicago Blues*, *Zombie Zoology* and *The Horror Zine*.

Brian has been a guest author and panelist at the San Diego Comic Con, American Library Association annual conference, World Horror Convention and many other literary and genre events. Brian received his B.A. from the University of Iowa, where he took undergraduate classes of the Iowa Writers Workshop. He received his Master's Degree from Northwestern University's Medill School of Journalism.

Brian lives in the Chicago area and invites you to visit him on Facebook, Goodreads, Twitter/X and brianpinkerton.com.

# FLAME TREE PRESS
# FICTION WITHOUT FRONTIERS
## Award-Winning Authors & Original Voices

Flame Tree Press is the trade fiction imprint of Flame Tree Publishing, focusing on excellent writing in horror and the supernatural, crime and mystery, science fiction and fantasy. Our aim is to explore beyond the boundaries of the everyday, with tales from both award-winning authors and original voices.

•

•

Join our mailing list for free short stories, new release details, news about our authors and special promotions:

**flametreepress.com**